BEWITCHED, BETRAYED, ENRAPTURED

Jessamine Stone's brother would marry her off to a covetous boor to salvage an impoverished estate. But Jessamine can love only Christian Haukinge—the handsome lord to whom she was once betrothed. Assured that she may wed her onetime fiancé if he consents to have her, the penniless beauty sets out to win Christian's affection once more—unaware that the rogue has been offered a tidy sum to break Jessamine's heart.

KISSED

Embittered over past injustices, Christian has good reason to despise the Stone family—and so ruthlessly agrees to the contemptible bargain. But Jessamine's sensuous spirit, her innocent trust, and her melting green-eyed gaze threaten to undermine his resolve for vengeance—and to heal his deep and scarring wounds with the soothing balm of unconditional love.

"Power and grace are Tanya Anne Crosby's trademarks. Richly sensual, eash tale is magnetic."
Stella Cameron, nationally best-selling, author of *Sheer Pleasures*

Other Avon Romantic Treasures by
Tanya Anne Crosby

ONCE UPON A KISS

If You've Enjoyed This Book,
Be Sure to Read These Other
AVON ROMANTIC TREASURES

A KISS IN THE NIGHT *by Jennifer Horsman*
LADY OF SUMMER *by Emma Merritt*
MY RUNAWAY HEART *by Miriam Minger*
RUNAWAY TIME *by Deborah Gordon*
TIMESWEPT BRIDE *by Eugenia Riley*

Coming Soon

RED SKY WARRIOR *by Genell Dellin*

TANYA ANNE CROSBY

KISSED

An Avon Romantic Treasure

AVON BOOKS ◆ NEW YORK

KISSED is an original publication of Avon Books. This work has never before appeared in book form. This work is a novel. Any similarity to actual persons or events is purely coincidental.

AVON BOOKS
A division of
The Hearst Corporation
1350 Avenue of the Americas
New York, New York 10019

First Avon Books Printing: December 1995

AVON TRADEMARK REG. U.S. PAT. OFF. AND IN OTHER COUNTRIES, MARCA REGISTRADA, HECHO EN U.S.A.

Printed in the U.S.A.

RA 10 9 8 7 6 5 4 3 2 1

This one's for Janet Heatley,
for eighteen years of friendship
Through boyfriends, to weddings,
to childbirth,
and the passing of loved ones,
you were always there . . .
through tears and laughter . . .
you still are . . .
Just wanted you to know you're appreciated

And to Keith . . . as always

What sweet thoughts,
what longing led them to this woeful pass?

—Dante

Prologue

England, Rose Park
April 1763

What *sort of man paid to have his sister's heart broken?*

Shaking his head in disgust, Christian Haukinge tossed the parchment aside, and reclined deeper into the leather desk chair, contemplating the inconceivable notion.

He didn't bother considering the issue it raised: What sort of man accepted such a vulgar proposition?

Damned if he didn't already know the answer to that one.

The scribbled letter before him bore no salutation, he noted—a deliberate rudeness, a flagrant omission of his title, he was certain—and his demeanor, as he retrieved the parchment, shifted from indifference to keen irritation. His gaze skimmed the page once more, settling upon the last paragraphs.

> . . . as she seems to have convinced herself no other beau will do, save you, fatuous as it seems, and has set her face against the new contract I have put before her, clinging to your annulled betrothal simply to defy my wishes, I am forced to offer this proposal. Please consider the above remuneration for your services; the amount is more than adequate for your brief employ, and, indeed, should prove quite useful in the refurbishment of your newly purchased estate. As to that, please accept my condolences.
>
> I am certain you shall wish to begin with all due haste, and look forward to your timely response in this matter. The sooner she has been suitably disillusioned, the sooner you might be compensated for your troubles. For the greater good, I do hope we might overlook the nature of our past relationship, and endeavor to assist each other in persuading my dear, misguided sister in choosing the right-minded course. The advance will assure you see it my way. Accept it in good faith.
>
> I shall enlighten you further when we are face-to-face.

Signed simply, Stone.
For the greater good.
Bloody bastard.

Christian's lip curved with contempt—and then a thought occurred to him: If Stone knew he'd purchased Rose Park, doubless, his own brother had wind of the fact, as well. Philip was likely choleric with rage, having to discover something of that nature second- or even thirdhand. Christian might have given much to glimpse the expression on his brother's face when he'd been informed of the fact.

Gazing out from his office window, at the unkept garden, he shook his head, and a rueful smile touched his lips. What a family he had; the elder a greedy thief, the younger a *contrebandier*. Sighing wearily, he reached back to rip out the satin tie that bound his hair, and then thrust his long fingers through the unpowdered length of it, muttering sourly beneath his breath.

Hell, at least he had no qualms over admitting the fact.

Then again, it might seem appropriate to bear *some* measure of guilt for his . . . *contrebande.* Too bad he couldn't seem to muster the sentiments. He'd burn in hell before he'd regret a damned thing. That in itself should have disturbed him, he supposed. But it didn't. Not in the least. He was what he was, and he felt absolutely no remorse for his . . . *enterprising.* It was the only way he'd known to advance himself. Supplies were needed in the colonies, and he simply transported those goods. Nor had he any falsely noble incentives to declare. His motives were quite simply self-indulgent.

He wanted money.

Aye, and he wanted respect.

He wanted land.

He wanted more than anything for the sons he intended to sire to all have equal shares of the empire he would build for them. Damned if he'd leave one alone to fend for himself in a world such as this. And nay, 'twas not so much the lack of title he abhorred, for he might truly have been happy in most any situation—save the one in which he found himself. Youngest son, nonentity. It was understood he was more than a commoner, yet he was less, *much* less, than the truly elite.

Aye, and imagine all that disdain without anyone having known of his greatest social flaw, even. His wry smile deepened. *What a field day the gentry would have if they were to discover his bastardy.*

All those years he'd settled for what little his father had cared to give him. Which was nothing, not even a momentary-lapse pat on the head, a "good show, son." *Nothing.* The only one thing he'd counted on, was his bequest of Hakewell, his mother's dower land. It was to be hers, until her death, and then it was to go to Christian. And God's truth, he'd been perfectly content to bide his time, however long that should be, for he cherished his mother and would have her live an eternity were it possible. But he *had* counted upon that estate someday. And then he'd been offered the betrothal with Stone's young daughter, and he'd found himself with such great expectations, such dreams. Security for his heirs.

Shattered, all of it shattered upon his father's death. The old man hadn't been gone more than a single month when Philip had set in motion Christian's disinheritance. All very discreet, of course. He'd finagled possession of Hakewell through legal loopholes and treachery.

Certainly Christian knew he might contest it, for Hakewell was his mother's to give, but Philip, the son of a bitch, had resorted to extortion, knowing Christian would not sully his mother's good name. And then he had run to Stone, of course, to inform him of the transfer of property, and with his bequeathal gone, Stone had annulled the betrothal at once; the sole reason for the contract to begin with was the single parcel of land. Hakewell. Without it, Christian was worth no more than a brass farthing.

In the blink of an eye, everything had been ripped away, and like a man caught in the throes of a riptide, he'd been helpless to do anything but let it bear him away.

No more. He was helpless no more. Never again.

His gaze returned to the letter in his hand, and his fingers closed about the parchment, crumpling it. He slammed his fist down against the hardwood desk.

He wanted revenge.

The certainty of it struck him full of force. Despite that he'd sworn himself against it— even after what had happened before—he wanted it, with a bloodlust that was almost palpable. Cold fury seized him and he determined, instead, to give the cocky young duke his due. The idiot had offered him a ridiculously low sum for this insulting task, as though he were a green boy fresh out of Eton with a bulge in his breeches and little in his purse. But that was not what rankled most. Rather it was the fact that he'd been presented the damnable proposition to begin with—the snobbery and contempt at the heart of every insult offered.

One too many from the almighty Stones.

Not good enough to wed the man's sister, was he? But good enough to—what? bed her?

So he would have his sister *disillusioned*, would he? For the greater good? Christian wondered what, precisely, that entailed. From the letter, he'd gotten the distinct impression that Jessamine Stone was not too receptive to her brother's choice of husband. He supposed 'twas her bastard brother's intent that once her little heart was duly crushed, she would more easily bend to his will. But to what end was Stone willing to go?

And why choose him, save to rub salt into his wounds? His eyes narrowed. God's truth, he had no wish to do Westmoor any favors, but there was some sense of justice in that he would be paid now to avail himself of what should have already been his.

Poetic justice.

Aye, he'd do it, all right, but if Stone thought he meant to honor the letter of the agreement, he was more fool than Christian supposed. His cobalt blue eyes glinted with ruthless determination. The truth was that

Christian had already ruined the father . . . He now fully intended to finish the business—*and he didn't give a bleedin' damn who was brought down along the way, virginal little sister included.*

He didn't bother to scribble a return note; it wasn't worth the effort to attempt to put words together. He peered up at the figure standing quietly in the doorway, awaiting his return message, and said with barely suppressed virulence, "Tell him my answer is yes."

And then tell him to go straight to hell, he added silently, and rose from his desk.

God help him, right or wrong, he was about to court Lady Jessamine Stone.

For the greater good.

Chapter 1

England, Westmoor
May 1763

Jessie Stone sat upon the small embankment, peering dreamily over the rim of an open book, scarcely able to keep her mind upon the text within. In passing the library, she'd chosen the much-loved volume, thinking to pass the time reading out of doors, but who could concentrate with so many thoughts cavorting within her head?

He'd come; Lord Christian had come.

Her brother had been expecting him this morn.

All this time, she'd never dared dream he would come flying to her rescue. And yet she'd so wished that he would! He was her very last hope!

The awful truth was that at twenty-two, Jessamine was a prime candidate for spinster-hood, and her dowry sadly lacking, as well. Silently she cursed her father for that. Secretly she was furious at him, though she'd never openly say so. It seemed ludicrous that she should be angry with a man for simply dying. But his untimely death, followed by the ugly rumors that surfaced afterward, had forced Westmoor into a monetary pinch, and thus had rendered her virtually unmarriageable.

Amazing how swiftly one's acquaintances withdrew when there was the scarcest nuance of scandal.

Still and all, there was the tiniest possibility that Lord Christian might yet desire her—if not her, precisely, then what little remained of her dwindling dowry. Perhaps it should trouble her that he might desire her for her money alone, but it didn't. God's truth, she would do anything—anything—to escape the fate her brother would mete her!

Including swear to a love she didn't feel.

She'd lied to Amos, and it did bother her just a little, but she would have done most anything to persuade him to agree to a betrothal with Lord Christian—anyone, in truth, to be free of Lord St. John. In her favor was the fact that Lord Christian had no grand title to consider. Nor had he any money to his name—proof was in the fact that he'd purchased such a tumbledown estate as Rose Park. In truth, he would be marrying up did he choose to accept Amos's paltry offer. And with that conclusion, her spirits lifted considerably.

And if he didn't desire her?

Well, then . . . still she might find a way to prevail upon him to assist her in finding safe passage to her father's cousin in the colonies. She had her mother's jewels to persuade him, after all. *And they had once been affianced.* He owed her something for that, did he not?

Aye, she determined, and refused to be disheartened. One way or the other, her greatest chance to escape Lord St. John lay with Christian Haukinge—and he had come at long last.

Her mood lighter than it had been in ages, she set the stiff, age-blackened volume down upon the grass to peer at the brook below. An old stone packhorse bridge spanned its shallow width. It had been there as long as Jessie could recall—put there by druids, her mother had claimed. Bathed in misty sunlight beneath the lush oaks and elms, this had always been her favorite place to come, whether to brood or shout huzzahs.

This instant she felt like dancing wildly.

The water seemed so cool and tempting . . . Surely no one would spy her if she removed her slippers and stockings to soak her feet . . .

How long had it been since she'd risked such a thing?

It seemed a lifetime ago she'd dared be so carefree.

Closing her eyes, she called to mind the day so long ago when her mother had caught her wading in nothing more than her pristine white shift. If she remembered very hard . . . she could still envision the scene within her mind's eye . . . almost hear her mother's sweet voice . . .

"Jessie love! 'Tis no place for a young lady to be cavorting all by her lonesome!"

She'd caught sight of Jessie's gown cast away upon the grass. "Good heavens!" she'd exclaimed. "What would your papa say!"

Bursting into fits of giggles, Jessie had flopped upon her belly in the water, splashing everywhere.

"Whatever shall I do with you?" her mother had asked, but Jessie had spied the smile she tried so hard to conceal.

"Watch me, Mother!" Sucking in a mouthful of water, Jessie held it dammed within her mouth as she watched her mother remove her silk shoes and wade in after her. When her mother stood before her at last, she popped her cheeks with her palms, spewing water all over her mother's fine gown.

Her mother had peered down incredulously at her ruined gown, and seeing the flustered expression upon her face, Jessie feared to have angered her at last, but suddenly her mother had lunged after her, a peal of raucous laughter bursting from her lovely lips.

Looking back upon it now, Jessie thought it might have been the disheartened expression she'd worn, for she couldn't begin to imagine what could be so humorous about an impish child and a ruined gown. And yet, how they'd laughed and frolicked that day.

Tilting her head back, she sighed, feeling the gentle warmth of the sun upon her face. She'd been six years old ... It was the year before her mother had died. More than a lifetime had passed since that day; now there was little left but precious memories.

God's truth, her brother ruled like a dreary little monarch. As her father would have then, he'd turn choleric with rage to spy her at such merrymaking. And truth to tell, she couldn't help but giggle at the expression she imagined he'd wear. A spark of mischief ignited. The birds twittered nervously in the treetops. What could he say, after all? He couldn't possibly be more callous toward her. What harm could come of it?

Impulsively she tossed off her slippers and stood, flinging up her skirts. Rolling down her stockings, she removed them, and cast them away with an impish giggle. And then drawing up her skirts, she knotted them firmly to keep from soaking the lacy hem. She was more than pleased with herself for forsaking her petticoat this morn. She'd had to sneak about to get out of the house, but the freedom it now gave her was well worth the undignified duck behind the server.

Nay, she wasn't fool enough to run about in a mere shift at her advanced age, but she could see nothing wrong with wetting her feet—to blazes with Amos!

She started down the incline at once, humming cheerily.

*   *   *

Christian found himself reluctant to intrude upon her delightful diversions and so he sat, admiring her unheeded as she whirled and frolicked like a doe in the fields. Kicking up a slim leg, she showered water into the air, laughing huskily when it rained down upon her face.

He smiled despite himself.

She made quite the charming picture.

Too charming.

He didn't want her to be refreshingly sincere and guileless. He wanted her to be coy and artificial . . . so that he could loathe her as he did her father and her brother.

Christ, why was he doing this?

There was too much to be dealt with to be engaged in paltry revenge.

So what if he'd been betrothed to the green-eyed witch? So what the hell if the betrothal had been wrenched from him solely because he'd been disinherited? Damn Amos Stone! For with the death of that blackguard's father, Christian had been more than prepared to forget.

The fool had dared provoke him yet again.

God's teeth, she wore no petticoat.

The revelation slammed into him without warning. Desire slid through his veins like warm brandy.

Provoked by his body's response to the sight of her, he spurred his mount down the incline, some part of him bent upon spoiling her revelry. He entered the brook without hesitation, his mount's hooves splashing, churning water, angrily grinding stones beneath the crystalline surface.

With a gasp of surprise, she spun to face him. "My lord!" she cried out.

He arched a brow, for it didn't escape him that her eyes widened in recognition. And then suddenly she was gazing up at him, her expression one almost of adoration.

Bloody hell.

"My lord," she began again, and her eyes turned liquid with gratitude. "I just cannot believe you've come!"

Christian knew she was addlepated—had to be. There was no way she could know *who* he was, and *still* look so bloody damned grateful to see him. But then, she didn't know, did she? All she knew was that her brother had supposedly written him and reinstated the offer of matrimony, only with a considerable lesser dowry. "Aye, m'mselle," he said, "did you think I would not?" But he didn't smile to reassure her.

She shook her head, and tears sprang to her eyes.

Damnation. There was no need for her to weep, was there? Taken aback by her unexpected reaction, he scowled, not quite able to tear his gaze away from her liquid green eyes; how singularly beautiful they were. *As they'd been that day so long ago.* They'd haunted him then. Bewitched him still.

He forced his gaze lower, to her full, sensual lips, and concluded that his business with her brother might not be so unpleasant, after all.

Quite the contrary. She was possibly one of the fairest women he'd ever laid eyes upon. Not beautiful, precisely, though something about her made him feel she was—those eyes . . . and those lips that seemed made for kissing.

She was a bold little thing, he decided, staring back as she was. And she certainly wasn't helping matters much, because the longer she stared, the greater her danger of being soundly and ruthlessly kissed. He was tempted.

After all, why postpone the inevitable?

"My lord," she said softly, demurely, "I swear I shall ever be in your debt!"

"Really, m'mselle?" He couldn't keep himself from baiting her. "Won't you tell me just who it is you think I am?"

She stiffened suddenly, peering up a little anxiously. "Why, Lord . . . Christian . . . of course . . ."

She sounded so beautifully anxious, so very uncertain, that Christian found himself grinning down at her. "None other," he confessed, "though how you placed me so quickly, I shall never know." *Why was it that he felt suddenly so relieved? pleased, even?*

She smiled sweetly, and it pricked at his heart. "I've a very good memory, my lord."

So did he, to his misfortune. "Indeed, your memory must be excellent, *chérie*, for that was well over five years ago." *And blazoned upon his mind and soul as though 'twere yesterday.*

"Why, yes! It certainly is," she replied, somehow missing the wrath in his tone. "I can even recall what you were wearing that day, my lord."

He cocked a brow at that, and was about to ask what it was he'd worn to have caught her notice so well, but she seemed to startle and shy away suddenly.

Chapter 2

Jessie's cheeks flamed.

What a ninny she must appear to be! Nibbling anxiously at her lower lip, she chided herself for her blather.

The truth was that she *had* recognized Lord Christian at once, though, in fact, he was not at all the man she recalled. She couldn't help herself, she found herself staring unabashedly, regarding his windblown locks with both fascination and scandalized horror. Gone was the genteel boyish quality she remembered, and with it every last pretense of civility. Whereas decent men wore dignified headpieces and powder, he wore only his natural dark mane, bound at his nape—a style that was more than a few years passé—and heaven help her, her first impression of the man before her was that he held himself accountable to no one.

So why had he come?

It didn't matter, she told herself. Though the years had changed him much, all that truly mattered was that he stood before her now, and she was heartily grateful despite a new tide of misgivings. *Please, Lord,* she prayed, *let him have come for me!* All her problems would then be solved.

If only he would stop staring at her so . . .

"I-I was reading, my lord," she blurted, unsettled by his unwavering regard.

"Really?" The tiniest smile curved his lips, and entered his eyes. "You appear to be reading," he said somewhat sardonically, and gazed down pointedly at her bare feet. "Perchance you have a book beneath those pretty little toes of yours?"

Jessie's cheeks burned hotter as she stared down at her bare feet.

Good Lord, she truly was a ninnyhammer! Mortification squeezed the breath from her lungs. "Nay, my lord!" she cried, her gaze flying back to his. "It's just that, you see . . . I-I left the book upon the bank! I-I was . . ." She fanned herself unconsciously. "It was rather hot, you see!" Lord-a-mercy but it was uncomfortably warm of a sudden. Feeling more than a little foolish, she turned at once and began to make her way out of the brook. "I should go now!" she declared.

"Not on my account, I hope."

Jessie didn't stop, couldn't find the courage to do so; she continued instead toward the bank. Lord, but this was too lowering by half!

"I was rather enjoying the sight of your revelry," he said behind her, and Jessie's stomach lurched. She halted abruptly, turning to peer up at him, chafed. Just how long had he stood watching before making his presence known?

"That really was too bad of you!" she reproved, reminding herself that she needed him still, and couldn't afford to offend him— the cad! And yet she didn't at all appreciate his lack of courtesy. "I must have been woolgathering," she assured with somewhat less vehemence. "I never even heard you approach, my lord."

His blue eyes glinted silver, though he said nothing to refute her subtle accusation, and for a long instant the silence between them lengthened as Jessie scrutinized him.

He wore a midnight blue riding coat, with immaculate white breeches that clung to his thighs so snugly, they were almost indecent. His waistcoat was blue, and his shirt a crisp white, with frilly cuffs that flared from beneath the sleeves of his coat. To his credit, his stock was neatly tied. And truth to tell, save for the dusty black boots, and his Bohemian hair, he appeared quite respectable, quite patrician, and not at all the nefarious rogue Amos portrayed him to be.

And yet there *was* something about him not quite civil . . . something menacing even . . .

Her eyes narrowed as she followed his gaze to her hem—her knotted hem—and her gasp was audible as she suddenly recalled her state of undress. At once she scrambled to untie the knot in her gown, and settled it hastily over her limbs, letting the fragile hem she'd taken such care with only moments before soak up the brook water.

Her mortification escalated.

She lowered her gaze at once, focusing upon his boots, completely at a loss for words now. She didn't dare look elsewhere—certainly not up into his too handsome face, for it seemed she was destined to remain apple-cheeked this morn. "M-My brother," she stammered, "h-he'd not approve—I-I should go!" She turned at once to leave.

"But, m'mselle," he protested, " 'twas your brother who suggested I might find you here."

Jessie spun once more, her gaze flying upward in surprise. "Amos directed you here?"

"When he couldn't find you at the house." His smile was somewhat cocksure.

Jessie tilted her head. "How . . . very forthcoming of him . . ." It wasn't her brother's way at all to abet the foe—and foes, they were in the matter of Lord Christian. It couldn't be helped; she'd dared to hope for something more than her brother was offering her—Lord St. John! God's truth, but he would condemn her to a fate worse than death with the man. She couldn't bear it. Her proposed intended was little more than a detestable boor—and more, the thought of his hands upon her made her physically ill. She had to prevail. She was determined to prevail.

And so was Amos.

She peered up at Lord Christian, unconvinced.

"I did get the distinct impression he doesn't care for me overmuch," he added offhandedly.

Jessie choked on the truth of his admission. Assured now, she felt compelled to reassure him, too, despite that he seemed not the least disturbed by the notion. "Why should you think such a thing, my lord?" she asked.

He shrugged. "A feeling, I suppose." And yet the glimmer in his eyes told her it was so much more. His gaze was all too knowing, and she found she couldn't perpetuate even the tiniest untruth under his keen scrutiny, not even a wee one for his own benefit.

"Yes, well . . . I suspect he may not, after all." Curse Amos and his condescending ways, for the last thing she wished to do was to discourage Lord Christian's suit. She so desperately needed his aid! "Even so, my lord," she confided a little resentfully, "I'm certain he's harmless where you're concerned."

He made some choked sound. "Harmless?" His lips twitched with what Jessie thought might be amusement.

She nodded, her brow furrowing. "I believe so, my lord." She couldn't very well tell him that her brother was a pantywaist, now could she?

"I dunno, *chérie*." He smiled down at her, his eyes glinting with mirth. "I rather thought him a formidable fellow. Had me quivering in my boots this morn, hinting of pistols at dawn and infernal regions." The gleam in his eyes intensified, and Jessie cast him a dubious glance, for 'twas impossible to believe the man before her had ever quivered before anything, or anyone. Ever. He was jesting with her, she thought . . . though she couldn't be certain.

"Really, my lord," she countered, "you mustn't take my brother's mettle so much to heart. The truth is that he trusts no one." She lifted her chin, meeting his gaze. "Not really . . ."

Christian acknowledged the fact with a curt nod, and she averted her gaze.

"In any case, he must have thought you quite harmless, too, my lord, or he would never have directed you here to me, I'm certain."

The chit was too trusting by far, he decided. Didn't she realize he might have said anything to gain her trust, even the truth?

Then again, wasn't that what he desired? To gain her faith. Certainly it would make his task here all the easier. So, then, why should he care whether she was easily duped?

He didn't.

His jaw clenched, and then she lifted her gaze fully to his, and he spied the flare of temper and uncertainty she tried so hard to conceal.

Anger for him, or for her brother?

"No offense was taken, I assure you, m'mselle. My word. 'Tis only fitting your brother be mindful of his sister," he advised, feeling it his duty. "Not all men are so honorable, you see."

She peered up at him and arched a brow in

challenge, irritation still evident in her uncommonly luminous eyes. "Nor are they all such terrible lechers as my brother would have me believe," she surprised him by saying.

Christian lifted a dubious brow.

"I don't believe they all are," she asserted, and blushed profusely.

"Really?"

She nodded, a little less certain now. "Truly," she persisted.

He watched her flush creep lower, to the region of her décolletage, and his gaze lingered upon the square-cut neckline of her rose colored gown. Subconsciously her hand fluttered to her throat—an alluring gesture—and he compelled himself not to think of what it might feel like to press his lips to that burning flesh.

Heaven; it would feel like heaven.

The only sort he was ever like to know.

"I . . . I really should go," she declared once more, and again moved toward the bank, backing away slowly, as though she were no longer quite certain whether to flee or to stay, to trust him or nay. He found he didn't wish her to leave him as yet, and so he allowed her the comfort of distance between them.

He waited until she was seated high upon the bank, beneath the old elm, and was well on her way to replacing her dainty slippers to her feet, and then spurred his mount after her.

Chapter 3

Jessie observed him guardedly as he hobbled his mount, trying to convince herself she truly should go. Instead, she sat rooted to the spot, berating herself for her foolish fancies.

What made her think his coming had anything to do with her? In all likelihood, his brother was in residence at Hakewell, was all, and Lord Christian was visiting.

And yet . . . had he not come calling this morn? Had he not said? Dare she hope?

Her thoughts reeling, she snatched up her silk stockings, knowing there wasn't time to don them before he turned from tending his mount, and hid them beneath her dress, keeping an eye to his back, lest he spy her and she be mortified once more. She couldn't bear it.

"Won't you sit?" she asked him somewhat

breathlessly, when he turned to face her at last. Good Lord, where had that come from?

She needed his aid, she reminded herself, and wouldn't get it by scurrying home with her proverbial tail tucked between her legs. His brows lifted at her request. "I-It . . . pains my neck to have to look up so," she explained lamely. Lord, she felt like a paper-skull spouting such flummery.

Hidden though they were, she felt her stockings beneath her limbs like smoldering embers against her bare flesh. This was no good—this was not right! She prayed fervently he would refuse her, for she seemed to have lost the good sense to ask him to go.

" 'Twould be my pleasure," he said, and sat dutifully upon the grass beside her. Jessie was both relieved and mortified at once. What would she say now? Whatever would they speak of? He plucked a pale blade to worry between his teeth, and Jessie smiled diffidently, fighting the urge to bound to her feet and hie away like a timid schoolgirl.

God's truth, but his face was arresting up close—startlingly so, with his deep-set blue eyes. His jaw was thick but lean, his cheekbones high, and against his swarthy coloring, his face was shadowed by a day's growth of whiskers, but it was the intense, fiery burn of his cobalt blue eyes that made her shiver and helplessly drew her attention.

Propping up a knee, he leaned backward upon one arm and began to suckle the tender blade. Jessie watched him, feeling both encouraged and titillated by his presence when she knew she should be heedful instead.

She wanted to imagine he'd come for her. Her knight in shining armor. She'd always dreamed he would someday. And though she'd never have admitted it to anyone, it had truly distressed her to know that he'd not cared enough to challenge her father's mandate all those years ago.

It didn't matter; he was here now, and there was hope.

Christian watched as she lifted up a small leather-bound volume, her lips curving in the most damnably tempting smile he'd ever beheld.

He could scarce keep himself from wondering at her thoughts as her smile deepened to reveal perfect white teeth. Like rose-blushed porcelain, her cheeks were stained faintly with color, and the long, lustrous strands of her hair were swept up at the sides, arranged to fall in an artful tumble of midnight curls. A few escaped confinement—evidence of her delightful romp in the brook.

He stared like a besotted youth, and only belatedly came aware of the soft rhythm she tapped upon the small volume.

His gaze focused upon the book.

Indirectly the book reminded him of his reason for calling today: her brother's damnable proposal. The terms of their bargain had been spelled out for him within the library this morning. Ironically, it was some five years before, in that very same room, that the old duke had breached yet another contract with him, and that revelation had a rather sobering effect.

He was more determined than ever to exact his revenge.

What did he care about some fresh-faced miss? She wasn't his concern. She lifted the book to her breast, hugging it shyly, and guilt pricked at him nevertheless. He ignored the stab, thrusting his damnable conscience away, suffocating it with his anger.

She smiled softly. "You see, I truly *was* reading, my lord." She presented the book as evidence. "*Adelard of Bath, Questions on Nature.* Do you know the text, by chance?"

Christian's brows lifted. "I wasn't aware it was proper reading material for a young lady," he said bluntly.

Her brows drew together. "Whyever should it not be?" She sounded quite affronted.

"Have you by chance read them all?" He was convinced she had not. Had she bothered, she'd never have brought up the manuscript at all. She'd more than likely be sitting upon the blasted book—as she was those stockings of hers, hiding them from his scrutiny.

Her legs were bare.

His heart quickened at the thought. God, but he felt like a beardless youth with sweaty palms sitting beside his first lover. What the devil was the matter with him?

"Not all of them, of course," she was saying. "But I've never found a one to be improper in the least. In fact," she informed him somewhat impudently, "I find them to be rather clever speculation and very much worth contemplating!"

"Clever?" Christian suppressed a chuckle, sensing she was perfectly serious. He found, at the moment, that the last thing he wished was to offend her.

"Yes, of course," she persisted. "Very clever speculation, indeed. Such as . . ." She tried for a disaffected tone, but he anticipated the coming challenge. The shrewd little wench, she was baiting him, he realized. "Do you never ponder, my lord, whether beasts have souls? Or . . ." She cocked her head coyly. "Why the seats of imagination, reason, and memory are found in the brain? *or* why the waters of the sea are salty? *or* why certain rivers are not?"

She glanced up at him, and seemed encouraged by his expression.

"Or," she continued, her tone flippant, "*why men get bald in front?*" Unable to contain a giggle, she then continued, "Or, for that matter . . ." Her lips twitched in forewarning. "It simply boggles the mind to consider why men were not born with horns or other such weapons on their person! Do you not agree, my lord?"

She graced him with a heart-winning smile suddenly. Dark, sooty lashes framed eyes that fairly glowed with merriment, and the effect was nothing less than stunning. It momentarily snatched Christian's breath away. He chuckled and cleared his throat, struggling in vain to ignore the lust that held him firmly in its grip now. "Are you quite certain of that fact, m'mselle?"

Her brow furrowed softly as she pondered his question. *God, but she was an innocent.*

"How can you know," he persisted, "whether I, in truth, have no horns, or *other* such weapons upon my person? I very well might."

Once again her blush crept to her bosom. His gaze followed, too tempted to resist. "My guess," he ventured, smiling darkly, "is that you do not." He lifted his gaze. "Furthermore, my lady scholar, not all of those inquiries in that little book of yours *are* suitable material for naive and impressionable young women, clever speculation or nay." By her expression, he surmised she was precisely that, naive, for she seemed truly unaware of some of the baser texts within the pages of her little book. "Such as," he added offhandedly, "why women, if they are more frigid than men, are more wanton in desire."

"Oh!" she gasped. "But I've no recollection of that one at all! And you, my lord, are truly debauched to have brought it to my attention!"

"You think so? I meant only to make a point, *ma belle.*"

"Yes! I truly do!" she scolded. "You are quite debased, sirrah!"

Now, why did he suddenly feel like a wretch? "Well, then, accept my humble apologies, if I've managed to offend. It is a failing of mine, I fear." He thought he sounded appropriately remorseful, and he must have, for she eyed him discerningly, and smiled slightly.

"Truly, my lord . . ." She flipped the book about, examining the back, and then again met his gaze, her eyes bright with curiosity. "Is such a question asked of Adelard?"

Inquisitive little vixen. His lips curved in unadulterated pleasure. "Certainly."

She gasped and discarded the book at once, setting it down between them. "Well then! I would think it safe to say 'tis Adelard and his inquiring nephew who are the depraved ones! And you, my lord, are ultimately absolved!" She gave him a coy little smile, blissfully unaware of how close she was coming to being thoroughly and lustily kissed.

God, but he was tempted.

Strange as it was, he felt inordinately pleased with her blind defense of him. It had been a long time since anyone had defended him at all—deservingly or nay. " 'Tis most kind of you to absolve me," he said with a heartfelt chuckle. And to his amazement, he found himself genuinely enjoying their singularly peculiar conversation. He held her gaze an instant longer, reluctant to release it as yet, wholly mesmerized by the beauty of her pale green eyes.

She wasn't wholly unaffected by him, he knew, for her blush was no longer one of chagrin. Her head tilted slightly, instinctively, and she leaned so far forward that her face was dangerously near his own. Christian had to constrain himself from leaning forward and brushing his lips against her soft pink lips. He wondered how she would taste. Sweet, he knew she would be sweet. Sweet as the tender blade between his teeth.

She was the first to glance away, her gaze returning inevitably to the book lying between them upon the ground.

"I *was* searching for something in particular," she explained a little breathlessly. "You see, I seem to recall that Adelard wrote of reason as a guide, and of authority as a halter. Are you perchance familiar with that particular passage, my lord?"

Flicking away the blade of grass from his lips with his fingers, Christian lifted the small volume from her hands. It wasn't an original copy, but ancient, nonetheless. "May I?" he asked, and awaited her consent before opening it.

"Of course, my lord." Her eyes flashed with gleeful anticipation.

He smiled and held her gaze as he quietly flipped through the fragile pages, until he located the text in question. And then he read aloud to her, his voice thick, " 'For what else should authority be called but a halter . . . ' " He cleared his throat. " 'Indeed, just as brute beasts are led by any kind of halter, and know neither where nor how they are led, and only follow the rope by which they are held . . . ' " He paused for breath, cocked a brow at her, and thinking he meant it as a challenge for her to finish if she could, she began her recital where he left off.

" 'So the authority of your writers leads into danger not a few who have been seized and bound by animal credulity!' He also claims that reason has been given to individuals, so that with it as the first judge, he may distinguish between the true and the false. Do you not agree with him, my lord? I mean that reason has been given to each of us," she clarified. "Should we not think for ourselves, men and women both?"

He lifted a brow. "*Très magnifique, m'mselle.* I should have liked to say I knew the text so well myself." He closed the book and handed it back to her, wondering at such a pointed question. "As to your query, aye. As Adelard suggests, 'unless reason be the universal judge, it is given in vain to *individuals.* And *whosoever* does not know or neglects reason should deservedly be considered blind.' I believe that fully of men and women both. Are you a dissenter, then?" he teased.

"Oh, nay, my lord!" she replied at once. "Though, at the moment, I believe my brother quite thinks so."

"I see. And why is that?" Her eyes, which had been fastened reverently to his, slid to the book now balanced upon her lap.

She blinked, and then peered up into the treetops. "Well, I suppose . . ." She sighed. "I suppose 'tis because we are of such different minds, he and I." She lowered her gaze to meet his eyes. "You see, he would be immensely pleased did I simply don his thoughts."

He gave her a commiserative smile. "Any thought in particular?"

"Not especially," she replied, then more firmly. "Nay."

Christian lifted a brow. "I see. Well, then, you're quite certainly entitled to your own mind, little one, though I doubt Adelard of Bath intended for you to use his writings as evidence to the fact. I rather think he'd turn in his grave to know he's inspired a young maid's insurgence. You see, in Adelard's time, women weren't considered individuals at all. Just as they wondered whether beasts had souls, so, too, did they wonder about women."

"How dreadful! Say it isn't so, my lord!"

"Ah, but 'tis the truth," Christian asserted. And then he had to chuckle because she looked so absolutely horrified at the prospect. She didn't seem to realize they weren't so far from those times even now.

"Imagine!" Her eyes were wide with incredulity. "Women without souls!" She shook her head despairingly, and shuddered. "Whatever could they have been thinking, my lord? If women had no souls, how then, pray tell, does a male child end with one?"

Christian chuckled, and shook his head. "I've no idea a'tall," he told her. "It does seem a rather ludicrous notion, does it not?"

"Indeed!"

She said the word with such impudence that his shoulders at once shook with mirth. It was on the tip of his tongue to tell her she was delightful, but at the temptation, he sobered. It wouldn't serve to be losing his head over the winsome chit . . . something he was beginning to suspect would be quite easily done.

She was beautiful, aye . . . but she was something more he'd not anticipated . . .

Chapter 4

*K**indred spirits.*

Jessie lay fidgeting upon her bed, thinking that they saw so much through the same eyes. Uncanny was what it was. But comfortable, too. She sighed dreamily, for Lord Christian seemed simply too wonderful to be true.

And he was monstrously wicked, too.

Her maid had long since retired for the eve; eager for the day to end and the morning to arrive, Jessie had dismissed her even before her hasty bath was complete. Only now that she lay within the darkness of her room, sleep stubbornly eluded her.

Exhausted, but too exhilarated to be frustrated by it, she resigned herself to her wakeful state, sat up, and tossed the coverlets aside. She rose and made her way to the window, drawing open the draperies just enough to allow her to survey the night sky, so full of brilliant, winking stars.

Mayhap he was too good to be true . . .

She peered down into the garden below, at the little bench she'd occupied so regularly this past week. Christian had called upon her every day. They'd done little more than sit, chaperoned by Hildie, and converse. To her wonder, it seemed he truly enjoyed her company, as well as her conversation. Unlike Amos, he seemed to encourage her to speak her mind at every turn, and never took sport in ridiculing her for some perspective he did not happen to share. Instead, he made it a point to ask why she'd come to such a conclusion, and then he'd weigh her explanation before offering his own, thus leading her into refreshingly direct discussions. She found she so enjoyed his company—respected him, too, for he had such noble views.

She was near certain now that he was courting her—near certain because she truly had no idea how one went about a courtship—a true courtship, that was. Not one the likes of which Lord St. John had embarked upon. That, she thought grimly, had been little more than a business proposal of sorts, with herself as the article of trade. She was heartily thankful that Christian had responded to her brother's missive, for she could never have borne Lord St. John as a husband. Never.

Mayhap she wouldn't have to.

Hope surged, and she smiled softly, releasing the drapery. She made her way back to the bed, slipping beneath the cool blankets, and closed her eyes, unable to think of anything other than Christian. He was everything she'd imagined he would be and more, gentle but strong, thoughtful yet amusing. God had surely favored her, she reflected happily, for to her mind he was as noble a soul as ever had existed upon the face of the earth. More so than the heroes of legend, for Christian was flesh and blood, and *he* had come to her rescue even after having been so wronged by her father.

Aye, he was her knight in shining armor come to save her from the cruel and ruthless world . . . and she . . . she was the damsel in distress for whom he would battle friend and foe in the name of love.

Love.

Mayhap it was possible after all.

Sighing wistfully at the fanciful notion, she sent a hasty thank you heavenward and snuggled deeply within the blankets.

Please, Lord, she prayed, *if this is a dream, don't let me wake.* Sleep discovered her smiling serenely.

"Please! oh, please!"

A harried sigh was Amos's response, together with a most disapproving scowl as he rifled through the morning's correspondence. He chose a particularly large envelope, tossing the rest aside, and sprawled backward within his big chair, hiding behind the envelope, as though to escape her.

She wasn't about to give up. "Please," she beseeched him. Still he sat, peering over the top of the envelope, his green eyes, so like her own, glittering with annoyance. Jessie suppressed a shudder at the cold feeling that swept over her. "Just this once," she pleaded. "And I'll not ask again—I swear it!"

He tore open the envelope with a vengeance, sighing a masterful reproduction of their father's disapproving lament. "Very well, Jessamine. Do as you wish. Extend our invitation to the miscreant." He didn't bother glancing up. "Tomorrow eve, if you must."

Jessie stepped away from the desk in surprise, eyeing her brother with disbelief. "Yes?" Her voice caught with glee. "You said . . . *yes*?"

Amos gave her his full regard at last, though his expression was liberally laced with resentment. "Can you not hear, girl? Yes! Do! Invite the cur to dine with us, if 'tis your wish, but leave me be just now!" Unfolding the doubled parchment he'd extracted from the envelope, he apprised her, "And I shall hold you to your word; do not ask this of me again."

Wide-eyed with disbelief and too delirious to stop herself, Jessie hurried around the desk to give her brother an affectionate hug, the first such embrace to pass between them in years.

Amos recoiled from her at once. Grasping her upper arms, he peeled her from his person. "Jessamine! Jessamine, please! Recall yourself at once!"

Jessie retreated, stung. "Yes, yes, of course. I . . . thank you, Amos. I don't know what came over me," she said as stoically as she was able, and then turned to go, her eyes misting. She didn't know why it should surprise her so each time he rebuffed her, yet it never failed to do so. And yet, this once, she had a concession from him, at least. She refused to feel dispirited.

He'd not always been so heartless, and she couldn't help but ponder what could have changed him so—though she had a very good notion as to what it was. Their father. Always it came back to their father. Francis Stone had lived the most unapproachable of lives, and Amos, in trying to prove his worthiness, was fast becoming a perfect replica of him.

Her older brother, Thomas, who'd been two years Amos's senior, had been their father's indisputable favorite. Poor Amos had lived in the shadow of that fact, trying so very hard to measure up, even unto the end. All for naught; after word had arrived of Thomas's death, their father had simply lost the will to live. *She and Amos had not been enough to keep him.* It had happened so quickly that Jessie sometimes wondered whether her father's death had, indeed, been a *natural* passing. But then, just as quickly, she discarded the ugly notion. His physician had declared it to be his heart, and that's what Jessie wished to believe.

Though now it confounded her that her father had worried Amos would never measure up to the title, for Jessie thought Amos was more like Francis Stone than any of his three children—Thomas included. Aye, like their father, Amos would take pains to insure his victory, she knew. But in this matter of her life, Jessie vowed to fight him unto the very end.

She found herself smiling, for at least she had tomorrow evening. For that she had her brother to thank. He didn't like to lose, she knew, but mayhap in time he would come to forgive her. If he saw that she was happy . . .

She was miserable.

God forgive her, but she had the most overwhelming desire to turn her goblet of good Madeira over Eliza's gaping bosom. There was absolutely no denying it, the evening was a miserable disaster. Jessie had hoped her brother would come to admire Lord Christian as she had, but that was not to be.

Eliza, to the contrary, seemed to have taken to him *quite* well, she thought sullenly, and if she continued to admire him so openly, she'd cause Amos's antipathy to wax irreversible this night!

Amos sat in resolute silence, regarding—or rather, disregarding—their guest with an air of disaffected aloofness, while Eliza never averted her eyes from him, even for an instant. Understandably, it was becoming more and more difficult for Amos to retain his air of indifference. Jessie's sole comfort was the fact that Christian seemed not to note any of the tumult surrounding him. That, or he simply could not be offended.

"M'lord," Eliza purred, taking a dainty sip from the finely etched crystal goblet she held. She waved the glass beneath her nostrils, sniffing deeply of its sweet contents. "You haven't said what it is, precisely, you plan to do with... your new estate." She leaned further, swinging her goblet airily. "You will refurbish it, of course, but have you decided upon a particular design as yet?"

Christian's gaze shifted from Amos's choleric face to that of his beautiful, simpering wife. "I'm afraid I have not, Countess, though tell me... have you an interest in that sort of thing?"

If he truly wished to avenge himself upon Westmoor, Amos's flirty little wife was extending the perfect opportunity. *If it weren't for the simple fact that he found her golden good looks and rehearsed elegance quite irksome at the moment.* God's teeth, for the pained expression upon Jessie's face, he wanted to strike her dumb—he who had never laid a finger upon any woman in anger.

"Oh, yes!" Eliza assured breathlessly. "Perhaps, my lord, you might even find me"—She smiled prettily, puckering her lips in blatant invitation—"of some assistance when the time comes?" She cocked her head suggestively. "We *are* neighbors, of sorts, after all?"

"Perhaps," Christian yielded, his lips curving. "Perhaps I shall, madame." His gaze returned to Jessie, and he found her expression apologetic. He smiled, reassuring her. Her features softened in response, and his heart squeezed. 'Twas inconceivable that she should look at him so adoringly. Incomprehensible, and God help him, he found himself reluctant to tear his gaze away.

"What I would like to know," Amos interjected, his tone bursting with rancor, "is how you intend to finance such a venture. Correct me if I am mistaken, sirrah, but you haven't the first resource from which to draw the necessary funds to undertake such a monumental task—less to complete one!" Provoked by Christian's inattention, he persisted, " 'Tis my understanding that Rose Park is just short of desolation, sir, a miserable estate, if ever I've seen one."

Tearing his gaze away from Jessie, Christian arched a brow. Rose Park might not be the grandest estate, but it was his now, regardless that some would say he'd gained it by disreputable means. His lips turned faintly at the corners. "So then, you have seen the estate?" He smiled, knowing bloody well Stone had not personally set eyes upon the property—his whoreson agent had.

"Well," Amos dissembled, glancing warily at his sister and taking a deliberately casual bite of his lemon-seasoned sole. "Not precisely . . . Let us simply say I have it from a very reliable source—but you have yet to answer my question, Haukinge. Have you the funds?"

"Amos," Jessie interjected, "perhaps 'tis none of our concern?"

Back to the business of championing him, was she?

Christian watched as Amos turned to pierce his sister with a frown. *Bastard*. His gut wrenched. Well . . . perhaps this time she might appreciate reinforcement. Christian, for certain, had digested more than enough for one evening. He waited until Amos was finished berating his sister and then met and held his gaze. It was curious how similar in color his eyes appeared to Jessie's . . . and how very different. Hers fairly sparkled with life and warmth, while Amos's were cold and removed. Wholly devoid of compassion.

"Well, now, I'm afraid I must disappoint you," he said. "While 'tis certainly true I've no real English assets—"

"Why, of course you do!" Jessie argued in defense of him. She glared at her brother. "You've Rose Park!" She gave him a fleeting nod and then turned once more to glower at her brother, daring to rebuke him on Christian's behalf.

Christian nearly laughed outright at the militant expression she wore—*the vixen*. He found himself wishing, not for the first time this night, that she were sitting beside him, not across the blasted table. What he wouldn't give just now to take in the essence of her beside him, inhale it into his soul. The thought alone aroused him.

"So I do," he relented, chuckling low. "Though as your brother can attest, Jessamine, Rose Park cannot as yet be considered an asset, per se. It is, in fact, a liability at present, though rest assured. Simply because I've no English land to speak of is not to say I've no assets at all, and Rose Park shall not remain a liability for long."

"Truly?" Eliza asked, intrigued now in earnest. "How very exciting!" She cast Amos a tight little smile, and then turned to regard Christian with slitted eyes. "I doubt my husband was aware of that fact, m'lord. Do tell us more. I do so enjoy discussing one's . . ." Her gaze slid to her husband as she emphasized with raised brows. ". . . *assets.*" Leaning seductively forward, she managed to display a sight more of her abundant cleavage.

Christian choked upon his Madeira.

Amos puffed visibly with impotent rage.

So, too, did Jessie, though rage, it seemed, was too mild a word for what she was experiencing.

She was saved from having to squander her good Madeira when Amos coughed rather indiscreetly. 'Twas evident Eliza had forced her brother beyond his limits. He rose abruptly, raking his chair backward as he stood, and went directly to his wife. He lifted her perforce from her chair, and didn't bother to excuse himself; rather, he simply dragged Eliza from the room. Their snarling voices trailed them all the way down the corridor, and up the spiraled stairwell.

Jessie was both relieved and mortified. Risking a glance at Christian, she found him smiling charitably. "My lord, I'm so sorry!" she exclaimed at once. "Truly! I never thought it would turn out so." And then her face fell, for who did she think she was fooling? How else could the evening have ended, considering Amos's animosity toward Christian? "I'm sorry," she said once more, feeling guilt acutely.

His smile deepened, putting her at ease. "No need." His eyes sparkled with good humor. "I rather suspect your brother's wife is in dire need of whatever it is he is about to give her."

Jessie laughed softly. "I assure you, Eliza can be quite difficult, but Amos would never harm her. He's not a brutal man. In truth, I sometimes wonder if he feels anything at all. He's so—"

"I wouldn't be too concerned," he broke in. "In fact, I would venture to say he's feeling a wealth of emotions just about now." Lifting his goblet of Madeira, he swirled the contents, raising it casually to his lips. Jessie found herself staring as he quaffed the last of it. Her gaze returned to his monstrously wicked eyes; they were so dark a blue and fairly twinkled with devilment. And then again, her gaze fell to his lips and she found her breath strangled. His mouth curved into a devastating smile, and something fluttered deep within her—a feeling not wholly unfamiliar to her these days.

"At any rate, I believe your sister-in-law has a little surprise in store," he said softly, his tone hinting at something . . . something, though she had no idea what. And yet, that same something within quivered at his words. Suddenly she didn't know what to say. After conversing about everything, from philosophy to freckles, she found herself dumbstruck in his presence.

"Are you, er, finished, my lord?"

"Finished?"

"With your meal?"

"Ah . . . yes, thank you. I believe I am. And you?"

Jessie nodded, her heart pummeling against her ribs. The richness and depth of his voice never failed to affect her. He rose abruptly and came about the table, halting at her side to proffer his aid. "Allow me to assist you, then," he offered gallantly.

Her heart was vanquished so easily.

She gave him a shy smile and then her hand, her gaze never wavering from his magnificent face. "Thank you, my lord," she whispered. She stood, grateful for his assistance, for she felt disconcertingly giddy this moment—and it was not the Madeira, she was certain, for her goblet remained filled to the brim.

"M'lady?"

Startled by her maid's diffident inquiry, Jessie spun toward the door. At her despondent expression, Jessie's brows collided. "What is it, Hildie?"

"Well . . . 'tis like this, mum." Hildie's eyes skidded uncertainly to Christian's imposing form, then again to Jessie. Seeming to have mustered her courage, she stated more firmly, "His lordship won't be returnin' to the table; he bade me tell you . . . well, you see, 'e's requested Lord Christian . . ." Her gaze shifted once more to their guest. "Well, mum, that 'e's to leave straightaway."

Jessie's spirits sank. "So early?"

"Sorry, mum, but that's what 'e said."

"I know, Hildie, I didn't mean—thank you." Instead of leaving them, Hildie lingered in the doorway, waiting nervously. "You may go now, Hildie," Jessie directed, though not unkindly.

Hildie shook her head. "Oh, no, mum, I can't! His lordship also said I was to stay wit' ye until the—er, ah . . ." She glanced discreetly at Christian, looking quite anxious. "Until *he* was off and away."

"Jessamine," Christian said, " 'tis past time for me to go." He squeezed her fingers tenderly, and it was only then that Jessie realized he was still holding her hand. She stood there, gaping stupidly. What must he think of her to be so bold? He bent to whisper in her ear. "Don't look so glum, love . . . I assure you I am not so easily offended." He winked at her then, and Jessie's heart turned over. More than anything, she wanted him to stay, but she had little choice in the matter. Amos had requested that he leave, and Jessie had absolutely no say in her brother's home.

Reluctantly, and without another word, she escorted him to the door, opened it, and leaned into it as Christian moved past her. He stepped out into the balmy night, and there, on the topmost step, he paused, and turned to face her. The intense look in his deep blue eyes snatched her breath away.

What if she asked him to stay? to meet her in the garden? Would he agree? Lord forgive her, but she wanted to ask that of him more than anything. Was she mad? Truly she had to consider the possibility, for she was certainly not herself these days.

"My lord," she began, disheartened to see him go so soon.

He placed a finger to her lips, shushing her, as though he knew what she would ask and sought to save her from herself. She swallowed the rest of her words as he leaned forward, brushing her mouth with his warm, velvety lips. He kissed her, and the world ceased to exist for the space of an instant.

He kissed her.

Closing her eyes, Jessie inhaled sharply at the intimate contact, moaning softly. Sweet heaven, he'd kissed her. If she thought her heart raced before, it pounded fiercely now. Lord, how she longed to draw him back again . . . to feel that quickening within her . . . to breathe in the heady, masculine scent of him.

Her eyes remained closed long after his lips had left her own.

"Good-bye, Jessamine."

She opened her eyes and blinked to find he was standing apart from her now, regarding her with heavy-lidded eyes and a somewhat rueful smile.

"Good . . . night," she whispered, her voice catching. Something about the way he'd spoken his farewell made it seem so final, and her heart twisted.

Giving her a brief salutory nod, he turned from her, and she watched him disappear into the shadows. Not until he was gone did she close the door to face her indignant maid.

Chapter 5

‿‿◠◯◯◠‿‿

When Jessie woke the next morning it was raining, scarcely more than a cooling mist, but enough to cast the day in gloom. It didn't matter. She was too happy to care.

Dressing carefully in anticipation of Lord Christian's daily attendance, she chose a deep forest green gown, one adorned with stark white lace at the neckline and sleeves. It seemed he was partial to green, for he complimented her grandly every time she wore the color.

Much too anxious to eat, she breakfasted on tea and a mere scrap of biscuit, then made her way into the library to find herself a book to read while she waited. Because it was still raining, she remained in the library as it was nearest to the front door. That way she'd be certain to hear the knocker when Christian called.

Never in her life had she bestowed so much hope upon one person.

Oddly enough, this morning Amos seemed resigned to Lord Christian's attendance at Westmoor . . . though truthfully, that gave her pause for thought. She could only attribute it to the fact that he and Eliza seemed to be reconciling themselves to one another after last night. Really, the two seemed a pair of ridiculous lovebirds—to go from one extreme to the blessed other? Jessie could scarcely fathom the difference between them this morn. She shook her head in utter bewilderment. Merely a week ago, neither of them would have spoken so much as a civil word to the other, yet the two had made sheep's eyes together all throughout breakfast. Who'd have imagined? It really didn't matter how they'd achieved it, Jessie was delighted for them—more so for herself.

By late afternoon, however, her joy had diminished somewhat. She'd managed to read full half her book before growing weary of it. When the print began to blur before her eyes, she snapped it shut, unable to concentrate upon a single letter, let alone make out the words. In truth, she wouldn't have been surprised to discover she'd been reading the volume upside down, so little did she recall of what she'd perused. She looked then, just to be certain, and was relieved to find it right side up.

Halfheartedly she skimmed another, but the truth was that she was bored silly, anxious, and a little bit disappointed he was coming so late.

What if he didn't come back at all? What if he'd changed his mind about courting her?

Sighing wistfully, she turned her thoughts to the kiss Christian had bestowed upon her last eve; she was at once encouraged by the memory. As though to savor it still, her fingers brushed her lips, caressing them absently in remembrance. His warmth somehow lingered there. She closed her eyes, and her heart thumped wildly.

She hoped, dear Lord, she hoped.

She wanted this so very much.

She started guiltily when the door to the library creaked open, and her hand flew from her mouth.

Eliza entered, her expression somewhat smug. Shutting the door behind her, she leaned against it. "Still waiting?" she said with an affectation of a sigh.

Jessie's stomach turned, for she recognized Eliza's mood.

"Really," Eliza carried on. "Even should Lord Christian *wish* to wed you, I should think you'd desire better for yourself, Jessamine. The man is a miscreant, after all."

Jessie bristled. "Why? Because he's a younger son?" God's truth, she'd never been anything but sympathetic to Eliza's plight, but of late her brother's wife had become implacable in her resentment. "What sin is there in that, Eliza? Amos, too, was a younger son once upon a time," she pointed out. "Though how convenient for him—*and for you*—that Thomas perished when he did." She couldn't help herself, Eliza's condescension grated upon her nerves.

Eliza's face flushed as she came forward, angry now. "Lord Christian is naught but a debaucher of women!" she retorted. "Mark my words, Jessamine, for I'll warrant he'll not stay overlong!"

Something in Eliza's expression gave Jessie pause. "Perhaps you know something I do not?"

Her stomach floated a little, for Eliza seemed to think on the question too long. And then Eliza narrowed her eyes, and her expression lost all trace of pretense. "I came to advise you, Jessie, so listen well ... You're fair enough, 'tis true, but Amos isn't foolish enough to give you a dowry to wed the likes of *that* man. Penniless, you'll be nothing to Lord Christian. Your brother knows it, too. Why else do you think he'd agree to such a farce, if not in hopes that once you discover the truth, you'll wed Lord St. John without further ado? I came to tell you that you're making a blessed fool of yourself!"

Jesse blanched. "Amos swore to me. I didn't expect much, but he promised. He'd not betray me so! I don't believe you."

"Now, who do you think sent me here?" Eliza asked, lifting her brows. "Amos would see Westmoor prosper, dear. If you must, then go ask him."

The ensuing silence was excruciating, for the

truth weighed heavily upon Jessie's heart.
Amos *would* do anything it took to win, she
knew. Even as a lad, he'd fought his battles
ruthlessly. Good Lord! She should have realized when she'd managed to convince him to
reinstate the betrothal that he'd only done so
because he'd never intended to play fair. Her
brother never gave anything willingly. She
should have known, and yet she'd been
blinded by hope.

As though she'd not already said enough,
Eliza broke in once more. "Do what you will,
say what you must, dear, charm Lord Christian to your heart's content. Though I fear I
must caution you . . ." She glanced pointedly
at Jessie. "You must *endeavor* to keep your virtue intact."

Jessie's intake of breath was audible. "How
dare you!"

Eliza offered a self-satisfied smile. "Obviously you take my meaning. You see," she
continued coldly, "Lord Christian will *not*
have you without a dowry, and I doubt even
Lord St. John, who is silly with lust for you,
would embrace a *soiled* wife. Unlike the others,
he'll take you penniless, but not despoiled.
He's much too proud a man."

Jessie rose from the chair. "How dare you
speak such things to me!" Her eyes stung with
tears. "You above all! Good Lord! Were it such
a simple matter as a mere lack of affection, I
might wed Lord St. John without a backward
thought, but I can barely tolerate the man!

He's old enough to be my father!" she added, somewhat hysterically.

Eliza simply shrugged. "As I've said before, *love* has little to do with anything. 'Tis a simple task to lie back and think of"—she offered a long-suffering smile—"more pleasant diversions. Really, I've no idea why you persist in this, Jessamine. Marriage is a contract, nothing more." She met Jessie's gaze. "Think, when has love *ever* had aught to do with anything, at all? Take Amos and me for instance . . . We've no affection between us at all, and we suit perfectly well."

Jessie's heart twisted painfully. "Do you, really?"

"Now, dear," Eliza advised balefully, "you might go into this union willingly, with your brother's blessing . . . or with his fury upon your head, though I daresay he shall prevail. Best you realize, at last, that he'll not be swayed in this matter. He *needs* this affiliation. *We* need this affiliation."

"He cannot make me wed if I am not here for him to command! Now, can he?" Jessie countered, feeling trapped, panicking. She hadn't meant to say it, but it was out now, and she found she meant it fiercely.

Eliza's brows lifted in amusement. "No?" She laughed softly. "And where else would you be if not here at Westmoor? Really, dear! Don't be addlepated!"

Jessie sat a little straighter. "Charlestown! I shall go to Father's cousin!" If she could but send a missive to the colonies, alerting her father's cousin of her arrival, then he would surely give her refuge against her brother. There was little love lost between the two, after all.

Eliza rolled her eyes. "Really, and how do you presume to accomplish such a feat? How would you go?" she asked. "Fly with the wind, perhaps?"

It was a very good question, though Jessie wasn't about to admit as much to Eliza. At the moment, she almost resented Lord Christian for leaving her to worry so. God's truth, she didn't know what she'd do without him. Swallowing the bile that rose in her throat, Jessie composed herself and said with as much aplomb as she was able, "I'm sorry you were forced into wedding my brother, Eliza . . ." Her limbs felt liquid as she moved toward the door. "But why you seem to fault me for it, I shall never know."

Eliza blinked at the accusation.

"You might inform my brother," Jessie added smartly, when she reached the door, "that if he persists with this—this—travesty of a union, he shall, indeed, have earned my hatred! As to Lord Christian, he will return, I assure you. I'll not marry that vile Lord St. John!" She opened the door and slammed it shut behind her, and prayed to God she spoke the truth.

Jessie Stone was blameless.

For two miserable weeks Christian kept himself otherwise occupied so as not to call at

Westmoor. He'd rebuffed every attempt Amos had made to contact him.

This morning he'd saddled one of his brother's Arabians, telling himself he meant only to ride.

The one blessing of this ill-begotten sojourn was that Philip and his nagging wife were not in residence. He'd made it a point to learn his brother's schedule and had bristled to hear that the place that had once meant so much to him was used so bloody little. It burned his gut, and only served to prove that Philip had taken his one and only bequest simply because he could. So much for putting his brother from his life.

God, what was he doing here?

Damned if he didn't have better things to do.

Such as securing a base port for his orphaned ships.

He clenched his teeth at the thought.

Word had arrived from Le Havre that one of his ships, the *Belle Terre,* had come into port there, and that the authorities had come aboard. While he'd been assured everything had been found in proper order, the officers of the vessel were now being interrogated. Procedure, he'd been told. Yet the thought of his men in the hands of the haughty French officials unsettled him—despite that he trusted his crew implicitly—mostly because after this incident, his ships would need to stay clear of France. At least till he discovered the cause behind this surprise inspection. Doubtless *some-*

one had pointed the finger at him, though *who* it was, he couldn't fathom.

The list of possibilities was endless.

'Twas fortunate that France supplied so little of his illicit trade. Most of what he procured there was transported quite legitimately indeed. As was the case with his English wares, but it was an inconvenience at least.

At worst it was treachery.

The drizzle that had plagued him most of the day had subsided, and the scent of wet loam rose with the heat-mist, lingering in the air, filling the senses. It was a familiar odor, though not a comforting one, for it forced Christian to consider his losses. Soothing to him was the scent of the sea; salt-mist so thick, it could be tasted upon the wind. Aye, he could nearly smell it now. He lapped at his lips and could almost taste the spray.

He closed his eyes, diverting his thoughts.

Soon enough, he'd be back aboard the *Mistral*. Even now, the ship was being prepared for his return. His lips curved as he thought of his newest acquisition. She was, by far, the largest of his vessels, a beautiful but costly ship made of sturdy live oak, and he counted himself fortunate to have her. The demand for well-crafted vessels was high, and Carolina-wrought ships were sought most of all for their exceptional durability. Their workmanship was unsurpassable. The *Mistral* was one such prize.

In his absence, she was being coated with pitch and tar; she'd be scoured and repainted.

Hell, he'd even commissioned stained glass for his cabin windows—extravagant, aye, but he spent far more time aboard his vessels than anywhere else, and he'd have one place for himself that didn't scream of meagerness. He inhaled deeply, anticipating his return, and the scent of sodden earth jolted him rudely from his pleasures.

At some point during the course of their first visit together, he'd concluded that vengeance against her brother was pointless.

Jessie would doubtless be the one to suffer its consequences, and the last thing he wished was to hurt her. After his last evening with her, he was more determined than ever not to wound her sweet little heart.

She deserved more.

So much more than he could offer her.

Christ, but he'd managed even to convince himself that he'd never intended to follow through with her brother's asinine proposal to begin with, that curiosity, and curiosity alone, had prompted him to accept when he should have spat in the bastard's face instead. And having convinced himself of that much, he'd determined never to see her again. His curiosity had been appeased, after all, and there was simply no point to it.

He couldn't have her.

Didn't want her.

Of that, too, he endeavored to convince himself.

It hadn't quite worked that way. Like some besotted youth, he'd gone to see her again and again—even after that wise decision had been arrived at—bloody fool that he was! Who'd have figured he would find the chit so damned engaging?

Damn.

Grimacing at the turn of his thoughts, he focused upon his commerce once more.

Nay . . . England would never do as a safe harbor. There was no way he'd bring his ships anywhere near her with illicit cargo aboard. Even if he could pull it off, he wanted no trace of scandal to mark his future here.

Concern not for himself, but for his heirs, of course.

Perhaps the West Indies—or even Charlestown would do . . . though Charlestown had never really been a smuggler's haven.

The image of a black-haired child rose up to taunt him . . . hair as silky soft and shiny as a raven's wings, a daughter with eyes so luminous a green, they made his heart melt with a single glance.

His heart squeezed with a longing so keen, it was physical.

Snarling in self-contempt, he sawed the reins.

The truth was that the cab he had ordered had long since arrived. Nothing more required him to keep residence in this godforsaken place—certainly it wasn't fond memories that kept him. He'd written off the estate long ago. Along with his relationship with Philip, he'd banished every last trace of his former life from his heart.

So then, he was left with only one explanation for his lingering.

Jessie Stone; he was reluctant to leave her.

Now that he'd made her acquaintance, he found he could not so easily put her from his thoughts, or his life.

He felt some measure of responsibility for her father's death, he told himself. He'd never expected the man to be such a weak-kneed, feckless fool. Nor had he ever expected to feel any remorse. Yet as much as he'd like to deny it now, he felt duty-bound to look after Jessamine's welfare. He'd purposely set out to devastate both her father's name and his resources.

And God damn him to hell, he'd succeeded.

What he hadn't counted on was the man losing a son, as well, and then taking his life over his losses. It had merely been his intention to give Francis Stone a small taste of what he himself had been dealt.

The man had proven a weak-minded fool.

And God's teeth, why the devil should he feel guilty for it?

He shook his head in self-disgust, his jaw working, for the fact was that he did. Pivoting his mount about, he headed towards Westmoor, ignoring the warnings that sounded like foghorns in his head.

God damn him, but he had the distinct feeling he was going to sorely regret this.

Jessie marveled that no matter how oft the colt was brought outdoors, it reacted as sur-

prised and delighted with the warm sun upon
its back as it had upon its first outing. The instant she detached the leading rein, it darted
away, bucking and twisting in a dance of eu-
phoria. Then suddenly it stopped, ears perked,
only to dance again without warning. She giggled softly at its antics. There was no question
that the animal was altogether enchanted with
life.

She only wished she were, too.

Her knight in shining armor had become a
somewhat tarnished figure.

Nearby, the dam stood nibbling at the grass.
Every so oft she'd glance up to eye the colt,
and nicker softly as though to reproach him—
a useless gesture, for the colt merely dismissed
her gentle rebuke, and her whinny managed
only to attract Mrs. Brown's attention.

Mrs. Brown, the old goat, had been a faithful companion to many a brood mare, and
seemed to have grown particularly fond of the
stable's newest addition. The faithful animal
seemed content as long as she had something
to nibble, grass, leaves . . . the mare's mane or
tail. Jessie smiled. Once, even, the goat had
managed to swallow a goodly portion of her
skirt before she'd even realized it stood behind
her.

Just now, Mrs. Brown's ancient face appeared between the fence slats, head cocked
inquisitively. As Jessie watched, the goat
shimmied beneath the fence to join her com-
panions. Hoisting herself up, Jessie sat upon
the fence-slat to watch the goat and mare sniff

proper greetings to one another. Afterward, as
though they'd shared some great parental confidence, the mare nodded and Mrs. Brown
turned to scrutinize the spirited colt with a
commiserative bleat. Despite her glum mood,
Jessie found herself smiling at the amusing
exchange, for they were not unlike a pair of
gossiping old maids.

Christian spied her at once, sitting upon the
stable fence, her back to him.

He didn't bother dismounting. She was so
enthralled with the young foal gamboling before her that she didn't seem to realize his
presence even once he was directly behind
her. She laughed suddenly, the sound low and
musical, and warmth spread through his
veins.

"Good morning, m'mselle," he said low.

She swung about, nearly toppling from her
perch upon the fence. "My lord!" Regaining
her composure, she cast him a reproachful
glance. "You startled me. However do you
manage to appear so suddenly?"

Christian swung down from his mount,
forcing levity, offering a wink and a smile. If
she asked him to leave, he didn't know what
he'd do. "My apologies if I've disturbed you,
chérie."

"Not at all," she said, somewhat aversely,
looking almost like a sullen child perched with
slumped shoulders upon the fence. There was
no chance, however, she could be mistaken for

a child, for her feminine wares were nothing if not conspicuous.

She turned away to watch the colt. "I wasn't expecting you," she said. "In truth, I thought perhaps you'd taken your leave of Hakewell, for 'tis been an age since I saw you last."

Christian felt certain she wasn't aware just how much she had disclosed with her carefully worded grievance.

"I simply had business to attend, is all," he lied, and hobbled his mount to the fence, then hoisted himself up to sit beside her, facing her, his back to the enclosure to better see her.

Devil hang him if she didn't have the most beautiful eyes.

They were his undoing.

"Didn't you miss me at all?" he whispered.

For a long instant she merely stared, and he could see clearly the confusion in her eyes. He'd done this to her, he realized. Without even trying, he'd begun to do her damage already. What more injury might be done if he stayed?

He should leave, he knew. It was the right thing to do, but he couldn't . . . wouldn't.

"I suppose I did, my lord," she confessed, and her eyes turned suspiciously liquid. He cursed himself roundly. She ducked her head, her cheeks flushing prettily, and Christian reached out to lift her chin with a finger. God's teeth, but one could be lost in those exquisite green melting pools.

Their gazes held.

He stroked her chin with his thumb. God only knew, he didn't deserve her assurance, but he needed to hear it, even so.

"I'm glad to know I'm not so easily forgotten," he said, his voice as gentle as a caress.

Jessie shivered, her breath catching softly at the intensity of his look. She gaped stupidly. His eyes . . . they seemed to be staring into the very depths of her soul . . . One brow rose slightly, and he smiled, a roguish smile, as he lifted her hand, placing it to his chest.

"Do this wretched heart o' mine a kindness," he whispered. "Tell me again, *chérie* . . . that you missed me . . ."

Jessie's heart skipped its normal beat. She prayed her blush wouldn't deepen and give her away. Of course, she had, so much so that some part of her had nearly died with grief in his absence. He might have sent word—might have told her that he intended to return. Rather than let her speculate and worry. Rather than leave her to fend off Eliza's smug "I told you so" looks. Her heart tripped painfully when his sensual lips broke into a grin, and she felt the telltale warmth creep down to the tips of her very toes. And yet she couldn't tell him what he wished to hear.

She couldn't let him see how much his inattention had hurt her.

How much his return meant to her.

She forced a lighthearted smile. "I-I was watching the colt."

He glanced over his shoulder at the animal in question, then turned again to scrutinize

her. Staring meaningfully into her eyes, he
whispered slowly, "Exquisite creature."

"Yes . . . yes, he is," she agreed.

His mouth quirked with amusement, and
she wondered what she'd said that was so
amusing. "The dam was a gift from my father," she explained, "the colt newly born of
her."

"Really?" His grin turned crooked. "That
was quite generous of your father, Jessamine,
but I wasn't speaking of the colt at all, you
see."

She was exquisite, Christian thought.

Her hair was caught today at her nape in a
brilliant yellow bow; a few of her dark, shiny
curls had found their way loose and now fell
in abandon, framing her lovely face. Her soft,
pale cheeks were flushed from too much sun.
In her bright saffron muslin gown she seemed
a ray of sunshine herself.

As though she only now grasped his meaning, her gaze fell demurely, and it was all he
could do not to lean forward and kiss those
soft lips as he craved to do. He had to remind
himself she was gentle born, not some dock-
side miss to be mishandled. For most every
second of the last two weeks he'd fantasized
about seeing her again, kissing her—a new experience to him, this idle daydreaming. He decided it had been much too long since he'd
lain with a woman, for even now he found
himself helpless to follow his baser instincts.
Her sweet innocence fed his lust; like kindling
to burning coals, it set him afire, brought him

to a full and painful arousal. He wanted to make her smile, he realized. He didn't relish seeing her this way.

"Jessie," he said, "I'm sorry if I've neglected you these past weeks . . . I wanted to come. I swear that I did. I simply couldn't." And it was the truth, nothing but the truth. "Forgive me?"

Jessie wanted to believe him, she truly did. He'd still not released her hand, she realized. She nodded at last, unable to deny him the words he wished to hear when he looked at her so. "Yes," she confessed softly, and her heart quickened painfully as he lowered his face to hers suddenly. "Yes, I do," she said.

He smiled. "Thank you," he said softly. "God's truth, but I thought of you every moment." He stared deeply into her eyes. "May I kiss you, Jessamine?" he asked suddenly, unexpectedly.

Her heart lurched, and she stammered, "Y-You wish to . . ."

"Kiss you," he finished. "Very much so . . ."

Jessie's heart pounded within her throat as he drew away a fraction, watching her with smoldering eyes. His covetous expression was her undoing. If she'd even harbored a thought of resisting, it was fled now. His gaze flicked provocatively to her lips, and he came forward once more, his hand touching her cheek as their lips met softly.

"I've craved this every moment we've been apart," he murmured.

God help her, but so had she . . .

Jessie ceased to breathe at all, and the shock of his lips upon her own prompted her to clamp her lips tightly shut. He made a sound, part chuckle, part groan, as though her absurd reaction had somehow pleased him, and then he cradled her face within his callused hands, pecking one corner of her mouth first, then the other, ending with the bridge of her nose.

Breathe! Jessie commanded herself. Breathe, ninny! But she couldn't, and then as his mouth lifted and descended once more, grazing hers, moving seductively over her trembling lips, molding insistently with her own, her unease quite literally vanished. With subtle but coercive pressure, he coaxed her lips apart, and liquid fire spilled into her mouth. Never in her life had she been kissed so exquisitely, so thoroughly. Indeed, never in her life had she been kissed at all.

"God . . . you are so lovely," he whispered into her mouth.

Jessie shivered as his tongue slipped boldly between her lips once more, the feel of it as erotically soft as warm, wet velvet upon her bare flesh.

She knew she should protest.

It was the right thing to do.

"I—"

"Hush, Jessamine," he whispered. "Don't deny me this . . . a kiss and no more . . ."

Chapter 6

Heaven help her, but she wanted this too. *A kiss and no more.*

Jessie was helpless to do anything but nod weakly as his tongue delved within the depths of her mouth. It was the most tender moment of her life. She was completely powerless to do anything but wrap her arm about his waist and hold on lest she melt from his embrace into a molten pool upon the ground. She could feel his warmth even through his coat, and his heart pounding against her own.

Abashedly she realized that her hand was exploring the breadth of his back . . . and worse, she was trembling. Mortified, she tried to still her quaking by pressing her hand more firmly against him. She was startled to find that his heart hammered fiercely, too. It was more than evident to her that Lord Christian had kissed many a woman in his life, and Jessie had been afraid he would find her wanting. And yet . . . if she wasn't mistaken . . . if she wasn't imagining, *he* was trembling, as well . . .

Or rather . . . it was his coat that trembled . . . Her brows drew together, for the movement seemed to commence . . .

She groped downward. At his coattail? Her curious fingers moved downward and encountered a warm, fuzzy face.

Mrs. Brown!

Understanding dawned, though even as she acknowledged the sloppy sound of Mrs. Brown chewing upon Lord Christian's frock coat, there was a sudden tug. It happened so quickly. Unwilling to take Jessie down with him, he released her at once and went flying backward. With wide, incredulous eyes, Jessie watched as he tumbled into the enclosure at her feet. Startled, the goat bleated and leapt away, a small morsel of Lord Christian's coattail still caught within her twitching mouth. Lord Christian, for his part, remained sprawled before her as dust settled upon his dark coat and breeches.

Prompted by his stillness, Mrs. Brown ventured back to glare down into his dazed face. He recoiled as she lowered her nose to sniff indignantly at him. Jessie couldn't help it; his dumbfounded expression brought a peal of laughter to her lips. All the tension of the past weeks dissolved at the sight before her.

"What is that?"

"That!" she told him, her voice strangled

with giggles. "That—" Lord help her, but she could not quite manage her hilarity, his expression was so comical. "That," she tried again, "is Mrs. Brown!"

"Mrs. Brown?" He eyed the goat balefully, and Mrs. Brown scurried away, decidedly uneasy with the look he gave her.

Jessie was teary-eyed with laughter when next he spoke.

"A bloody goat!"

"Yes, my lord." Jessie managed an appropriately sober nod, and reached up to dab her misty eyes with a finger, only to burst out laughing once more.

To his credit, he managed a chuckle as he admonished her, "If you'd not wished to kiss me, m'mselle, you might simply have said *no*." He arched a plaintive brow.

"But, oh," Jessie cried, her merriment rekindled. "'Twas so much more effective this way! Do you not think so, my lord?" She burst out laughing and Christian's hand darted out to catch her ankle. With very little effort, he snatched her down into his embrace.

Laughing, she tumbled down atop him. "My lord, nay!" she shrieked, scandalized, her gaze darting about.

"What?" he asked much too innocently.

Her laughter ended abruptly as his hand slid about her waist, securing her where she sat.

Her beautiful eyes wide with confusion, she had no notion what a tempting morsel she made, Christian decided.

Supporting their combined weight with one arm, he slowly compelled her forward. Her intake of breath was audible, and her breast rose enticingly with the effort, tempting him beyond reason, bewildering him so that he momentarily forgot his resolve merely to kiss her. Closing his eyes in an attempt to regain his composure, he caught the heady scent of lilacs—perhaps from a sachet secreted beneath her underclothing—and he was at once thankful for his tight breeches to conceal the evidence upon which she was so innocently perched.

Seeming to recover her senses, she squirmed, trying to remove herself from his lap, but his hand tightened about her arm, stilling her movements. He groaned and she froze, meeting his gaze. She tried again to rise, but with a firm hand to her back, he brought her forward for another kiss instead.

Ah, but Christ, he couldn't help himself.

He thought to make it brief, just a quick peck, but when his lips touched upon hers, and she parted them so sweetly for him, he nearly lost his will to stop. Her mouth was too warm, her breath too sweet. He kissed her hungrily, savoring the moment like a man starved.

When he retreated suddenly, Jessie felt the loss acutely and tried to draw him back. He murmured assurances as the rising breeze touched the moistness he left behind, sending shivers down her spine. Her breath stilled completely as his lips brushed against her throat. A shiver of anticipation coursed through her as he nibbled her there. Good lord, she knew she should make him stop, but she could no more do so than she could commence to breathe again. She whimpered as his fingers tightened about her arms, drawing her closer.

Shamelessly delighting in all he was doing to her, she arched backward as he continued to nip at her throat, but that instinctive movement did more to separate them than to bring them closer.

Christian's breath caught as he found his mouth at the level of her breast, a blatant invitation to his parted lips. He was so close now ... So many times he'd fantasized about loving her this way ... He closed his eyes, commanding what was left of his self-control. All he needed to do was move a fraction forward. Only a fraction ... and then suckle ...

But it would frighten her, he knew.

As much as he wished to believe she was wise to his needs, that she shared them—that she knew where this petting and fondling would lead—he recognized innocence when faced with it. She was too bloody naive to even know how to restrain her newly awakened passions.

Damn, but he wanted this.

His pulse quickening, he moved forward a fraction, and then cursing himself to blazes, shifted, moving away from the tempting morsel she offered. Somewhere in the back of his mind, he knew that if he didn't lift her from his person this very instant, she would soon discern the lump she was perched upon so unsuspectingly was no simple lump, at all. Worse, he might completely forget their surroundings and be tempted to make love to her here under the darkening sky.

She deserved better, he reasoned desperately, searching diligently for the impostor gentleman within—the one who seemed so eager to be all that she desired.

Perhaps the man had fled? He hoped, and yet, he felt inclined to seek him out once more.

They would doubtless be discovered before the first raindrops fell—which would be any moment if he scented it aright. He peered up at the sky.

If not that, then Mrs. Brown might decide to take exception to his loving her and nab his rear.

If not Mrs. Brown . . . then perhaps one of the other two occupants of the enclosure. The last thing he desired was teeth marks upon his arse . . . or pistols at dawn.

Or mayhap that was precisely what he wished.

To face a pair of barking irons.

Sighing regretfully, he caught Jessie with both hands at the waist—and fought the incredible urge to slide his hands upward, cup them about the tantalizing flesh she'd only just tempted him with.

Blast it all, he *was* going to sorely regret this visit. Tonight when he lay alone in his bed.

"I believe I scent rain," he said thickly, his

voice sounding strangled to his own ears. "Much as I've enjoyed this..." He eyed her meaningfully. "I fear I must be off before it pours, m'mselle." And then slowly, though reluctant to do so, he lifted her from his person, cursing roundly to himself as he did so.

Jessie nodded, though she seemed not to have heard a word he'd said. Christian knew the very instant she regained her wits because her face flushed a rosy pink. He couldn't quite bring himself to apologize, however, for he wasn't the least bit sorry for what little had passed between them today.

In truth, he might have preferred to have had something of which to be repentant. Still, he didn't wish to embarrass her more than she likely would be when she realized what liberties she'd allowed him, so he remained seated upon the ground and lifted a knee to conceal his amatory state.

When he made no move to rise, Jessie seemed to forget her chagrin at once, eyeing him solicitously. "Oh my! Are you hurt, my lord?"

Shaking his head at her naïveté, he chuckled ruefully. *Christ, but he was going to suffer tonight.*

"Here, let me help you!" She extended her hand in aid.

He waved her away, clearing his throat. "In an instant, Jessie. I'm just a wee bit ... *stiff* at the moment." He peered up at her, gauging her expression, and smiled grimly. "The fall," he suggested.

"But you're not hurt?" she asked, her tone filled with concern.

Enormously relieved that she'd not understood his lecherous jest, he said, "I assure you, m'mselle, I shall live." *To his misfortune*, he thought. At her doubtful expression, he rose as proof. "See." He grinned then, seizing her by the chin, and raising her face to place a perfectly chaste kiss upon the bridge of her nose. He turned her about so that she couldn't spy his arousal.

She seemed reassured, but even as she turned to smile up at him, the first raindrops struck her full in the face. She mopped them away with a sleeve, and laughed softly. "I do believe it *is* going to rain, my lord," she told him, her humor restored. "I commend your unerring nose." She bolted toward the gate. "Follow me!"

He didn't dare.

He waited until she was out of the gate and racing toward the shelter of the house before bothering to move. And then reluctantly, he scaled the fence. Seizing his reins, he mounted his horse.

Realizing at last that he wasn't following behind her, she halted abruptly, whirling about.

"Don't stop!" he shouted. "Get yourself to the house, lest you be caught in the downpour!"

She stood, nevertheless, rain soaking her, reluctant to leave him, sheltering her face with her hand. Instinctively he understood why, and it warmed his heart.

"I'll call again tomorrow," he swore, and then added, "My word!"

She smiled.

Wheeling his mount about, he cast her a backward glance. She was still watching, despite that it was raining harder now, and he pivoted his mount to face her. His steed pranced impatiently, eager to go.

He advanced upon her suddenly, and said impulsively, "Meet me by the brook . . . noon tomorrow?"

Her brow furrowed. "I . . . I don't know . . ."

"Noon," he said again, and prayed she'd refuse him.

She nodded and he smiled down at her, giving her a final salutory wink.

"Till then, my love," he said, and turned to leave before she could rethink the wisdom of what she'd agreed to.

Before his damnable conscience could intrude.

Chapter 7

❧⟋⟍❧

It proved a far from easy feat to keep her rendezvous with Christian the next afternoon.

Dressing hastily and for comfort, she stole away from the house, not daring even to secure a mount, lest her brother discover her destination and follow—or worse, prevent her from going.

Foolish mayhap, but Jessie knew she'd be in good hands once she was with Christian.

True to his word, he materialized by the brook precisely at noon—equipped for a picnic, of all things! Jessie was delighted that he'd taken the time to consider so much.

She'd worried for naught.

Once again they whiled away the hours conversing, and Jessie sighed contentedly as she listened to him. He was so wonderful, so very wonderful—magnificently handsome, too.

Languishing in the heat of the day, he'd removed his frock coat. It lay forgotten now upon the grass. His crisp white shirt, with its perfect pristine ruffles and folds, he wore recklessly unbuttoned at the neckline, long having discarded the stock. Jessie found herself staring at him more oft than not, powerless to dispel from her mind the burning memory of his kiss; it kindled a strange warmth within her every time she thought of it.

Plucking a small yellow blossom, she peered up at him through her lashes, praying he couldn't discern the wickedness of her thoughts. She twirled the bloom between her fingertips, wondering how long it would be before he would try to kiss her again.

Would he?

Did she wish him to?

Her cheeks burned as she acknowledged the truth, impossible as it was to deny. She'd broken the rules of propriety by coming alone to this secluded place without a chaperon. Why else would she have done so, but in hopes that he would kiss her . . . if only once more? She cast him another surreptitious glance, and her heart fluttered wildly.

God have mercy, she yearned for it, even, as one would hunger for food or thirst for drink, or even want for sleep. *She was consumed by the desire for it.* His kiss had somehow awakened some unfamiliar yearning within her, and even when she'd fallen asleep last eve, tossing and turning, it had not fled her.

Lord help her, she'd dreamed of him even then.

Seeing the adoring look in her eyes, Christian felt his stomach knot.

God's truth, but she seemed to see in him only what she wished to and nothing more.

What might she think if she knew him for what he really was? If she knew what base thoughts burned through his mind, what sordid desires slithered through his veins?

Christ, the things he wanted to do to her even now as she gazed up at him so worshipfully would shock her to her core. He could think of little more than taking her within his arms and initiating her beautiful body into glorious womanhood.

Only, for the first time in his life . . . there was something more than mere lust that compelled him. And still . . . His jaw turned taut, for it was merely a matter of time before she discovered his true nature.

She might as well know it of him now.

This moment.

Before he might be tempted to lay his heart at her mercy. And God save him if that ever came to be, for if he allowed it . . . she had it within her power to crush him beneath those precious feet of hers. Suddenly he felt the need to shock her. "What might you think, Jess, if I revealed to you that I was bastard born? Would you still look at me with such reverence?" The words had come bluntly, his tone hinting at all that was loathsome about his life.

A vision came upon him of himself as a superstitious peasant warding away evil with a makeshift cross. If it weren't such a pathetic image, he might have been amused. Was he so desperate to save himself from the devotion so evident in her beautiful eyes? Christ... they had the power to reach so deeply into his soul... so deep... the power to touch his very heart. Somehow... she made him want to be all that she believed of him.

All that he was not.

And more.

He couldn't hurt her, he realized. He *wouldn't* hurt her.

She looked stricken by the unexpected revelation. "Is it true?" she asked, sounding horrified.

He laughed derisively, casting her a dispassionate glance. "Aye."

"How—" She shook her head, refusing to believe it. "However did you discover such a thing?"

"It doesn't matter?"

"Of course it matters!" Her brows drew together. "They might have been lying, don't you see!"

Christian shook his head soberly, wondering belatedly over the wisdom in telling her such a thing. To reveal this, his darkest secret, was to open a vein for her to draw on. That someone other than himself and his mother— he refused to acknowledge the rest of his family—should possess the knowledge of his bastardy would make him vulnerable as he'd never been before.

"Nay, Jess."

She seemed dumbstruck, and then sputtered, "Y-Your father?"

He wasn't certain what it was she was asking. "Maxwell Haukinge?"

"Nay," she said softly, and looked disconcerted. "Does he know?"

He nodded, understanding. "Ah, well, yes . . . I believe he does." Something in her expression compelled him to go on. "Though, I believe he would as soon hang himself from the tallest masthead rather than defame my mother's good name. My captain, you see, is the man who sired me, and loved my mother."

For a long moment, there was silence between them. When she spoke again there was only concern in her tone, and he was warmed by it. "When did you discover the truth?"

He inhaled sharply. "As a lad. I didn't learn *who* until about a year ago." Gazing at her sweet face, he wondered why he felt compelled to drive her away when he craved more than anything the sweet fulfillment he suspected she could give him.

Try as he might, he couldn't find the answer.

"Please," she entreated softly. "Tell me of it . . ."

He cocked his brows uncertainly. Inconceivably, there was no condemnation in her voice, no loathing in her eyes. God, it felt so good to reveal himself to her. A strange calm threatened to steal over him, and for the first time in his life he felt he could trust, *truly trust,* another human being.

Plucking a grape from the platter before them, he pitched it at her. It fell halfway between them, and he retrieved it, pitching it again. "There's isn't much to the tale . . . nothing sensational to speak of." He went still, remembering. "I simply looked into his eyes and knew."

He shook his head and reached out to pluck another grape, placing it within his mouth. Plucking another, he fed it to Jessie. She accepted his offering with a sad smile, urging him, with her silence and her persuasive green gaze, to continue. Her eyes . . . God . . . how they seemed to reach into his soul and draw out the words, never mind that they'd never been spoken before now.

Uncomfortable with her scrutiny, he lay back upon the blanket, locking his hands behind his head, and peered into the treetops as he continued, "It was the strangest thing," he said, "but for the space of an instant, the years were stripped away from Jean Paul . . . and 'twas as though I were left gazing into a looking glass at my own reflection, blue eyes and all. Somehow, I just knew."

Staring past the lush greenery into the clear azure sky, Christian waited for her to speak—to say something, anything—words that would give him some small hint of how she felt about his shocking disclosure. When she said nothing for a long moment, he rolled to face her. Propping his head upon his hand, he stared into her eyes, hoping to see into her heart. What he saw there in the shimmering depth of her eyes gave root to his burgeoning sense of peace. Once again he felt compelled to go on; the need to purge himself of the blackness was strong, and it seemed that she, and she alone, had the ability to absolve him with her soul-cleansing gaze.

"My brother has gray eyes," he told her softly, "as did *our father*. My mother has beautiful brown eyes, so deep and dark, they seem almost fathomless. And I, well, I was the only one in the brood with eyes of blue—and God . . . at that moment, Jessie . . . looking into Jean Paul's face . . . his eyes . . . so many things became comprehensible at last."

"What sort of things?" Taking a grape for herself, she offered another to Christian, as he had done for her. He repaid her gesture with a lopsided grin.

"For one . . ." He took it, but placed it against her own lips, and smiled when she accepted it so easily. This ease between them felt good—better than anything had in all his years. "Jean Paul appointed himself guardian over my mother and me when first we took up residence with my grandparents in France—a fact that had always bedeviled me, that this man, so in love with the sea, would bind himself to a woman and child not his own. It made no sense at all."

"Do you think, perhaps, he did so out of guilt for his part in your mother's . . . predicament? She left England, I know. Only 'twas never known precisely why."

"She was banished by my father, actually—we both were." He glanced away, uncomfortable with the emotions that surfaced in that instant. "She was glad enough to go, I think. I always thought she was in love with Jean Paul, though for my sake she masked it well." His gaze returned to her, gauging her expression. Nothing. He could discern nothing. "For her parents, as well, of course; she would have spared them any injury." He plucked another grape, squeezing it gently, anticipating her reaction; veiled disgust, revulsion perhaps.

He was unprepared for sympathy. "How very sad. I'm so sorry for you," she whispered.

The grape burst, spurting juice everywhere. She cried softly, wincing as it sprayed her face. Wiping a droplet from her lip with a fingertip, she held his gaze, smiling wanly. Christian tossed the grape over his shoulder. Sympathy was not precisely the emotion he'd sought from her. "Don't be. I was rendered quite speechless by the discovery at the time, I assure you, but I've no contention in my soul over it a'tall. I welcomed the knowledge of Jean Paul as my father wholeheartedly, embraced it even, for it made so many things bearable."

"Truly?"

Their gazes met and held; stark blue and magical green.

Jessie's look was so compassionate, her eyes so luminous with concern, that Christian experienced the sudden inexorable urge to kiss her distress away, to assure her that he'd come away from it unscathed. Years of mistrust compelled him to say instead, "You must swear to me, Jessamine, that you'll never repeat a word of what I've revealed to you. I only wished you to understand that I'm not the exemplary man you think me." He lifted her delicate chin with a finger. "Every time you look at me, *ma belle vie*, I see . . . I see reverence. Trust me when I tell you I'm the very last soul upon this earth to deserve it."

"Nay! Never say so! You are—"

He lifted a finger to her lips. "Hush, my love," he commanded her. He brushed a wayward curl from her face. His fingers caressed her sun-flushed cheek, moving to the silky thickness of her hair, gliding through it reverently, catching finally at the blue satin binding that kept her wild curls so neat and tidy. He drew the ribbon free, releasing her glorious hair.

Without warning, he drew her down beside him and rolled atop her, pinning her beneath him in one easy movement. She didn't protest. Her breath caught and she cried out.

There was no fear in her lovely eyes, none at all, and relief surged through him. God help him, he doubted he could restrain himself much longer. This moment, he wanted more than merely to soothe his troubled spirit. He needed to appease his body's beastly hunger. He went about each day in a semiaroused state, and in her presence it became unbearable. What manner of hold did she have upon him that he would subject himself to such monstrous torture? That he would feel driven to protect her from himself? He wanted her so desperately that he actually ached with his need of her, and still he restrained himself.

Jessie knew she should object—indeed, knew she must. But Lord, how she wanted him to kiss her again! Her soul ached for it. Her mouth craved the feel of him.

Would he taste again as he had yesterday? A heady mixture of brandy and musky maleness that she'd savored again last eve while she'd dreamt of him. Even her body seemed to cry out for it now.

A knot formed in her breast, constricting painfully. Nay, she'd not stop him . . . she very much desired this—nay! needed it. Swallowing her dutiful words of protest, she let him move atop her, and sighed . . . What a wanton she was that she would allow him such wicked liberties.

Unbidden, Eliza's words invaded her thoughts. *Do what you will . . . say what you must. Charm him to your heart's content. But I warn you . . . keep your virtue intact.* As his lips touched her own, she began to quake. A single tear escaped, unnoticed, for he was kissing her at long last and did not see. It didn't matter, she didn't want him to stop—she'd die if he did. She clung to him as though her life depended upon it. And she thought that it might.

Feeling her shudders, he whispered softly against her throat, "Have no fear, *mon amour.*"

He stopped, peering down at her, and swore, "I shall take nothing you do not freely give."

Oh, but *that*, dear God, was precisely what she feared. This moment, everything she had was his to take—everything! She wanted to give him all that she had.

"Open your eyes for me, dearling."

She obeyed him, opening shimmering eyes. The hunger evident in his gaze made her heart fly into her throat.

"My God, but they are the rarest of jewels," he whispered softly, passionately. "You are . . . so lovely . . . so very lovely . . ."

His hand slid firmly to her waist, then to her hip, exploring . . .

Remembering the way she'd looked standing in the brook that first day, barefoot and wide-eyed, Christian hardened fully. A vision of slim calves and shapely thighs besieged him and a shudder coursed through him as he bent to kiss her lips once more, all the while gathering the hem of her gown into his fist, drawing it up to expose her beautiful legs to the warm, sultry sun . . . to his touch. Once again she'd forsworn her petticoats, and he whispered a prayer of thanks—ignoble as it might be—that she seemed to shun that one vestige of propriety. She wanted this, too, he told himself—and Christ! he thought he'd die without it.

Her hand flew out to stop his ascent—instinct, he thought, for she didn't end the kiss. Though he rarely prayed, he did so now, fervently. If she denied him . . . if she said nay . . .

that damnable part of himself would feel
honor-bound to stop. And God's teeth, he'd
not be able to bear it.

Her lips were soft, too soft, pliable, warm
creamy silk... He kissed her feverishly,
groaning in relief when she forgot about her
elevated skirts and her hands moved to ex-
plore his back. He smiled with fierce satisfaction as her fingers bored themselves
passionately into his flesh. God help him, he
battled the urge to strip her quickly and ravish
her where she lay. Damnation, but he couldn't
bear this maddening torture much longer.

He was no gentleman, for God's sake, no
saint, merely a man—*and not a bloody honorable
one at that!*

Sliding her skirts higher, he shifted upward, groaning as he pressed his aching anatomy into the sweet, warm hollow between her
thighs. She lifted against him, though timidly,
as though unsure of herself or her intuitive reaction to his blatant invitation, and he felt himself swell against her.

It was all the encouragement he needed.

She might not have understood the provoc-
ative inquiry, but her body certainly did. She
wanted this as much as he did... and who
was he kidding? *He'd love to oblige.* His tongue
swept into her mouth, moving as he craved to
do in other regions. She tasted of grapes...
smelled of lilacs, and woman... so fresh a
scent, so pure. Her body quivered beneath
him, and heat surged through his loins, tight-

ening them. Shoving aside the cautioning voice of reason, he set free the fiend within.

She was sweet . . . so sweet . . . too sweet . . .

Somewhere at the back of her thoughts, Jessie heard the voice that cautioned her to stop, but she knew she'd not heed it. She was lost, her body no longer her own to command. Her breath came in strangled gasps as Christian rocked seductively against her. Thunder stole into her heart. Instinctively she gave back motion for motion, feeling the hardness between them, and not truly understanding anything more than it gave her body pleasure to seek it.

Heat flowed, like warm honey, into the most secret core of her being. Her senses flowered, making her bold. Each time she pressed back, the return pressure deepened, until she could think of nothing but appeasing her body's sensational new hunger. Fully clothed, their bodies writhed together upon the blanket, off the blanket, rolled onto the fragrant green grass, undulating in time to some age-old inner rhythm.

It happened so quickly. Somehow, she came to be on top of him, and he stroked the back of her thighs beneath her gown. Her heart thudded to a halt when his fingers slid to her bare bottom, pressing her more firmly against him. Then, just as quickly as they had lit there, they slid between her slightly parted legs, skimming lightly over that hidden region below, now so filled with heat. A jolt of pure, delicious sensation burst through her, snatching her breath away, tightening her breasts till they ached.

As she buried her face into the crook of Christian's neck, Jessie's lips moved of their own accord upon his muscle-corded throat. He groaned, as though in pain, and it startled her so that she froze.

"Nay," he rasped, breathing heavily now. "Not now . . . don't stop now . . ." He pressed her face against the quickening pulse at his throat, urging her back into carnal oblivion.

Moaning softly, Jessie parted her lips against his heated skin, tasting him against her tongue.

"God . . . yes . . ."

She nibbled him as he'd done to her, and it drove Christian insane with lust.

His body quivering with restraint, he seized her hand, folded it tightly within his own. His senses dimmed by the inferno at his groin, he slid her fingers between their bodies where he most craved her magnificent touch, pressing her delicate little palm against himself suggestively.

He needed her now—God, but he had to have her! He was beyond reason. Too long he'd denied himself.

She was too sweet . . . too tempting . . .

Whimpering, Jessie swallowed the lump that appeared in her throat, yet she couldn't have removed her hand had she tried. She knew an overwhelming desire for completion. Though a completion of what? She had to know. A quivering seized her.

She trusted Christian, she reasoned. He'd saved her life ... and he'd surely save her from the rest of the world. He wanted her in the way that a man wanted a woman, and the knowledge made her lie eagerly before him. He would do nothing to harm her; she knew it deep down in her heart.

And he was giving her pleasure as she'd never imagined possible.

His lips seared her flesh, kissed her boldly. When he moved down, nibbling her breast through her bodice, she felt a shock of pure rapture seize her.

Whatever he would do to her, she would gladly allow it ... anything ...

Christian slid his hands up her skirts, and her shudders intensified. Beneath his callused fingers, her bottom felt like warm satin.

"Chr-Christian ..."

He shuddered at the sound of his name upon her lips. "Shush, dearling, *let me love you* ..."

Chapter 8

L et me love you . . .
   The plea seemed to echo through Jessie's very heart.

She adored him. He was her savior, her protector. Anything he wanted of her, she would give him willingly, gladly, madly . . . She was mindless with need for him, for all that his touch promised.

His hand found that place between her thighs, and he stroked it lovingly. Jessie's emotions worked with her body, spiraling her into oblivion. She could think of nothing but the sensations he was rousing within her as his finger slipped daringly within her, then stopped abruptly.

Christian froze, cursing roundly.

He'd known it was there, but had blatantly ignored the prick of his conscience. Now it shrieked at him like a banshee out of a mistral wind. She opened her eyes, silently questioning his hesitation, and the screeching intensified as she gazed up at him so expectantly.

Christ, he couldn't do this to her.

He couldn't do this to her!

She trusted him, respected him, saw only the good and honorable in him . . . and he . . . he couldn't fail her. Sweat slid from his brow as he reined in his lust—a near impossible feat, for he was nearly over the edge.

Still, he hung on, mentally haranguing himself out of his lascivious designs.

Damn . . . he'd asked that she meet with him here today for this very purpose . . . and she had come to him . . .

Still, she was an innocent, and *she* would be the one to pay if he accepted what she so willingly offered.

God curse him, he wanted to hurl caution to the wind; he hurt so badly. She needed him—he could see the passion in her luminous green eyes.

He clenched his jaw. She needed the release he knew he could give her. He needed to give it to her, by damn.

He intended to give it to her.

He stroked her body, gently but insistently, and felt her respond with abandon. Her face screwed in the most erotic expression he had ever had the pleasure of beholding, her eyes closed, her jaw clenched.

"I-I love you!" she gasped.

The unexpected declaration lashed him as soundly as a physical blow. Pleasure so keen, it was pain that shot through him, and yet he wanted her to speak it again, and again . . . and again. Working feverishly to bring the declaration to her lips once more, pleasuring her, he swore to deny himself, and suffered as he watched the rosy flush of sexual rapture blossom upon her cheeks. Her bottom lip caught firmly between her teeth and she concentrated so intently upon the pleasure that she drew the tiniest trace of ruby red blood.

Leaning forward, he lapped the salty droplet away, healing her mouth with his kiss.

He couldn't help himself; he kissed her eyes, then her nose, her mouth . . .

Again his conscience shrieked at him. She trusted him to keep her safe—safe from his lechery. He would loathe himself did he rob her of her virginity, her virtue. He would despise himself beyond bearing if he hurt her. His finger slipped within her body once more, as though to be certain, but the filmy barrier remained to taunt him.

He grimaced, shuddering.

Bloody damn, but he could not do this to her . . . Still, he could not leave her wanting either. Struggling with the needs of his own body, he worked to give her the release she required now, taking pains not to damage her maidenhead in the process. He'd brought her past the point of return, and it would be his penance to go without for himself.

His penance.

"Oh, my God!" she cried out, unaware that

she had, and then her body shuddered in release.

Christian, aching as he was, watched the emotions that played across her face, and felt strangely triumphant in that instant.

She lay unmoving for the longest while, her expression sullen, her eyes closed tightly against the brightness of the day.

A hand moved out of her skirts—Christian's, Jessie acknowledged with growing mortification.

She flushed as strong fingers smoothed down her garments, repairing them. Desperately she tried to understand what had transpired between them, but shame washed over her, warming every inch of her body.

Why could she not have listened to her conscience? *to Eliza?*

She could scarce bear to open her eyes and face him now. What must he think of her? Was she defiled? If not precisely defiled, what then was she? If she was now disgraced, what could she do? Never would she think to lay the blame upon Christian's shoulders, for she had silently invited him—nay, pleaded for him—to take whatever he would of her. Dear God, would he depart from her life now that he'd taken the only one thing of value she'd had to offer him? Eliza had said he would. She felt sick with dread. Confusion.

"Jess?"

Her eyes flew open to meet his. He was looking at her strangely. Was it pity she spied in his gaze? disgust?

Her voice failed her. She choked on her emotions. Did she really wish to know what he was thinking? His expression was such a peculiar one. Why had he come into her life? she wondered. Before she could stop herself, she asked him, "Why did you come, my lord?"

For an instant, Christian was taken aback by the innocent question.

The look in her eyes told him she had no inkling what it seemed she was asking. A rueful smile curved his lips, for he *hadn't*, didn't she know.

"I meant to say . . . I know . . . I know that my father—"

"I'd as soon not discuss your father," he snapped. His jaw worked, and then he said, softening the angry sting of his words, "If you don't mind . . . not now."

"O-Of course," she whispered. She closed her eyes.

Seeing her anguished expression, the way she turned from him, Christian felt his gut twist. After a moment, her long lashes fluttered open, and she turned to him, revealing shimmering green irises. He wanted so much to reach out and wipe the corners of her eyes with his thumb—before the regrets could come. He didn't think he could bear it if she cried. If possible, her eyes became greener, brighter, in the wash of unshed tears. Their gazes held, and then hers skidded away.

He swallowed the lump that tried to strangle the words into oblivion. "I came," he began, hating himself for being so callous with her feelings. She turned to him expectantly, her chin lifting, her eyes alight with hope as she awaited his response.

Ah, Christ . . . he had the greatest desire to kiss those eyes closed once more lest she discern the fateful emotions that warred so violently within him, to feel the silky curl of her lashes against his lips, to soothe away her troubles once and for all. She didn't deserve the grief that lay in store for her . . . the heartache he was sure to give her. Damn her brother for an uncaring ass. She needed someone to protect her.

The question was . . . could he?

When he was the greatest thing she had to fear?

"I'm—" His voice caught at her hauntingly tender expression. She went so still that he suspected she'd ceased to breathe altogether. God damn him to hell, the reassuring words would not come, no matter that he desperately wanted to speak them. "I'm not certain," he finished, shaking his head, gritting his teeth against the lie. Her shoulders slumped and her eyes swam with tears as he said again, softly, "I don't know why I came, Jessamine."

Bloody hell if he didn't.

Tossing down the last swig of his brandy, Christian poured himself another, emptying the second decanter for the night. Disgusted with himself, he set the snifter down and lifted the container, staring down into its crystalline depths as though somehow he might find the answers revealed to him amid the acrid-sweet fumes within.

What the devil was he supposed to have said to her? *I came, Jess, my love, because your whoreson brother offered me a tidy little sum to break your goddamn little heart?*

Turning the decanter, he examined the beautiful etchings, a delicate floral scrolling pattern. The extravagant bit of glass had graced Hakewell's library for as long as he could recall . . his father's . . . his father's before him . . . damn them all to hell.

Damning himself as well, he hurled the decanter at the lapping flames across the room, aiming too high; it struck the mantel with a deafening crash, shattering into a profusion of multicolored pieces.

He shouldn't care—had trained himself not to—but the simple truth was that he was fast losing his heart to the little twit. God's blood, but he should wed her and end the torture once and for all.

Wed her.

The thought wasn't altogether unappealing. Scowling, he resisted the urge to glimpse over his shoulder to be certain there wasn't some demon angel perched there, whispering noble suggestions into his ear. There was nothing noble about him, and he'd be doing her a disfavor, bringing her into his life . . . his world . . . his disgusting secrets . . .

Secrets that could destroy him.

Secrets that could devastate her.

The firelight cast the room in an eerie light, basking all it touched in deep orange-red hues. Squinting against the shadows, he slouched backward into the elaborately carved damask chair, surveying the room before him. Upon entering, he'd drawn the curtains to let in the muted afternoon light, but the sun had long since set and the night mist cast an opaque veil over the half-moon rising.

His gaze shifted from the window to the vast shelves of books occupying the far wall. This should have been his study. His, and not Philip's. Everything might have been different then, if only his brother had not stolen his birthright. Aye, for then he might have wed the late . . . great . . . son of a bitch's daughter all those years ago, without the dissent he was now plagued with.

Damn.

Retrieving the snifter from the desktop, he swirled the amber liquid within, envisioning his life as it might have been; the anger that might have been forsaken, the loathing he might not have felt . . .

He imagined coming home to sweet Jessie, imagined her waiting, tucked prettily between the sheets—their bed. He imagined taking her the first time, the second time, every time thereafter. His lust was rekindled just so easily, if indeed it had ever been extinguished; blazing white heat shot through his veins.

Christ, the ways he would have her . . .

God, what did he care what had passed before? what might have been? She still could be his . . . if only he might cease brooding long enough to ask for her hand in marriage.

And she needed him. St. John desired her for one reason, and one reason alone . . . because Christian had been denied her. It hadn't hurt matters much that she'd turned out to be such a beauty. Still . . . even were he not the reason . . . everyone knew the way St. John dealt with his women, bloody whoreson that he was. Why would a wife be treated differently? Christian felt an incredible violence stir within him, imagining St. John's hands upon her—anyone's hands, for that matter.

If he were to hurt her . . .

He couldn't live with it.

But what if Jessie's fool brother thought to deny him?

Again.

His eyes narrowed thoughtfully, for he'd simply have to see to it that Amos Stone didn't refuse him.

And what will you do if he doesn't cow? a voice within taunted. *Drive him to suicide as you did their father?* Clamping his jaw shut, he moaned low, as though to deny the nagging presence that was bent on giving him conscience.

He was what he was.

And if Jessie didn't wish to wed him . . . well, then . . . so be it. He could leave despising her for it, and all would be again as it was. Tossing down the last swallow of liquor, he shook his head, shuddering away the effects, and thrust the snifter none too gently across the mahogany desk. It slid, stopping just before plunging over the edge. It hung there, suspended, contrary to the laws of nature, more of it resting off than on. The sight of it wrung a wry smile from his lips.

Damned if he didn't feel as though he was going off the edge himself.

"Wake up," demanded a frantic Hildie. "Wake up, m'lady!"

Jessie lifted the covers over her head, shielding herself from her maid's scrutiny. She moaned. "Go away. I feel sick!" And it was true, for she'd spent long hours worrying herself that way over her appalling behavior with Christian. She'd practically thrown herself into his arms, after all. *She'd ensured her own ruin yesterday afternoon, and ruined, she was.*

"Sick?" the maid worried, gently shaking Jessie's tightly bundled form.

"Please . . . please, just go away!" Jessie felt like weeping. God's truth, but she never wanted to show her face again!

The maid sighed regretfully. "I would, lovey, if only I could, but ye've a guest downstairs to be attending. Amos said to fetch ye, will ye nill ye."

No, Jessie fretted silently. No, no, no—not Christian! She couldn't face him, as yet— didn't want to! A whirlwind of emotions swept through her all at once. She sat reluctantly, clutching the coverlet to her bosom. Shame descended upon her like a storm, and she worried that Hildie would discern the difference in her. Surely it would be apparent in her eyes. Her face? She felt as though her loss of innocence had somehow physically changed her.

She felt different.

"Lord Christian?"

Hildie shook her head regretfully. "Nay, m'lady. 'Tain't Lord Christian, at all. Come, now, up and dress yourself."

Her brows drew together. "Who, then?" Since their father's death, few had called at Westmoor. Even their closest acquaintances had ceased to visit after hearing the ugly rumors of Francis Stone's death, never mind that they were as yet unfounded.

Hildie mumbled something under her breath, and though Jessie hadn't heard a word of the maid's disclosure, her sorrowful expression made Jessie's suspicions rear. "Who is it that's come calling, Hildie?"

The maid peered at her anxiously. "Lord St. John, m'lady . . . all the way from Charlestown, he has."

Chapter 9

Christian's mouth felt parched. His head ached—effects of the liquor, no doubt, though perhaps in part it was also a result of the momentous decision he'd come to last night.

God's teeth, but he was glad for Quincy's aid this morn, he thought, as he observed the wrestling match between man and boot.

White-haired Quincy had come to him along with Rose Park—a shabby, run-down estate and a dilapidated old man. *Fitting pair.* Still and all, Christian felt a certain attachment to the decrepit old fool, as he did to Rose Park. Knowing no one else would have hired him in his advanced days, Christian had kept him on. It seemed old age made Quincy an unwanted relic to be discarded as useless, and Christian felt a certain empathy for his plight.

He winced as the boot was shoved onto his

foot, at long last, with more force than was credible. And then his brows collided as Quincy suddenly gave an offensive snort. He watched incredulously as the old man lifted his thin upper lip, spraying spittle through his teeth. The repulsive sprinkling landed squarely upon Christian's right boot.

Christian reconsidered at once. "God's teeth, man! What the devil do you think you're doing!"

"Buffing your shoes, m'lord." Using his faded sleeve, Quincy proceeded to buff the spittle from the tip of Christian's boot.

Christian groaned.

" 'Tain't nothin' quite the likes o' it, to tidy a man's leather."

Christian grunted a response, too distracted by other matters to protest further. "If you must do so in future," he added, "do it when I'm not about to witness it!"

Quincy chortled, and Christian grimaced, pressing his hand to his forehead to still the hammering in his brain. Raking his fingers through his hair, he willed himself to bloody blue blazes—perchance *there* he would be less tormented!

"Ye goin' again to Westmoor this morn, m'lord?"

Christian eyed the old man with an arched brow. "Aye," he relented.

"To see the little miss?"

God's blood, but he was turning bold. He frowned as Quincy grunted knowingly.

"That's quite enough polishing for the one boot," Christian announced querulously.

Quincy peered up from his handiwork, nodding with pleasure. "Certainly, m'lord," he said after a moment's deliberation, and then left off with the polishing to retrieve the boot that was still lying upon the wooden floor. He rose to his knees, extending it for Christian's foot. Christian proffered it, bracing himself for the impact of Quincy's weight. Grunting, the old man shoved, but the boot proved more stubborn than he, and Quincy thrust again, harder this time. Caught unexpectedly, Christian was propelled backward over the bed. In the blink of an eye, Quincy leapt upon the mattress with him and stood above him, battering the upturned sole of his boot, threatening it physical harm. For a long moment, Christian could only stare, his expression screwing in disbelief. And then he came to his senses. "Enough already. Get off!" Then, more forcefully when Quincy made no move to obey, "Get the devil off my bed! I'll put the damned thing on myself," he groused.

Quincy ignored him still, shoving more forcefully, and the boot rewarded him by popping into place at last. That done, he lifted a sleeve and spat upon it.

Christian rolled from the bed, coming to his feet at once. "Damnit all! 'Tis not my boots in need of acceptance, but my bloody proposal! Stay clear of me with that spittle-sodden sleeve of yours!"

"But, m'lord!" Quincy objected. And then

his eyes bulged. "Proposin', you say, m'lord? Marriage? Well, now—"

"Not if I don't make it out of this room in one piece, I won't!" Christian slapped at his coat and trousers indignantly. "And I've already told you once, spit on my goddamned boots if 'tis your bloody wish, but *not* in my presence!"

"But, m'lord!" the old man interjected, all the more determined now. "Ye just can't go with one boot shiny as a copper and the other dustier'n me gran's attic—specially not today. 'Tain't right," he objected. "What would the little miss say?"

Christian glared fiercely at him. And then, shaking his head with mute disgust, he slid into the nearest chair. *What would she say?* he wondered, and cursed softly. He massaged the taut cords of his neck. If Jessie didn't agree . . . Christ, he loathed the thought of making a fool of himself over some slip of a girl. Quincy stared expectantly, and he sighed wearily, proffering his boot. "Do it, then," he said sullenly. "Quickly."

Grinning, Quincy at once dropped to his knees before him, snorted, and spat, then set about the task of buffing with quiet determination. "You won't be sorry, m'lord!"

No? Damned if he wasn't already, Christian thought morosely. Damned if he wasn't already.

*   *   *

Lord St. John was a balding, self-loving bore, with more hair than wit—and he didn't have much of that!

Jessie thought if she heard once more about how influential he was, she was going to rip out his three remaining hairs, one by one. Botheration! And this was the man her brother would have her spend the whole of her life with? She shuddered at the thought.

"Really," Leland was saying. "You'll love Charlestown, m'dear—so much like London, it is." He gave her a meaningful smile, and boldly tapped her skirt with a finger.

Jessie started at his touch, jerking away. "Truly, m'lord?" She choked back the contempt from her voice. She loathed London! And she detested the man sitting beside her all the more! The very sound of his voice made her shudder. She hugged herself protectively, hoping he wouldn't notice her disgust.

"Oh yes, indeed," he crowed, grinning with pleasure over her feigned interest. "Some like to refer to it as Little Londontown, even— named after old King Charles, it was."

Jessie turned from him slightly, rolling her eyes. "Aye, my lord, so I've heard. I believe I heard it from you, recently, in fact," she added, giving him a sweet little smile. She resisted the urge to ask him if he was addle-pated. He must be, for it'd been a mere quarter of an hour since he'd last recounted that very thing to her.

Botheration, what was her brother doing?

Why wasn't he back yet? He'd abandoned them so long ago. And where, she wondered crossly, was Eliza? Certainly she'd made herself visible enough for Christian. Jessie scooted forward impatiently, toward the edge of the settee.

Leland cast her a questioning glance, as though to discern whether or not she mocked him. Apparently resolving she did not, much to her dismay, he carried on with his incessant rambling. A discreet cough brought Jessie's attention to the doorway. "Griffin!" She sprung from the settee at once, grateful for the butler's interruption, and made her way to where he stood, leaning forward to hiss into his ear. "Where is my brother?"

"Er, yes, m'lady," he said, not truly answering her question. "He bade me tell you to remain here in the salon, and to assure you that he and Lord St. John shall return anon." Turning to Leland, he announced, "His Lordship awaits you in the Lib'ry, if you would be so kind to oblige, m'lord." Gesturing with a hand, he urged Leland from the room.

"Yes, of course," Leland replied. He turned to fix Jessie with a frightening smile. "I shall return in an instant, m'dear. Don't fret yourself over it."

Jessie cringed as she watched him go, and was filled suddenly with a terrible foreboding. Just what had Amos been up to for so long in the library when he knew full well that she was inappropriately ensconced in the salon with a man she barely knew? that her repu-

tation might suffer because of it? True, she had
managed to be alone with Christian, but never
with Amos's knowledge or approval. All but
for a handful of times, Amos had been made
aware of Christian's presence, and had made
certain that Hildie was near to keep a watchful
eye upon them.

Something was amiss . . . and bedamned if
she didn't intend to discover just what it was.
She waited until she was certain the way was
clear, and then headed to the library after
them.

Chapter 10

❦

"**B**loody hell!"
        For the last hour, Christian had tried in vain to convince Stone of his intent to wed his sister, but the son of a bitch seemed to have turned a deaf ear to his words.

"Damn you! I don't want your blood money, not now—not ever!"

"I was under the impression, Haukinge, that we'd come to an agreement concerning my dear sister already."

"Agreement, hell! You spoke, I listened, and you took my silence as an alliance!"

"I see," Amos said stiffly. "Well, then, just what is it you require of me, sirrah?"

Christian's jaw ticked with anger. *Bastard!* "*Jessamine,*" he said with quiet menace. "I wish your sister's hand in matrimony, and nothing more—as it should have been years ago!"

"Impossible, she's already betrothed—" Amos halted his explanation as the library door creaked opened, revealing a mottle-faced Lord St. John behind it.

"Well, now, there he is!" Amos smiled broadly. "Jessamine's intended himself!" With great satisfaction, he then decreed, "Lord Christian, you may take great pleasure in making the acquaintance of Lord St. John, lately of Charlestown. It is to him I have granted my dear sister's hand in matrimony. So, then," he concluded, "as you now know, your request is far from a reasonable one."

A cool nod was Christian's only greeting as he acknowledged his longtime adversary. His gaze swept over St. John, and his lips formed a snarl as he turned again to Amos Stone. "The pleasure has already been mine, I fear." Turning to Leland, he muttered a curt, "St. John."

"Haukinge," Leland replied disingenuously, "so very good to see you again."

"I'm certain," Christian drawled.

Shrewdly assessing the situation at hand, Leland said, "Amos is telling the truth, you realize. Dear, lovely Jessamine has agreed to become my bride." When Christian looked disbelieving still, he announced, "We shall be departing two weeks hence for the colonies and shall wed there. Unfortunately circumstances do not permit me a lengthier stay this voyage." Casting Christian a very meaningful glance, he explained, "Much has gone awry in

Charlestown, sir, much indeed—if you know what I mean—*and I know that you do!*"

Turning to Amos, Christian ignored Leland's carefully worded accusation. "I don't believe it. She would have said she was spoken for."

"Now, now, Haukinge," Leland interjected, his voice a sneer. He came forward to stand beside Amos. "Why should Stone lie to you? Why would I? I'm quite aware that you *frequent*"—the word was another insinuation—"Charlestown's harbor. Wouldn't it be a rather simple matter for you to investigate my personal affairs if you were so inclined?"

Christian's gut twisted. He had the lowering feeling St. John was telling him the truth. Why would Jessie have lied to him? Why would she have whispered of love when she knew full well she belonged to another man? Why had she so eagerly encouraged his suit? From what he knew of her, it didn't make sense. Then again, when had anything between them ever made a lick of sense? He managed a slow nod. "I take it, then, that Jessie knows?"

Amos smiled victoriously. "Well, of course she knows, Haukinge. How could she not know?"

Once again, the door creaked open and Jessie herself peered warily into the library.

"I knocked," she told them apologetically, glancing first at Leland, then at Amos. "Jessie knows what?" she asked quickly, and then suddenly she turned and gasped in shock as she spied Christian. "I did not realize you were here, my lord!"

Christian merely stared, holding her gaze, not trusting himself to speak.

"Is something wrong?"

A shiver swept down Jessie's spine as she scrutinized the occupants of the room. Christian's expression told her, undoubtedly, that something was indeed very wrong. The look in his eyes and his rigid stance told her all she needed to know; he was raging mad.

Botheration! She had no idea what Amos had said to anger him so, but he looked positively feral, ready to pounce. She swept the room with her gaze and inquired once more, "What is it that Jessie knows?" When there was still no reply to her question, she demanded, "Will someone please speak!"

"The fact that you are to wed Lord St. John, of course."

Jessie whirled on her brother. "But you said—"

"I remember well what I said," he returned quickly, flicking Christian a glance. "But the charade must now come to an end, I fear. I never imagined Lord St. John would come to collect you so soon."

Jessie's stomach twisted. "Charade?" She swallowed convulsively. "What charade, Amos?"

"Quite simple, sister dear. Haukinge came to court you only because I *paid* him to, and now I believe he's come to collect his due."

Her heart lurched. Jessie turned to Christian;

their gazes collided like fire and steel. "He paid you?" He didn't reply and she knew. "My God!" Her fingers flew to her lips. "He paid you!"

Eyeing her coldly, Christian answered her question with one of his own. "Have you agreed to wed this man or not?"

Their gazes remained locked for a long, painful instant, and then Christian shook his head when Jessie couldn't speak to deny it. Raking a hand through his hair, he hung his head backward, closing his eyes, and froze in that position when he heard Amos's next words.

"I'm sorry, Mr. Haukinge, but you really cannot have expected Jessamine would wed a bastard. Even if she would, it would be heinous of me to allow such a mesalliance."

Christian's head snapped upright, his eyes glittering coldly. He fixed his glare upon Jessie, though his question was directed at Amos. "What did you say?"

If he'd needed proof against her, then he certainly had it now.

Leland's eyes bulged. His gaze sought Christian's to verify the disclosure.

"I said," Amos repeated, "that it would be heinous of me to allow—"

"Son of a—" He hung his head backward. "Did she tell you that?" He lifted his head and turned to Jessie, demanding, "Did you?"

Jessie opened her mouth to deny it, but she was still stung by Amos's revelation. Nay, she'd not told him! But how dare he be angry with her when 'twas he who had committed the dishonor!

"Christ! Don't answer," he snarled. "I've had more than enough of your lies already. What a grand little actress you are! If ever you tire of playing the seductress, m'mselle, you might consider taking to the floorboards!"

Jessie felt as though she'd been slapped. Her eyes misted, and her heart felt as though it would shatter into a thousand tiny shards. She tried desperately not to weep before him. Weeping would accomplish naught, she knew, and yet, even as she restrained herself, a sob seemed to form of its own will. "How could you have?" she blurted miserably, "I . . . I never—"

"Shut up, Jessamine!" Amos exploded. Closing the distance between them, he seized her forcefully by the arm, gripping her hard in warning. "You've absolutely nothing to explain to this—this jackal!"

All eyes turned to Jessie, waiting.

She couldn't speak. Amos's grip warned her not to—nor could she seem to form the words.

Christian was the first to turn away.

Shaking his head with disgust, he clenched his jaw. Those pale green eyes of hers had a way of piercing his very heart. Impossible not to feel when they were fixed upon him, and he didn't want to feel just now. Outwardly his expression remained carefully bland, until he happened to spy the wounded expression she wore.

How could he ever have thought her pure?

Sweet? Caring? How dare she play the injured before him now? He didn't give a bloody damn who else was present, he wasn't about to leave this place without giving her a piece of his mind. And to think he'd nearly given her . . . everything—Christ, what a bloody fool he was! His eyes narrowed. "Tell me, my love, was it difficult to lie there beneath me and whisper love words, knowing all the while you belonged to another man?" His jaw clenched.

Her face drained of color, but he felt no satisfaction, only pain more intensely.

"So much for love, eh?"

Leland's face mottled with rage.

"Do not make intimations that can so easily be disproved, Haukinge." Amos shot a warning glance to Jessie, urging her without words to remain silent while he attempted to acquit her name.

Smoldering with anger, Christian taunted, one brow lifted in contempt, "Can it now?" He turned to Jessie. "Can it, I wonder, *my love*?"

He was daring her to deny it.

Jessie's face flamed at his mortifying disclosure. It seemed all eyes were upon her again, probing, questioning, gawking. God help her, but she could not deny Christian's insinuation, for she was, in truth, no longer innocent. Only that didn't seem to matter just now, she only felt the pain of his betrayal. How could he? She choked on a sob. "I . . . "

"You what? You *do* love me? Say it now, so

that all may hear your tender declaration, love."

Jessie stood silent, her heart breaking, her world collapsing around her. God, she thought she would swoon. Her palms dampened, and she wet her lips nervously, glancing at her brother, then at Leland, then again at Christian, not knowing to whom to turn. Tears welled in her eyes, blinding her to all but Christian's spiteful glare. His furious expression cut her as surely as a knife. Her hands began to quiver, but she could not speak. She didn't know what to say in response to all the hurtful things he was saying to her. Oh, God! She stifled a sob. Amos had paid him! And Christian, he'd accepted without compunction.

Her heart felt crushed beyond repair.

She couldn't bear it. Bile surged in her throat. 'Twas no wonder he believed she would betray him, for he *had* betrayed her. Her heart felt as though it would rend in two. And God help her, for she loved him even still. He stared, waiting, inviting her to humiliate herself further by professing an unrequited love, for he couldn't possibly love her in return.

Well, she wasn't about to satisfy him.

"You cannot say it, can you? Now, when it matters most! Christ! How witless of me to have ever believed in you!" His eyes came alive with loathing, as he turned to Leland. "My congratulations to you, St. John, on your impending nuptials. You richly deserve one another!" He started toward her. "Keep your stinking money, Stone, your sister has already paid me in full." His gaze locked with hers as he passed her, and he whispered for her ears alone, "Haven't you, love?" He left then, his footsteps echoing behind him. He opened and slammed the front door, taking with him the promise of Jessie's future.

If possible, Leland's face reddened even more as he turned to face her. The whites of his eyes seemed to bulge from his face. "Is it true?"

Even without Christian's presence, she could not answer.

"I shall not be the butt of every man's joke!"

What could she say? Nothing. There was nothing she could possibly say in her own defense.

Silence permeated the room.

Damned her.

"By God!" Leland thundered. "I shall not have that jackal's leavings! Not this day! Nor any other! Good day to the two of you!"

"Wait!" Amos demanded as Leland turned from him. "I can explain!"

Leland shook his head, not bothering to look Amos's way. "Nay, sirrah, you cannot! I shall be departing Westmoor at once. A good life to you both!" With that, he, too, left, slamming the door in his wake.

Jessie was certain the front door would split in two if it were slammed so violently even once more.

"Damn, damn, bloody damn!" Amos exploded. He glared at Jessie.

Left to themselves, the room became deathly

quiet. Amos shook his powdered and peruked head, hatred and disgust leaping from his eyes.

Jessie felt anew the condemning sting of tears.

"Does he speak the truth, Jessamine? Tell me, now!"

For a long moment she couldn't speak, and then she nodded, her lips quivering. Her hands trembling, she wiped away the blur of tears from her eyes.

Amos gave her a contemptuous snort and shook his head. "Do you realize what you've done?" he asked gravely. "I cannot believe you would do this to me—to Westmoor!"

His expression was frightening, his tone cold and brutal in its sharpness. She recoiled as he came toward her, raising his hand in anger. He stopped abruptly, held it in midair, as tears pooled and spilled from her eyes. Silently they coursed down her cheeks, onto her lips. She let them, not bothering to wipe the humiliating wetness away. Looking directly into her brother's vacant eyes, she realized then that there was nothing left of him there. They revealed not a trace of warmth.

"I thought he loved me," she sobbed brokenly, tasting the salt of her grief. "I-I thought you—"

His hand slammed down upon the desk and he glared at her as though to blame her for the violent reaction she'd wrought from him. "You thought too much!"

"Why, Amos? Why would you do such a

thing? I-I don't understand. Why would Lord Chris—'' She choked on the question, unable to finish.

'' 'Tis not so difficult to comprehend,'' he replied balefully, his words clipped and cool. "For the good of Westmoor, Jessamine, I would sell my very soul to the devil. And Lord Christian? 'Tis quite the simple deduction as well; he's the lowest of low, the scourge of society. 'Tis to be expected from the likes of him.''

Once again, silence fell between them. Only her sobs broke the hush.

She cried softly. "What will you do?''

Amos shrugged, his look cold, unreachable. "Precisely what I should have done to begin with. Send you to Charlestown, m'dear.''

She blanched. "But Lord St. John said—''

Amos eyed her coldly. "Have you no ears? Did you not hear? Nay, you'll not go with Lord St. John, but to Robert, instead!'' He shook his head lamentably. "I can do nothing more for you here—you have seen to that well and good! Robert may fare better than I.'' He observed the silent tears as they spilled down her cheeks and was unmoved by them.

"You've disgraced us! You've dishonored *my* name. Eliza warned you that Haukinge was a debaucher of women—a penniless one at that!'' he scoffed. "But nay, you would not listen. 'Twas also made known to you that he would not stay overlong once he knew you came to him without a dowry. I can only say I told you so.''

Jessie held her breath momentarily. Hope
stirred despite the pain. "He asked after my
dowry?" Pride seemed a forgone thing suddenly. If Christian had asked after her dowry,
he must have asked about matrimony. And
then it dawned on her suddenly what Amos
had said to him and hope surged. *You really
cannot have expected Jessamine would wed a bastard.* "Amos, did he ask to wed with me?"

"It never came to that. With no dowry, you
are nothing to him, and I made that clear from
the start—that you would be given none. He
never bothered to ask."

Jessie masked her face with her hands as an
anguished sob burst forth.

Amos watched a moment longer, and then
abandoned her, too. Just so easily, everything
was gone.

Everything.

There is no greater sorrow
than to be mindful of the happy time
in misery.

—*Dante*

Chapter 11

～○○○○～

Charlestown
1763

"*Sacrebleu!* I 'ave grown two heads, *mon ami?*"

Shaking the sweat-dampened hair from his face, Christian chuckled at Jean Paul's indignant tone. Seizing up the crowbar, he pried the lid from the largest crate before them. "You've still the one, old man, rest assured." He eyed Jean Paul reproachfully. "Just the same, I strongly suggest you refrain from calling me by *that* name."

Jean Paul's brows rose. "Since when do you take offense to *mon ami?*"

Christian eyed him narrowly. "You know very well what I'm referring to. The name I prefer is Christian, as you seem inclined to for-

137

get. Charlestown is not Boston, Jean Paul. *Comprends?*"

Wiping the sweat from his brow, he peered into the newly opened crate. "Damn. Not in this one either." He eyed Jean Paul pensively. "Are you certain 'twas loaded upon the *Anastasie?*"

"Quite certain," Jean Paul answered, frowning. "At any rate, had they found their way to France, we would have heard by now. I swear to you, *Hawk*, they must be here someplace."

"*Christian.*"

Jean Paul grimaced. "And that reminds me," he said, ignoring Christian's reproof. "That cantankerous old English fool you brought with you seems to 'ave taken offense to my sleeping in your chamber at the big house. I've told him it was only till you returned, that there was no place else for me as yet, but *non!* Again and again he moves my things into the unfinished rooms. *Ce type est un emmerder!* The west wing, no less! And it rained late last night!"

"Merely a drizzle," Christian countered, grinning, though he vowed to speak with Quincy at the first opportunity.

"*Mon cul!* Mayhap here! *There* it was more! Two inches of water on the floor where I slept—I swam instead! And this morn, my peruke was ruined!"

Christian chuckled. "Demme if you need that lice-ridden headpiece, anyway."

Jean Paul scowled at him. "And you should wear it more, I think! *Un jour . . .* For someone who doesn't wish attention called to himself, you have a curious way to show it."

Jessie had oft eschewed her petticoats, as well, Christian couldn't help but recall, and it occurred to him in that instant that he'd never thought to question it. On the contrary, he'd understood completely. It was her one small rebellion against authority. *His had merely been the first of many.*

"Very well," he relented, cursing himself for a bloody fool. Why couldn't he seem to forget? "I'll bring Quincy back to the city with me." He hung his head back to relieve the tension in his neck, massaging the soreness, and then with a grimace of disgust, turned his attention to the crate before him. "Here, old man... give me a hand with this."

"What old man!" Jean Paul eyed him reproachfully, but complied at once. "You are disrespectful to your elders, *mon fils!*" Together they shoved the heavy crate out of the way. "I could be your—"

"Father?" Christian sobered by the turn of their conversation. He turned to face Jean Paul, one brow arched in challenge. Jean Paul said nothing. The two merely stared at one another, gazes locked, and then the moment passed. Jean Paul glanced away and Christian bent to retrieve the crowbar.

"I could be," Jean Paul said suddenly, his declaration barely more than a whisper. Christian's gaze snapped up, meeting his father's eyes. Aye, he knew... but did Jean Paul? He thought so, and yet...

Jean Paul's expression shuttered suddenly. "What happened to you in England?" he demanded. "That is what I wish to know!"

Christian turned away, his jaw working as he moved to the next crate. "Nothing I care to discuss, old man."

"I know you too well . . . *Christian*." Jean Paul paused long enough to give emphasis to the word. "Something has happened to make you so foul-tempered. *Quelle barbe!* I see you not for months—and now, when I should be glad to find you are not fodder for the fish, or hanging from the French gallows, I can scarcely bear to look at you for that hideous scowl you wear!"

Christian grunted as he pried off the lid. "Then don't look."

"Never have I known you to take an insult so lightly! *Non*, the *Hawk* I know would 'ave simply taken what was his just due! *Jesu Christ!* I have seen you seize even that which was not your own! If they took something from you, why do you not just seize it back and cease all this brooding, at long last?"

Christian's head snapped up. "I'm not brooding, devil hang you!" His eyes narrowed in warning. He'd be damned if he'd have his affairs questioned by anyone—even Jean Paul! "Enough to say we didn't suit—we're cut of different cloth, she and I. Now . . . give it up, Jean Paul."

"Humph!"

Slamming the lid back into place, Christian muttered an oath. "Not here either!" Raking his fingers through his hair, he mused aloud, "They must've somehow been unloaded back on Adger's wharf."

Jean Paul's heavy brows lifted.

Christian shrugged, at once resigned to what must be done. "We'll have to go into the warehouse tonight, retrieve them before customs realizes 'tis there under their bloody noses."

"Just so?"

"What choice have we?"

"I suppose, not very much, at all," Jean Paul ceded. "But you have an obligation to attend the gala tonight—the oaf knows you're here. If you make no appearance, St. John will likely suspect and come searching. There have been rumors, Christian."

"I know, demme, I know!" Christian considered his options. "I suppose I shall have to pay a visit to the Wilkes club to see if Ben can't round up some of his boys. I'll go to the tavern just as soon as we finish here." His gaze returned to Jean Paul. "The two of you can handle it from there, can you not?"

Jean Paul considered a moment, his eyes narrowing. "*Oui* . . . I think . . . but there is no need to go searching." He nodded in the direction of Oyster Point. "Stone is there." He lifted his chin, gesturing over Christian's shoulder. "His men too. I can see them from here."

Christian pivoted. He went to the ship's railing to gaze out over the expanse of blue-gray water that separated the *Anastasie* from the

Charlestown battery. "What the bloody hell would have them congregating so damned conspicuously?"

Jean Paul came up behind him, clapping a cautioning hand upon his shoulder. "Daniel Moore, the new stamp collector, he's arrested two of Laurens's vessels. Have a care now, Hawk . . . the situation grows grave."

From her vantage point along the bay, Jessie could see clear to Oyster Point. In the harbor itself, hundreds of ships were at anchor—the breathtaking sight never ceased to awe her. All about, people scurried to and fro. Children played. Merchants peddled their wares, while elegantly dressed women walked simply to be seen—perhaps chattering about tonight's gala?

Glancing down at the envelope she held within her hand, she smiled knowingly. Kathryn Sinclair was absolutely anxious for Jessie to invite her cousin to attend the masquerade, and Jessie had promised she would attempt to persuade him. To that end, she'd gone to her cousin's wharf to inquire over Ben's whereabouts and had been told to seek him out at Oyster Point, though what he was up to away from the wharf so early, she just couldn't fathom. Nibbling her lip fretfully, she considered the rumors . . . but nay, she refused to believe them. Ben would never place himself at such risk.

Shuddering, she glanced up, gauging the sky. Even through the lingering storm clouds, the sun shone brightly, warming her. She hoped it wouldn't rain again tonight—more than that, she wished she wouldn't cease to breathe every time she passed this blessed street!

As so many times before, when she passed the brick facade town house she'd discovered belonged to *him,* she couldn't resist a glimpse. She was startled to find that today its black protective shutters were open wide to the fresh air.

Was he here, then? In Charlestown? After all these months? Her heart lurched at the possibility.

God curse the rotten scoundrel that he could do this to her even now! What was wrong with her? she wondered peevishly.

She knew what was wrong with her, of course! Now, at last, when she was able to walk the shell-paved streets without searching for *his* face in the crowd, he came to torment her once more!

Aye, she knew Christian had holdings in Charlestown. She had dreaded meeting with him—but he might have given her more time! Not that he would have concerned himself with her preferences. Rotten, deceiving wretch!

Mayhap it wasn't him at all, she reasoned. He might have loaned it, after all.

She certainly didn't *want* it to be him . . .

Did she?

Seagulls dotted the clear blue sky above, wailing as they swooped to the streets in search of scraps of food. Pigeons wobbled carelessly, dodging carriages and rushing feet, all oblivious to her sinking mood. She walked faster, no longer in the frame of mind to tarry. She intended to deliver the envelope to Ben, and then hurry home and lock herself within her room for the rest of her natural life!

And then perhaps not . . . Why should she? she thought crossly, resisting the childish urge to stomp her foot and scream. Why should she allow him to terrorize her into hiding away?

Well, she wasn't about to!

Botheration! Ben would likely scold her for delivering the invitation by hand when she could have easily sent a messenger instead, but she'd needed the walk and the fresh air—if it could be called fresh. Her nostrils flared slightly at the odor that rose to accost her. Many of Charlestown's streets were paved with crushed oyster shells, effecting a rather distinct odor that was saved from being fetid only by the sweet breeze of the sea. She glanced over her shoulder, at the brick-facade town house.

Was he in Charlestown, then?

Or were the servants merely preparing for his arrival?

For her peace of mind, she prayed it wasn't so. She forced her thoughts away from the town house and Christian Haukinge.

A carriage rolled slowly by, crackling noisily over the delicate shells. A white-gloved hand, followed by a shrill female voice, caught her attention. Waving in greeting, Jessie continued on her way. Despite her fears to the contrary, Charlestown had, in truth, proven to be the haven she'd sought. She'd worried so that Lord St. John would sully her name here, and that she would be labeled an outcast upon arriving in the city, but for whatever reason, he'd not so much as breathed a word of the *incident* to a soul. There were some, in truth, who still believed her betrothed to him . . . which led her to wonder that perhaps Lord St. John was as humiliated by the ordeal as was she.

She smiled softly then, with grim satisfaction, for Amos would likely curse himself to Jericho did he know that this penance of his was no penance at all. Her father's cousin and wife had proven so very good to her. For the first time since her mother's death, Jessie felt part of a true family. Her cousin Ben was more like a brother to her than Amos could ever have thought to be—even if he was a mite too accommodating at times!

Ben, who was merely two years Jessie's senior, had been her cousin Robert's sole child. Robert, Claire, and Ben had all afforded her such a warm welcome when first she'd arrived in Charlestown that she couldn't help but love them all dearly already.

Love.

She couldn't help it, she wondered if *he* would be at the masquerade tonight, and then cursed herself for her weakness to him.

"Jessamine! Wait!"

Frowning, Jessie turned to see that the carriage that had only just passed her by had circled and now drew up behind her once more. Kathryn Sinclair nearly toppled from it, and Jessie smiled as she acknowledged her newly found friend. "I should have thought you'd be home, diligently preparing for this eve."

"I'm to pick up my gown from Madame Legare," Kathryn announced, smiling brightly. She snatched off one of her gloves and toyed with it nervously, betraying her anxiousness. "And I was . . . looking," she confessed.

For Ben. Jessie's smile deepened. "I wish I'd known. I might have asked you to join me." She lifted the small envelope and displayed it to Kathryn's inquiring eyes.

Kathryn nibbled her lower lip, suppressing her glee. "Do you think he'll come? Oh, how I hope so! My heart positively aches for it!"

Jessie laughed softly, shrugging noncommittally. "You know Ben," she cautioned. "One can never tell, but I shall endeavor to convince him."

"And I just know you will succeed!"

Suddenly inspired, Jessie glanced over her shoulder, toward Oyster Point. "Tell me, Kathryn," she said, facing her friend once more, "are you expected home very soon?" She smiled mischievously.

Kathryn's gaze followed hers to the point, and she admitted, "I saw him from the carriage! And nay! God's truth, I was requested *not* to return directly, for it seems I've frazzled just about everyone's nerves." She smiled unrepentantly. "And poor Thom," she added with a grievous sigh. She waved a hand in the direction of her waiting coach. "I've dragged the wretched soul to every last boutique in this city and now am left with no choice but to return home to plague my mother and the servants." She sighed airily. "Unless, of course . . . someone should take pity on me, and take me with them to the point . . ." She smiled coyly, and Jessie laughed.

"Well, then . . ." Jessie gave her friend a shrewd smile. "Why not accompany me while I deliver this urgent missive to Ben?"

Kathryn's eyes lit with merriment. "Really? Truly? You'd not mind if I tagged along?"

"Of course not," Jessie insisted. "I'd be quite grateful for the company."

Chapter 12

"**B**oth, you say?"

Ben Stone nodded glumly.

"Devil plague the man!" Christian shook his head in bewilderment. "Whatever possessed Moore to seize them, at any rate? Charlestown has never been a smugglers' haven; why would he suspect?" The vessels in question had made the usual voyage between Charlestown and Laurens's property in Georgia, and though 'twas intended that trade between territories be cleared with customs first, there was no customs house near Laurens's plantation and so he'd not been able to comply with the requirement. Customarily such cases were overlooked, but Moore had for some reason refused to do so, and Christian was nonplussed as to why.

"Mayhap he simply intends to make an example of him?"

"Or perhaps 'tis a warning . . ."

"Perhaps," Christian ceded. "Then again, I suspect St. John may have had a hand in this matter, as well. He and Moore have been thick as thieves, and St. John and Laurens have little regard for one another."

"Nor does St. John care overmuch for you, Hawk," added one of Ben's cronies. "Swears he'll snatch you one of these days."

"Aye," Ben agreed, chuckling, "though I'd like to see him try."

"Never under—" Christian broke off suddenly, and stiffened.

Turning to see what had captured his attention, Ben chuckled and said, "My cousin . . . she seems to have that effect quite regularly, I'd say."

His cronies all murmured an agreement.

Christian eyed him pointedly and scowled at the rest of them. "*Your* cousin?" he said.

Christian knew the instant Ben detected his interest in her, for his brows slanted to a frown. His stance grew rigid as his own. "*Hawk*," he said, his voice low in warning.

Devil hang him! Even now the sight of her stole his breath away. He loathed himself for his weakness toward her. *Stone.* Damn, but why hadn't he put the two together? His jaw clenched. "Threats, Ben?" Even now, it was impossible not to want her. His gut wrenched with remembrance, even as he hardened his heart against her.

"Nay," Ben said evenly, "I just didn't realize. She's my cousin, Hawk . . . Go easy with her . . ."

Lifting her skirts, Jessie hurried across the sand-filled street into the clearing, smiling with delight at Kathryn's bubbling excitement. And then at once her heart lurched to a halt. She froze, her breath strangling in her throat as the tallest man in the gathering turned to face them.

Their gazes met and held.

Jessie's knees buckled a little at the baleful glare he gave her. Unknowingly she crushed the envelope she'd been carrying within her fist. If she weren't such a blessed coward, she told herself, she'd walk directly to him and slap the self-righteous expression from his face! But she *was* a coward, and the truth of the matter was that if she didn't turn now, and go, this moment, she'd surely shame herself. She felt Kathryn's hand upon her arm and was grateful for her steadying presence.

"What is it, Jessamine? What's wrong?"

He continued to stare, his smoldering eyes narrowing in condemnation, but he said not a word, nor did he move to address her. What had she expected? A greeting? I'm sorry? How've you been, my love? Nothing! she told herself. She expected nothing—and received less. 'Twould serve her best to simply walk away now. She spun on her heels and hastened away, with no answer for Kathryn's anxious inquiry.

Kathryn hurried after her. "Jessamine! Wait! What is it?"

Ben caught her as she crossed the street, his expression sober as he asked, "Him?"

Jessie couldn't find her voice to speak.

"Confound it!" Ben exploded.

"Who?" Kathryn asked, trying in vain to keep up with their hurried steps and fragmented conversation. There was only concern evident in her tone as she demanded, "Tell me, Jessamine! What has happened to upset you so?"

Still unable to speak, lest she burst into tears, Jessie shook her head. Ben was the only one person in Charlestown, aside from Christian and Lord St. John, who knew the truth about what had happened all those months ago in England. Only he hadn't known everything—he hadn't known precisely who was responsible. Even Ben's parents had been spared the awful truth. 'Twas the one thing for which she had Amos to thank, he'd spared her that much—more for his own sake than for hers, she was certain. She'd grown so close to Ben these past months that confiding in him had seemed the natural thing to do, but she could never bear for Kathryn to know her shame. Her cheeks colored even as she remembered that fateful afternoon beneath the elm tree, and her eyes misted, though she refused to weep.

Too many tears had been wasted already.

Ben seized her by the shoulders and spun

her about to face him, gripping her harder than she knew he meant to. "Was it he?"

Lifting her face to him, Jessie forced a nod, and leaned into his embrace, wanting him to shield her from so many prying eyes. She knew people were staring, though she couldn't see them through the blur of her tears.

"Ah, Jessie . . ." He enfolded her within his arms, and for a long moment there was only the comfort of his silence. "Are you well enough to make it home?" He cast a glance at Kathryn.

"I've my carriage," Kathryn offered.

"I . . . I'm fine . . ." Jessie forced a smile for Ben's sake, for Kathryn's sake. "I-I've no idea what came over me," she swore, mindful of Kathryn's critical regard, "but I-I . . . I'm fine now."

"Are you certain, Jessie?" Turning to Kathryn, Ben appealed, "Would you mind terribly excusing us? I should like to speak to my cousin privately."

Kathryn nodded, flustered. "Certainly," she said, sounding wounded, though she tried not to show it. "I shall go on, then." She turned to Jessie. "Are you certain you will be all right?"

"Yes, thank you, Kathryn. I truly am fine."

Kathryn managed a nod. "Very well, then . . . if you're certain . . ."

"Perhaps I shall see you this eve, Kathryn," Ben suggested, dismissing her once and for all.

Kathryn's expression softened at once and she smiled brightly. "Why, yes—yes, of course! That would be wonderful!" Her face aglow once more, she turned to Jessie. "Good-bye, Jessamine. Feel better." Leaning closer, she whispered a fervent, "Please!"

Jessie smiled weakly. "I shall," she assured her, trying to sound cheerful, though her heart was breaking into tiny wretched pieces. With a farewell wave for her friend, she turned to Ben, her eyes blurring with tears. "I'd no idea that you and Christian—Lord—that man— were so well acquainted!" she hissed at him, unable to help herself.

He frowned at her. "More importantly, I didn't realize *you* knew him so well, Jessie." His voice held no condemnation, only sorrow on her behalf.

Shame suffused her, and she averted her eyes. "I only wish I did not."

"You should have told me," he said, his jaw tautening. Peering up at him, she could see the fury flashing in his eyes. *"Haw*—" He broke off, glanced away, toward the point, and then back. "Christian will not trouble you. I swear it."

Jessie gave him a doubtful look. If Ben only knew what misery Christian could invoke with only a glance . . . if only he knew . . . but he couldn't know.

He smiled down at her, giving her a playful chuck beneath the chin. And then, as though he scarce could help himself, his fingers slid up and he stroked her cheek with the back of his knuckles. "Sweet, sweet, Jess . . . how they've hurt you—Christ, if only you weren't

my cousin . . ." He smiled down at her then,
and said lightly, "I believe I would marry you
myself and tuck you safely away." His expression sobered suddenly, his gaze shutter-
ing. "If you weren't my cousin," he added.

Something in his expression made Jessie uneasy in his presence suddenly. She peeled herself away from him. "And yet you are," she
reminded him firmly. She didn't wish to hurt
Ben's feelings, but it seemed of late he made
more and more such declarations. Didn't he
realize? Cousin or no, she could never love another man as long as she lived!

"Come," she told him, taking his hand and
leading him away. "Your mother will worry."

The noise was unbearable.
And the stench.
For the fifth time in as many moments, Leland St. John glanced over his shoulder at
the door, readjusting his tricorne. He'd forgone his powdered peruke for this meeting
in hopes of blending more easily with the
rabble of Dillon's tavern, but he felt exposed
without it. His tricorn was much too large
for his unclad head, as it had been made to
fit a gentleman's peruke, an item of dress he
was rarely without. He only hoped he wasn't
too conspicuous . . . that this meeting would
mete itself well.

A barmaid came to him and he shook his
head, sending her away without a word. It
seemed to him that everyone was staring in
his direction, and he fidgeted uneasily under

their scrutiny, ignoring them as best he could. Thankful for the dim light of the tavern, he seized up his full tankard, lifting it up to his lips and sipping hastily before stopping to glance once more over his shoulder at the door.

Filthy, the place was filthy!

He loathed the thought of drinking after all these stinking mouths—wouldn't be surprised to find they didn't even wash their cups. He eyed the tankard with unveiled disgust.

Again he glanced over his shoulder. A dark-haired man entered and peered his way, nodding politely before turning away, but it was not the man he awaited, and he cursed softly as a nervous spasm shot through the cords of his neck. Wincing, he squeezed his eyes shut against the pain and set his tankard down, resisting the urge to slam it, for fear of drawing unwanted attention.

Where the devil was McCarney?

Haukinge—damn his hide to hell—he and Hawk were one in the same, and Leland intended to prove it, once and for all. By God! The blackguard had managed to make him look the fool one too many times, and he intended to make him pay, at long last. He gritted his teeth in frustration.

The problem was that Haukinge was much too careful . . . his men too loyal—or terrified.

Still, 'twas merely a matter of time before he exposed himself. Merely a matter of time . . . Leland intended to be there when he did.

Dammit, where was McCarney?

"Ye look like a fool!" commented a voice at his back.

Leland leapt from his seat in startle. He swung about, dislodging his tricorne in the process. One hand flew out to catch it. " 'Tis about time! I've been waiting for over an hour! What have you brought for me, McCarney?" he demanded. "I expect you've summoned me for a better reason than simply to admire my dress!"

McCarney adjusted his own tricorne under Leland's watchful eye, then lifted Leland's tankard from the table, quaffing the last of his ale without bothering to ask.

"God's teeth, man! What have you brought for me? I cannot stand this accursed place!" He glanced about. "Come outside with me before I suffocate within this filthy pigeonhole!"

With a brief glance about and a shrug, McCarney followed Leland from the tavern. Outside, Leland made his way to where a groom held his mount, pausing a good fifteen feet away. There, he turned to McCarney expectantly.

"Ye want Hawk?"

Removing his tricorne, Leland crushed it to his chest, thumping an anxious finger against the brim of it. His lips slowly curved into a triumphant grin. "You know that I do."

McCarney paused long enough to create a moment of anticipation, and then revealed, "He's raidin' the warehouse at Adger's wharf tonight . . . ten, or thereaboots. Seems 'is men mistakenly unloaded somethin' of consequence late this morn . . . somethin' that *must* be removed by first light . . . Do ye take my meaning?"

"I do," Leland said. "And how did you discover this?"

McCarney's eyes gleamed by the light of the moon. "Ben Stone. He's roundin' up men for the job even as we speak."

Leland eyed the man suspiciously. "Why are you telling me this, McCarney? I know you're in league with them . . ."

McCarney sneered. " 'Tis nae secret ye've a grudge against the man . . . You ain't the only one. Anyhoo," he added, "I've heard ye're offerin' coin—might as well do fer money what I'd like tae do fer free."

Leland's curiosity was piqued. "Aye? And what's he done to you, McCarney?"

McCarney eyed him balefully. "Not that 'tis any o' yer concern, mind ye, but the jackal killed my brother—ain't aboot to forget a thing like that!"

Leland smiled, satisfied. "How touching . . . brotherly devotion, and all . . . but tell me, how do I know you're not making this up? I can't say I trust you."

"I don't give a brass farthing iffen you don't," McCarney said, his lip curling. "I'll get 'im on me own someday—tried once already, don't ye doubt it." He snorted and spat upon the ground at Leland's feet.

"You'll have to stand in line, I'm afraid," Leland said, producing a silver piece.

"That's not enough," McCarney announced, eyeing the coin greedily.

"But it'll do," Leland told him coolly. " 'Tis a good thing for the crown there are still men like you about, McCarney, unfettered as you are by noble sentiments." He flung the coin into the air and caught it, balancing the silver piece upon the tip of his thumb as he gauged McCarney's expression. "Tenish, you say?"

"Aye," McCarney answered, eyeing the coin.

Leland laughed, flipped him the silver piece, then turned and walked away.

Jessie was grateful for Ben's company, for the alley seemed strange and eerie. The lanterns, which were usually brightly lit at this hour, had for some odd reason all been gutted already. Only the full, luminous moon lit their path, and even that light was minimal, for the buildings along the narrow lane cast shadows that were untouched by the moon's glow. As she recalled the tales Claire had related to her last eve, a shiver coursed down her spine, making her shudder.

Sensing her unease, and the cause for it, Ben thought to console her. "Mother oft worries for naught."

"I don't believe that, at all," Jessie countered. "If what she says is true, then we have much to fear with those turncoats wreaking their havoc about. I wonder why the lights have been gutted," she added uneasily.

Ben's hold tightened upon her hand. "*They* might be dissenters, Jessie, but *turncoats*, nay."

Jessie twisted her fingers out of his painful grip, flexing them. She rubbed her hand, peering up at him. "Dissenters? I rather doubt I would put it so mildly," she told him. "Your mother told me they threatened to hang British officials! 'Tis treachery, plain and simple!"

"My mother embellishes. They wouldn't have hung the man. They simply intended to make a point—that and nothing more."

"By building gallows and hanging effigies of stamp collectors upon them? That, Ben Stone, is a threat if ever I've heard one. At any rate, why are you defending them?" Once again she peered warily up at her fair-haired cousin. His golden locks reflected the moonlight and seemed to glow. In contrast, his sun-darkened face was almost invisible to her, so deeply was it cast in shadow. "You're not in league with them, are you?" she asked when he didn't respond.

"Me?" He chuckled. "Now, dear coz, do I look like a *turncoat* to you?"

She scrutinized him a long moment as they walked. In the darkness she couldn't quite make out the color of his coat, but she knew it to be a midnight blue; only his crisp white stock stood out, reflecting the moonlight. He and Christian had much in common, she reflected suddenly, for they both seemed to flaunt fashion. Nor was that all they had in common. Smiling wanly into the shadows, she recalled that Christian, too, had teased her as easily as Ben did now, and the memory brought a sting to her eyes. "I suppose not," she yielded at last, "though if Gadsden and Pinkney are in league with those anarchists, who is to say what a turncoat looks like? Certainly not I."

For a long moment there was only silence between them; only the hollow sound of their echoing footsteps infiltrated it.

"True, coz," Ben agreed after a moment, snatching up her hand once more. "Though I wonder how it is you know so much."

"Your mother, of course," Jessie replied, laughing softly. "I declare, she seems privy to every last morsel of gossip in this province. You should have heard what she discovered today." With a trace of laughter still evident in her voice, she disclosed in a mock whisper, "It seems the notorious Hawk is sailing Carolina waters again. Imagine that! Do you know, Ben, that I have heard him referred to as the Prince of Smugglers, even? What gall! I can scarce imagine anyone wearing such an ignoble title so proudly!"

Ben's hand tightened upon her own. "Nonsense. Hawk has no business here—Charlestown is not like Boston, where smugglers are made welcome and praised for their fearlessness. I wonder where my mother would have heard such a thing."

Having arrived at their destination, Ben led her without delay onto the Sinclair veranda and halted there. The front door was open to the night. The sounds of festivity, laughter and music, drifted to them. Two men in Sinclair livery stood, each on opposite sides of the door, their expressions cast as though in stone.

Jessie was momentarily taken aback by the agitation in Ben's tone. Aided by the light from within, she studied the rigid planes of his face, wondering why he seemed so tense tonight. "Really, Ben . . . I've no idea where she might have heard—enough of that; come, let's go in!" She turned, tugging at his hand, and started to enter the house, but Ben drew her back.

"Wait . . . the night is much too lovely to go inside as yet. Keep my company an instant longer."

She stared at him through the shadows, not liking what she heard. "You aren't coming in?"

"Nay, I"—he sighed, looked away, then back—"can't."

"Oh, Ben! Kathryn will be so disappointed! How could you break her heart so!"

He turned away, staring in the direction of the harbor. "Give her my best regards," he said somewhat absently. Had Jessie not had her gaze centered on the harbor, as well, she might have missed the sudden flash of light that pierced the darkness. Even as she stared, there was another. And then another.

"I wonder what that was."

"Hmmm?" Following the direction of her gaze, Ben assured her, "Nothing, I'm certain 'tis nothing, sweet coz." He untied his stock and slid it off, looping it gently about her neck, drawing her close. "I'd best be going, at any rate. Go in and enjoy yourself. Kathryn will be waiting, and I shall return to collect you soon." With a wink, he added, "You'll save me a dance, won't you?" Jessie nodded, and he bent to kiss her forehead, abandoning the stock about her shoulders.

Leaving her with another wink, he leapt down from the veranda; shells crackled noisily as he lit upon the street. Jessie stood, watching as he slipped into the shadows. Since he'd left behind his snow white cravat, his garments blended consummately with the night. A feeling of unease swept through her as she watched him go. She ignored it, telling herself there was nothing to be concerned with—perhaps he was meeting a woman . . . Removing his cravat from her shoulders, she gazed at it pensively, and then deciding that must be so, she shoved it within her reticule and made her way past the servants, into the festively decorated hall.

Chapter 13

Moonlight spilled over the open veranda, lighting most of its length, but within the garden, beneath the oaks, there was only blissful darkness. It was precisely the haven Jessie sought, and she quickly made her way into the shadows, grateful for having escaped the crush without having gained anyone's notice.

Beguiled by the peace of her surroundings, she stood gazing wistfully into the lantern lit gardens as the soothing strains of a familiar ballad drifted through the air. For an instant she was lost in reverie.

If only things had been different.

Mayhap she, too, would be within . . . dancing gaily under the dazzling candlelit chandeliers . . . in his arms . . . gazing lovingly into his remarkable eyes.

But it was not to be.

And she was no child to muse away her life on shattered dreams.

Sighing wistfully, she drew the domino mask from her head and stared pensively at it. Most of the guests wore one in lieu of a full costume, for fine cloth was not so easily procured here. Her own was gold and silver to match her gown, and though it was truly a work of art, it looked rather dismal with its pouty mouth and exotic eyes. No matter, it matched her mood.

Christian Haukinge was a contemptible blackguard, a swine, a lecher. He was every woman's nightmare.

The problem was . . . she loved him still.

The music faded and she came aware of another sound in the distance—the gentle rushing of water from a garden fountain. It was such a peaceful, lulling sound that when the music recommenced, a minuet seemingly louder than before, it grated on her nerves and she went in search of the font. Following the well-worn garden path, she left behind the festive sounds of the masquerade and entered the serene quiet of the central garden. The font was there in the heart of the hedged enclosure, water spouting from its moonlit core, cascading into an illuminated pool. The scent of wild honeysuckle and roses wafted sweetly upon the air, filling her senses—making her forget, if only for the instant.

Hidden within shadow, Christian watched as she passed him. At the font, she removed her glove and like some bloody seductress, slid her bare fingers into the rushing curtain of water. She sighed softly as she brought the moisture to her skin, cooling her wonderfully soft flesh.

Damn him, but he couldn't seem to forget the feel of it.

Her performance was such a seductive one that he found himself at once aroused. And then again, he thought ruefully, it didn't seem to take much. He needed only remember the day they'd lain together under the elm tree . . . the way she'd trembled at his touch . . . the expression upon her face as she'd come to completion . . . It haunted him still.

He clenched his jaw and thrust the image away.

It served no purpose to remember now.

He glanced away, unable to bear the sight of her. The image of Ben Stone, the way he'd held her this afternoon, twisted his gut. He shouldn't care—didn't want to care—but devil hang him if he didn't. Like metal to a lodestone, his gaze returned to the font, drawn despite his resolve against it. He watched her sway seductively against the cement monstrosity, her face upturned to the inky sky as she caressed her neck with the moistened tips of her fingers. Inexplicable anger surged within him. Did she know he was watching?

He thought it likely so—no doubt another devilish form of torture she'd devised to torment him. All evening she'd danced so lightheartedly, smiled so brilliantly with all her beaux—as though nothing in the world troubled her.

And aye, she'd managed to make his heart bleed all over again.

Before he could be tempted to go to her, he sat upon the ironwork bench, watching. God help him, he was drawn to her like a drunkard to wine, knowing she was no good for him, and still . . . craving her with a need that was too painful to deny.

This time he would resist.

Closing her eyes, Jessie wished herself away from the smiling faces and blissful couples she envied so. Though she was glad for them, it was much too difficult to watch their gaiety when every promise of happiness had vanished from her life. Lord, how she wished she'd never set eyes upon him again—more than that, even, she wished she'd never known him at all.

If only she'd known then what she knew now—that he was a contemptible blackguard who cared only for his own mean pleasures. He'd used her heartlessly, without so much as a thought for her feelings.

With all her heart, she wished herself back in time . . . so that she might undo her mistakes—or, at the very least, prayed she would open her eyes and find it had all been a dreadful nightmare, that she would awaken and find herself capable of feeling again. Turning her face up to the stars, she squeezed her eyes shut and whispered a fervent, "I wish . . ."

"And what is it you wish, m'mselle?" a painfully familiar voice inquired from behind, startling her.

Her heart slammed against her ribs, and for a moment she was paralyzed with dread. Panicking at the thought of facing him again, she drew the domino mask over her head at once and spun around.

She had to search a moment to spy him. He was seated upon the arm of an ornately carved bench, his arms crossed, his legs spread before him, linked casually at the ankles. He stood slowly, flinging a lit cheroot upon the ground, crushing it beneath his boot before coming forward out of the shadows. He regarded her all the while with an expression of supreme boredom.

Please, Lord, she begged, *don't let him realize 'tis me.*

Her heart thundered painfully, and she glanced about anxiously, hoping for a hasty retreat. God curse them, her feet refused to move. And then it was too late, he was standing before her.

His dark lashes fell momentarily, masking his eyes, and then he glanced up once more, meeting her gaze directly. "You were wishing for?"

Her nerves were near the breaking point, and his scrutiny managed to fragment her composure completely. Should she lie? Should she run? The truth barreled out. "I-I was merely indulging in a whim, my lord. Woolgathering you might say." She frowned behind her mask, hoping he wouldn't read the truth behind her words.

His gaze left her as he considered her answer, and in that brief instant Jessie was able to observe him unheeded. He was as handsome as ever—God curse him for that. Dressed in black, he blended consummately with the night. *Like Ben.* Unlike the other guests, however, he wore neither costume nor mask. 'Twas the only reason she'd been aware of his presence. She prayed he didn't know it was her.

When he looked at her again it was with narrowed eyes, and his cold, unmerciful gaze took her breath away. In that discomfiting instant, she knew ... concealing her face from him was pointless. Her mask might have been made of glass, for all it seemed to conceal. His gaze converged upon the glove she'd removed from her hand, and then reverted to the font, lingering there an excruciating moment before returning to her.

His smile was chilling. "You make an alluring picture, my love," he said at last. "Tell me ... was that performance entirely for my benefit ... or would you by chance be meeting a lover?"

His question stung like a slap to the face. How dare he! Her eyes misted traitorously at his accusation. "I-I was merely seeking air," she told him, suppressing the urge to slap his wickedly handsome face. She wanted to kick at him, and rail at him, and might have given in to such childish ravings had her dress not restricted her so. She loathed these trappings, loathed the social order that forbade an open show of her anger. God help her, but she wanted to hurt him, as he'd hurt her!

"If you will excuse me, my lord," she said instead, her hands trembling. "I-I believe I shall leave you to your solitude—my apologies if I have intruded!" With halted breath, she stepped around him, but he caught her arm and drew her back. Jessie gave a cry of despair as he snatched the hood from her head. She snatched it back, her fingers tightening about the gold and silver cloth as a cruel smile touched his lips. His grip tightened upon her arm. "Release me!" She jerked her arm free, and lifted her skirts to bolt past him, but his hand shot out once more, seizing her wrist, jerking her backward.

Her heart lurched. "Please," she whispered, desperate to be away from him. "Please . . . let me go . . ."

"Nay, damn you!"

God help him, he couldn't. And damn him, too, because he shouldn't have to think of her every waking moment—because he shouldn't want to touch her even now—because he shouldn't know the compelling desire to hold her in his arms and kiss her senseless.

He'd come to the garden for a minute's solitude, away from her haunting green gaze, her ingenuous smiles, only to have that peace intruded upon by none other than his green-eyed tormentor herself. Had she thought to hide behind that silly mask of hers? Foolish—

one need only glimpse into those witch's eyes to know her. Only a blind man could not see.

"Damn you, Jessamine!" he swore again, drawing her to him and crushing her against him.

She cried out but did not resist him at once.

"Damn you, damn you . . . damn you," he whispered, lowering his face to hers.

"Don't!" she cried, and tried to break free. "No!" He paused briefly to look into her eyes, and then his gaze fell to her mouth, lingering there.

"Jess," he said, lifting a dark curl that had fallen from her coif and stroking it between his thumb and forefinger. He put his finger to her mouth, caressing her lips, wandering to her cheek, stroking it softly as he held her gaze.

Shivers coursed down her spine. Jessie wasn't aware he released her until both of his hands tangled within her hair. His fingers curled about her neck, holding her steady for his kiss.

Her shoulders slumped in defeat as his lips descended once more. "Nay," she beseeched him, trying in vain to avert her face; he held her imprisoned. "Don't . . . don't . . . please . . ." She whimpered.

"Jessie," said with a groan, urging her to face him, forcing her to acknowledge him.

The sound of his voice was low and tormented, undoing her completely, and then his mouth met hers with savage determination, coaxing her trembling lips. Like liquid fire, his tongue slipped within to brush hotly against her own, and a jolt of almost painful pleasure surged through her. His other hand slid down to splay across her back . . . pressing firmly, forcing her to acknowledge the rest of him as well.

God help her, she responded wantonly to his tender coercion, letting him take whatever he would in that instant. He tasted of brandy, his mouth so warm and sweet with the taste that she could almost feel the burning liquor gliding down her own throat. He smelled of it, too . . . the scent heady to her senses. Her hands dropped helplessly at her sides, and the mask and glove slipped forgotten from her fingers.

"Jessie," he murmured. "Jessie, Jessie, Jessie . . ."

She shook her head, some last vestige of her pride clinging to reality. What was wrong with her that she would weaken so? Even after all that he'd done to her? A sob caught in her throat as she acknowledged the truth. She was in love with him—would always be in love with him—regardless of what he was, regardless of what he'd done to her.

And she loathed him for it—herself even more!

With a strength she didn't know she possessed, she broke free. "Get away from me!" With trembling fingers, she swiped his kiss from her lips. Glaring at him, she bent to pick up the discarded mask at her feet, overlooking the satin glove that lay just beneath it. He stepped forward, and she raised her face to look into his eyes. "Stay away from me!" Her eyes misted traitorously. He reached for her and she twisted away. "No! I loathe it when you touch me!"

It was a blatant lie, and they both knew it.

He arched a brow. "Really?"

Her heart pounded.

"It seemed to me you wanted that kiss as much as I," he taunted. He reached out to place a finger beneath her chin, raising it slightly. "Don't dare deny it, love."

She slapped his hand away from her face. "I am *not* your love!" she hissed. "You don't know the meaning of the word!"

He stiffened. "And you perchance do?" A muscle twitched in his jaw, and she backed away another pace, ready to bolt if he advanced upon her again, but he merely stood, glaring at her with that soul-searing gaze.

Six months ago, that very same blaze in his eyes had broken her heart. Now it only infuriated her. And fury gave her the courage to ask the one thing she needed to know of him. "What sort of man are you, that you would accept payment for breaking a woman's heart?"

For a long instant he merely stared at her, his jaw working, and then he answered, "What kind of man is your brother that he would invite me to do so?"

"I am not asking you to defend my brother's honor!" she countered. "Merely your own! And I ask you again—what kind of man are you that you would take payment for such an ignoble deed? Certainly no gentleman!"

Again he stiffened. "If you find me no gentleman, m'mselle . . . it is because you are no lady." He laughed then, the sound harsh, and stooped to retrieve her glove from the ground. His accusation wrenched at her soul, for she very much feared 'twas so. He brought the glove to his lips for a heartless kiss, and tossed it angrily at her breast. Then he turned and walked away, leaving her to stare after him in mute rage.

With trembling hands, she replaced her hood and mask, and after a moment followed him into the house, hoping he intended to leave, because she, as yet, could not. She cursed Ben to perdition for leaving her here at his mercy. Her heart continued to pound traitorously. She found Kathryn still on the dance floor, laughing gaily, and so she stood aside, watching the shimmering silk and satin dresses promenade by. After a moment—or it might have been a lifetime—Lord St. John appeared at her side. Silently she wished him to blazes, as well, but managed to give him a pleasant smile, nevertheless.

"Jessamine, m'dear," he crooned. "You look absolutely ravishing this eve!"

She resisted the urge to kick him squarely in the shin. "Thank you, my lord," she said sweetly. "However did you know it was me?" She extended her hand in greeting, and he brought it to his lips. Behind her mask, she recoiled at his touch. Only after everyone else in Charlestown had given her such a warm welcome had Lord St. John even bothered to call upon her, fickle fool that he was—not that she wished him to, mind you, but he seemed to flow with the tide of public opinion, wanting her one moment, despising her the next— much like someone else she knew. Her gaze searched the room.

"You," he murmured, kissing her proffered hand, "are simply unmistakable, m'dear."

She sighed. "And why is that, my lord?" she asked through clenched teeth, thankful for the mask that concealed her expression of disgust.

"Why, your eyes, of course," he declared. "They are the rarest of jewels, you see . . ."

At his declaration, Jessie fought to hold back the tears. Christian had once said the very same thing to her, and she wondered irately just how many women had been privy to such disingenuous drivel. *How many others had Christian whispered such endearments to?* The very thought left her bereft, furious too.

Once again her gaze swept the room, this time meeting his over a snifter of brandy. He raised the glass in silent acclaim. She could scarce read his face from the distance, but she suspected he was congratulating her upon Lord St. John's renewed quest for her hand. The man *was* becoming a boor in his pursuit of her. This week alone, Lord St. John had called upon her near a dozen times, and each time she'd claimed an attack of the vapors. Nothing seemed to dissuade him. He simply came again, and again, and again . . .

She averted her gaze, pretending interest in Lord St. John's one-sided discussion. It was insufferable that *both* men who had caused her so much anguish all those many months ago in England should be here now, so many miles away, making her miserable once more. God was surely punishing her!

Chapter 14

"**A**nd where is Ben tonight?" Leland asked, his gaze turning with unconcealed disgust toward Christian. *McCarney had lied to him.* "Jessamine? Are you listening, m'dear?"

"Hmmm? I beg your pardon, my lord," she answered sweetly. "What did you say?"

"I was inquiring over your cousin," he said, silently cursing her. It had not escaped him the way *their* eyes continued to meet across the room—never mind that their expressions were full of veiled contempt. The woman could barely listen to him for *his* presence. *How many times must he forfeit to Haukinge?*

"I really don't know, my lord," she replied, sounding bored.

Leland gritted his teeth, wanting to smack her for her cut of him once again. He forced himself to remain calm and shook his head gravely. "Well ... I daresay ... I do hope he doesn't find himself near the docks this eve ..." He'd come to believe in her innocence, and that as much as anything had kept his tongue stilled about the *incident*, but with the way Haukinge watched her now, as though she were a coveted lost possession, he had to consider her part in the affair all over again. He smiled then, for what sweet justice it would be to woo Jessamine from under his very nose.

"Oh? Why is that, my lord?"

If she would only cooperate, blast it all! Why, he pondered irately, was Haukinge not with his men tonight? His eyes widened with feigned disbelief as he bent to whisper low, "You mean to say you've not heard?" He glanced at Haukinge. The man was rabid, he could see. Leland could feel his tension tangibly, even with the distance between them. His gaze returned to Jessamine. Perhaps he wouldn't lose this round after all ... Perhaps he could use their mutual attraction to his advantage ...

Jessie shook her head, her brow furrowing.

"Well, m'dear, they've seized two of Laurens's vessels! It seems Daniel Moore, who is a very, *very* good friend of mine, I should say, had reason to suspect him of smuggling. And that is not all! Moore has also received word that the infamous Hawk will attempt to smuggle in arms this very night—perhaps even as we speak—to those blasted rebel traitors he abets. Imagine that!" Watching her expression, he continued, "I daresay 'twould serve those devils well if each and every one was assigned the gibbet tonight!" Gazing at Jessie speculatively, he then added suggestively, "I do hope your cousin is wise enough to keep his distance from those rabble-rousers . . . and, of course, the docks . . . at least for tonight . . ."

Jessie's heart began to race wildly. "Of course, my lord! Ben would never!" She tried to mask her concern from Leland, smiling and saying, "In truth, I expect him any instant."

"Do you?" He smiled softly, his expression oddly triumphant.

Jessie smiled wanly in return, though her blood ran cold. If Lord St. John spoke the truth . . . then Ben could very well be with them now—she just couldn't bear to think of the price he might pay. She couldn't help but recall the lights flickering at the dock, nor Ben's rapt attention toward them . . . as though he were watching . . . a signal? She shuddered at the notion.

"Good," he said, "good, because I daresay Adger's wharf is no place to be tonight." Jessie followed the direction of his gaze to where Christian stood, and wondered at the fact that Leland made it a point to raise his chin in greeting, when she knew they despised one another. When Leland's gaze returned to her, he was smiling victoriously, and another shudder seized her.

"Dance with me, dear," he said, giving her no opportunity to resist, for he took her hand and led her without delay amidst the dancers.

Unwilling to create a scene, she went, though her gaze strayed once more across the room.

Christian watched them, his fury barely suppressed.

It was obvious by the expression upon St. John's face, and by the way the bastard's gaze kept straying in his direction, that he had burned Jessie's ears with information intended for him. Maggot. He smiled in disgust. Little did he know that he was investing in the wrong stratagem; Jessie would never willingly come near him—particularly after what had transpired between them in the garden. She'd studiously avoided his gaze since.

Damn St. John. Damn her.

Well, he felt compelled to oblige—if St. John wished to convey information through her treacherous lips, he was certainly willing to hear it. He moved purposefully through the dancers and bent to whisper in her ear.

"Might I have this dance, m'mselle?"

Startled, Jessie swung about to discover Christian behind her, smiling coldly, though for once, not at her, but at Lord St. John. Lord St. John's gaze, too, held some private, undecipherable message, and she shuddered at the feeling that came over her suddenly—as though somehow she were caught in the midst of some war raging between them.

Releasing her, Lord St. John smiled as he stepped away. "Of course," he said, relenting much too easily.

Jessie started to protest, but he gave her no opportunity. Without awaiting her assent,

Christian swept her into his arms, leading her away from Lord St. John.

"I don't believe I recall agreeing to dance with you, my lord," she said evenly. "You're rude, to say the least!"

He smiled without mirth. "You flatter me, *ma belle*. Now, tell me . . . what were you discussing so privately with Lord St. John."

"Of all the arrogant, vain—" She gnashed her teeth. " 'Twas none of your concern!"

"M'mselle," he said, smiling down at her with all the devastating charm that had once been her downfall. Nothing about his tone or expression hinted at the threat she sensed in the address. "I will know this moment what you discussed," he demanded, "or I promise that you will sorely wish you'd stayed at home this eve instead of coming out to parade your"—his gaze swept down, lingering over her carefully exposed bosom—"assets," he finished. "I didn't realize you had so much. You would do Eliza proud, I think."

"How dare you! Arrogant cur!" Jessie gritted her teeth and glared at him. "What makes you think our discourse was any of your concern, at any rate, my lord?"

"Let us simply call it mother wit, *love*."

Jessie's eyes burned with contempt. "I asked you not to call me *that*!"

Christian grinned a slow, unrepentant grin. *"Pardonnez-moi, ma pauvre petite."*

"Nay!" she spat. "I will not!"

He gave her a wintry little smile, but said nothing.

A thought occurred to her suddenly; much as she despised the fact, she knew that Christian and Ben were acquainted . . . If Ben was, in truth, in danger, she would need someone's aid. There was nothing she could accomplish alone, especially at this late hour of the night. The sad truth was that there was no one else she knew to ask for help save Christian. Still, she loathed to ask anything of him. "Very well!" she relented. "He said there was to be trouble on the docks this eve . . . that Ben should stay away!"

"Really?" His gaze was as cold and unyielding as steel. "And?"

"That the notorious *Prince of Smugglers* himself would be raiding the warehouse at Adger's wharf! He—"

Without warning, Christian seized her firmly by the arm, turning her about. She gave a small cry of pain and he released her at once. With a hand at her back, he forced her off the dance floor, walking so close behind her that she could feel the heat of his body. "Do as I say," he whispered for her ears alone, "or so help me God, you will live to regret it."

He led her directly toward their hostess, made a hasty apology for their early departure, and within moments, they were out the front door.

"How dare you tell her I was ill!" She spun about to face him. "My God, you are a despicable liar, as well!"

Christian shook her hard in warning. "Shut up! Shut up, and listen to me, before I lose what bloody little patience I've left! You'll take my carriage and go directly home, *tu me comprends?* Directly!" His tone brooked no argument. He waved a hand, signaling his driver.

"I cannot go now!"

He jerked her arm, warning her without words to be silent.

She stumbled slightly, tripping over her skirts. "Oh! You! Give me one accursed reason I should do as you say—just one!"

His lips curved contemptuously as he peered down into her face, his eyes shadowed. "Because, my love," he spat, "you care too bloody much for your cousin to see him hang, that's why!" Shoving her into his carriage, he hailed the driver off, and then disappeared into the darkness, toward the docks.

"Jean Paul!" Christian's angry summons slashed through the darkness of the warehouse.

"We found it, Hawk. Here!" As proof, Ben swung the lantern quickly over the wooden crates in question.

Pistol in hand, Christian made his way quickly to where they stood.

"The rest have already been hauled aboard the ship."

"Good—get the bloody things up and get out of here! *St. John knows.*" Christian belted his pistol to help with the crates, but no sooner had he seized up one end when there was a muffled hiss from across the room. Within seconds, a thunderous report ripped through the air. Jean Paul's end of the crate crashed to the floor; he took a single step, floundered, and then collapsed upon the crate.

"Halt in the name of the Crown!"

Two more shots rang out and the lantern Ben was clutching swung sharply through the darkness, plummeting downward. It shattered against the splintered wood, bursting into flames.

Chapter 15

~~~∽◯◯∽~~~

Pacing the confines of her room, Jessie was torn between fury and fear—and then she heard the cry and fear won.

"Fire!" came the cry once more, and a chill swept down her spine.

Racing to the window, she peered down below just in time to hear the man call out once more. *"Fire! Fire at the warehouse!"* He scurried down the street, bellowing at the top of his lungs; one by one, windows lit along the shadowy lane. Across the alley, a man came stumbling out in his nightwear. Sprinting into the middle of the street, he snatched off his nightcap as he ran, waving it wildly, hailing the crier, who was even now turning the corner to Church Street. More doors burst open. Within moments the narrow lane became congested with the curious and alarmed.

A loud rapping at Jessie's bedroom door

187

startled her away from the window. "Miss Jessie! Miss Jessie!" cried the voice behind it.

Jessie hurried to the door, thrusting it open to reveal a pudgy, sweet-faced black woman. "Miss Jessie!" the maid squawked. "They's a man downstairs, waitin' fo ya at the back doe—he says that Mastah Ben is in trouble! He tole me to fetch only you, not Mastah Robert! He says that you is the only one who can help him! Should I wake Mastah Robert?"

Fear clutched at Jessie's heart; she shook her head. It might be Christian! "Not yet; let me see what the man says."

Leaving the door open for the maid to enter, Jessie turned to snatch up her cloak from the wooden peg upon the wall. Too distraught to worry over her appearance, she flung the cape over her shoulders and slipped her feet into the soft blue leather slippers she'd discarded earlier in the eve.

Immogene appeared scandalized. "Ain't you gonna dress, Miss Jessie?"

"Once I've discovered what the man has to say, I shall." She hurried past the fretting maid, into the corridor and down the elegantly carpeted stairwell.

"Well, I'm comin' wit' you, then!" Immogene hurried down after her, adding, "Ain't fittin' fo a woman to be runnin' round wit' nothin' on but her nightie!"

"I'll be fine," Jessie swore. "Just see that Claire and Robert are told about the fire."

"Fire?" Immogene halted behind her upon

the stairwell at once. "Lawdy, Miss Jessie, what fire?"

"The warehouse, though I don't know which one as yet! Just go tell them!"

Immogene turned, hurrying back up the stairs, and Jessie raced through the corridor, into the dark kitchen. Thrusting open the back door, she found a short, dark-haired man standing upon the back steps. *It wasn't Christian.* The look he gave her made her wrap her cloak more firmly about her.

"Name's McCarney," he told her, his thick brogue made more prominent by drink. She could smell his fetid breath even from where she stood. "I've come ta fetch ye for Ben, lass. He's been hurt."

"What do you mean hurt? How?"

The man's gaze shifted nervously.

"Has it something to do with the fire?"

He seemed to hesitate a moment, then nodded. "Aye," he yielded at once, "the fire."

"Dear God!" Jessie exclaimed, turning and starting back into the house. "Please, Mr. McCarney, wait while I fetch my cousin Robert."

"Nae, ye don', lass!" Without warning, he seized her by the cloak, jerking her backward. He pressed a whiskey-steeped hand against her lips and nostrils.

Jessie choked, and opened her mouth to scream, but he shoved his fingers down her throat then, gagging her as he forced her into the concealing shadows.

The door slammed shut as she struggled

free of him. Twisting away from him, she ran back toward the safety of the house, opening her mouth to cry out for help, but suddenly the sound of shattering glass rang in her ears. Something wet and sticky trickled down the side of her face. Jolted by the blow, she wavered and fell back into his arms.

The last she heard before blackness took her was an indecipherable Irish curse.

"McCarney, you whoreson! What the bloody blue blazes have you done to her?"

"She wouldna come," he said without remorse. "She was aboot t' go and tell her cousin—couldna let her do that, now could I?"

"You didn't have to strike her so damned hard!" Taking Jessie into his arms, Christian shoved McCarney away.

"I dinna draw blood!"

"God's teeth!" Christian snarled. "She's dead to the world. What'd you hit her with?"

McCarney frowned. "My whiskey flask, and y' can well believe I was no' too pleased o'er wastin' it, either—paid good coin fer it, damn it all!"

"Well, you'd bloody well better pray she wakes up."

"She's breathin', ain't she?"

Christian eyed him speculatively as he placed Jessie gently down within the skiff. Her cloak was twisted wildly about her—damned, if she didn't look like an Indian corpse being readied for a burning. Untying it, he carefully unraveled it, and removed it.

"Christ!" he muttered, dropping the cloak over her at once to shield her from Mc-Carney's greedy eyes. He turned to fix Mc-Carney with another glare as he came to his haunches beside her. "What the devil did you do, McCarney, take her from her goddamned bed?"

McCarney shook his head, his eyes flashing insolently. "Nay! She came t' the door just sae!"

Damn her, Christian cursed silently. "Let's get out of here." It was a wonder they'd escaped at all. He shook his head in disgust. Someone had cost him dearly this night—damned if he wouldn't find out just who. First Jean Paul—Christ, if his father died . . . He forced his thoughts away from that possibility. And then Ben. Now Jessie? He couldn't bear it if she was hurt.

Within moments the boat was launched and gliding soundlessly down the Cooper River, toward the shadowy harbor. Jessie groaned, placing a hand to her head, and relief surged through him as he watched her revive. And then she lifted that beautiful green gaze to his, and he had the sudden urge to toss her overboard, so much revulsion was evident there.

"You!" she hissed, scooting away from him as though he were a slug in her bed. She drew herself up, glaring fiercely at him. "I should have known! God, I should have known! You're a despicable liar, Mister Haukinge!"

Mister, was it?

He'd fallen that far from grace, had he?

Again she scooted backward, and stood, rocking the boat with her hysterics. Her cloak slid away, revealing the dark tips of her breasts through the pristine white night rail she wore. His jaw tautened. He glanced over his shoulder, scowling. "Turn around, McCarney!" Turning again to Jessie, he apprised her, his tone firm, "Be still, or you'll topple the boat."

"You're a liar!" she shrieked. "Where's Ben? God, he's not hurt, is he? What a paper-skull I am! God—oh, God, where are you taking me?"

Christian frowned. Why wasn't there more ruching, or lace, or bows—or some other goddamned thing on the bodice of her night rail to conceal her from view! A memory besieged him; the day he'd pulled her from the fence . . . how he'd wanted to taste her then. He shuddered, thrusting the sultry image away. "Cover yourself, Jess."

She didn't seem to have heard him. "Where are you taking me!"

"Goddamn it, Jess!"

"God! I loathe you," she hissed. "Where are you taking me?"

"Despise me all you like," he allowed, reaching for the cloak that lay pooled at her feet. "Only cover—"

Thinking he meant to grab her, she recoiled, shrieking, her hands flailing as she lost her balance. The boat tipped precariously. Christian reached for her, snatching her down before she could tumble overboard. He brought her safely to her knees. She fought him, shoving wildly, and when that didn't work, pounded his shoulder with the butt of her hand.

"Be still, dammit—you'll topple the boat!"

Her eyes burned with green ire. "*I* can swim, Mr. Haukinge—can *you*?"

A faint smile quirked at Christian's lips. Impertinent wench! She ceased her struggles at last and glared at him as though she could will him to burst into flames—the irony of it all was that she could. *He burned for her even now.* "Aye," he told her, "I can, though I'd prefer not to."

"I don't much care for what you prefer! I demand you return me to my home this very instant!"

Christian shook his head regretfully. "I cannot, I'm afraid." He smiled slightly as he suggested, "Though you might always hitch a ride with the gators, if you like."

"Gators!"

As Christian intended, she went perfectly still within his embrace. He nodded. "Out there." He nodded toward the darkness.

She immediately searched the shadows. "You lie! I see no gators!"

"Ah," he said, "but are you willing to chance it?" He released her then, to prove his point. For a moment she peered hard into the blackness, into the moon's reflection upon the water, as though to discern whether or not he spoke the truth. There was an ominous splash in the distance, a swish of water, but nothing was discernible through the darkness. Assuming Jessie had heard it as well, he was unprepared for what she did next. He caught her once again as she lunged toward the water, forcing her flat upon her back. He had to lie full upon her in order to still her completely.

Anger clouding her judgment, Jessie fought him, pummeling him with her fists and shoving with all her strength. He seemed as heavy as a mountain—indestructible as one, as well—and the only thing she seemed to accomplish was to rock the boat. Feeling utterly helpless, she boxed his left ear with an open palm.

"Ayyee! Devil hang you, woman!" Christian caught her wrists, pinning them ruthlessly to the planks. "Damn you! Didn't you hear me? There are gators in these waters! Do you really loathe me so much, Jessie, that you'd prefer their company to mine?"

"Aye!" she spat. "At least with them, I know what to expect! *You*, Mr. Haukinge, are an impostor of the worst sort!"

Chapter 16

❧◦◦❧

She didn't know the half of it.

He felt the urge to lash back at her, to make her heart ache as much as his did, but he found he couldn't bear to do that. There had been far too much grief already this night. He had no idea if Jean Paul even lived at the moment, he only knew that by now they would have reached the *Mistral*—that he and Jessie, too, must reach the *Mistral*. He desperately needed her help. "Jess . . ." God, he loathed the thought of telling her. "Ben *was* shot tonight."

Her expression transformed before his eyes, from fiery abhorrence to liquid fear. "Shot?"

"Aye . . . and Jean Paul, too."

"The same Jean Paul?"

Christian nodded slowly, his jaw taut. "Aye."

"Is—" Her voice broke. She shook her head, choking on her words. "Ben . . ."

Christian knew instinctively what she was asking. "He was alive when last I saw him," he told her, trying to be merciful, but truthful. "I've no idea how he fares just now."

Jessie's eyes glistened with tears as she stared up at him. His anguish deepened as he acknowledged her tormented expression. "If I release you," he asked softly, averting his gaze momentarily, "will you promise to sit quietly?"

She nodded dumbly, and Christian removed himself from atop her at once. Comfort was there within his grasp—within her arms—but they were not alone, nor did he feel she'd welcome his embrace. She sat slowly, hugging her knees to her breast, staring numbly into the darkness. Unsure of what to say to ease her, Christian retrieved her cloak, tossing it about her shoulders.

"How?"

She couldn't seem to bear to look at him.

"You'll have to ask Ben," he told her softly. "If he wishes you to know, he'll tell you himself."

Jessie nodded glumly, and Christian wondered if he was making a mistake involving her. Could she be trusted? Though she'd betrayed him once already, the truth was that he had little choice in the matter: Jean Paul needed someone to nurse him, Ben, too, and Jessie, inexperienced as she might be, was all that was available to him. He could trust no one else—sad state of affairs, but these were treacherous times. He told himself she had every reason to keep silent . . . for Ben's sake. And judging by the sorrowful look upon her face, he had nothing to fear; she cared for her cousin.

The question was . . . *how much*?

His gut twisted at the thought of the two of them together.

Night sounds filled the air. Frogs and crickets that only moments before had been silent croaked and trilled so loudly that their din overwhelmed all other sound.

Hugging herself against the crisp night air, Jessie turned to meet Christian's gaze. He was watching her with an odd intensity, his dark hair gleaming in the moonlight. His jaw taut, and his mouth set determinedly. However much she loathed him, now was not the time for it, she decided.

Ben needed her.

"What of Jean Paul?"

"Alive," he revealed with a shrug that tried to conceal his pain. "I really don't know." With a glance toward McCarney, he shook his head and repeated softly, "I really don't know."

The *Mistral* was anchored offshore, far enough that there was no light to guide them, yet close enough that they dared not use a lantern for fear of discovery.

The faint glow of a single lantern illumined one of the portholes of the *Mistral*, and by that light, Jessie could make out the rope ladder that had been left for their use. McCarney maneuvered the skiff alongside it, and with a curt nod and a wave of his hand, Christian motioned for her to climb it. She hesitated and he asked her, "Perhaps you'd like to remain with McCarney, instead?"

That veiled warning sent Jessie up the ladder at once. God's truth, but she had no wish to be alone with that man ever again! Certainly he'd not needed to employ such appalling violence to gain her compliance. He might have simply tried explaining Ben's predicament. She would have flown to his aid!

She reached the top rung and started to feel Christian's hand suddenly upon her, steadying her until she was safely over the railing. She'd not realized he was following so close behind. Even as she planted her feet firmly upon the decking, he heaved himself over the side after her. He said not a word, guided her instead, toward the feeble light belowdecks. He led her within a cabin at the midway point along the dusky passage.

Clasping her cloak together, she froze upon entering the room, tendrils of fear clutching at her heart. Two cots occupied the small cabin room. Jean Paul lay so very still upon one, Ben upon the other. Christian at once went to his father's side, his profile as rigid as steel as he stooped over him. His jaw twitched, only slightly, though enough to reveal his pain. Jessie's heart ached for him.

Taking a deep breath, she followed within. Ben turned to face her at once.

"How do they fare?" she heard Christian ask.

"Jessie!" Ben exclaimed. "What the devil are you doing here, coz?"

Jessie's eyes misted as she dropped to her knees beside him. "Where . . . where were you shot?" Her voice faltered with joy and relief. Her fingers trembled as she took him by the hand.

Ben's gaze skidded away. He closed his eyes for the briefest instant, his jaw working. "Who . . . who told you?"

Jessie's gaze reverted to where Christian knelt, examining Jean Paul, and then quickly returned to Ben.

Ben sighed, understanding her silent message. "It merely grazed me," he yielded at last, turning to show her a small gash at his temple.

"Balderdash!"

Startled by the exclamation, Jessie immediately searched the cabin for the bearer of the voice. A white-haired man rose from beside Christian and started toward them, shaking his head. Bending purposely over Ben, he very unceremoniously yanked the coverlet from his limbs. Pointing to the wound upon Ben's leg, he asked, "Does that look like a scrape to ye, mum?"

Jessie gasped, for Ben was bare beneath the blanket. She forced her gaze to remain, for the wound seemed hideous and she wanted so desperately to help. It was evident that he had bled a great deal, for there was blood encrusted upon his leg and a fair amount soaking the pallet beneath him. Yet it no longer bled, and for that she was deeply gratified.

Casting the old man an angry glare, Ben snatched the blanket back before Jessie could see more. He flushed, but noting her horrified expression, he turned again to the old man. "What the devil do you know!" he snapped. "What are you trying to do? Frighten her to death?"

Amazingly, the old man glowered back at him. He snorted. "Tryin' to save yer ungrateful hide, is all," he grumbled. "What do ye think she's here fer, anyhow?"

Returning his gaze to Jessie, Ben assured her, "Really, coz, 'tis not as bad as it appears." He gave a resentful nod in the old man's direction. "The slug's already been removed— and *not* too gently, I might add! 'Tis why it looks so bad and bled so much."

"I see," Jessie replied. "Who removed it?"

Turning to pierce the scowling white-haired old man with an indignant glare, he ground out, "Take one guess!"

"I'm certain, Ben, that he was only trying to help." She shook her head, trying to keep at bay her emotions. "At any rate," she told him, her eyes questioning, " 'tis not his fault you were wounded tonight, was it?"

"Crotchety pain-in-the-arse old man!" Ben grumbled, but his eyes misted suspiciously. He averted his gaze.

"Please . . ." She glanced up into the old man's gentle brown eyes. "Bring me water and rags, and accept my apologies for my cousin's discourteous behavior. It must be the pain that dims his sense of gratitude."

The old man stared at her a long moment, clearly unused to such apologies and evidently bemused by her defense of him. He nodded suddenly and scurried away to do her bidding.

"You know not what you're doing, abetting that man," Ben said, still unable to look at her.

"Shush," she said. Reassured that anyone as contrary as Ben was too mean to die, she turned her attention to Jean Paul. In truth, she had no idea what else to say to her cousin, for she was seeing a side of him she'd never known existed. Nor was she entirely certain she wanted to know what had occurred tonight.

Christian moved away as Jessie neared, but she noted the way he watched her so intently. He didn't trust her, she knew. Well, she didn't care. She ignored him as best she could, turning to peer down into the slumbering man's face. Her eyes widened and her gaze immediately returned to Christian. The resemblance between them was remarkable. How, she wondered, could Jean Paul not know Christian was his flesh and blood? Deciding they were a pair of stubborn old fools—and that they deserved one another—she turned again to Jean Paul.

Placing the back of her hand to his nostrils, she felt his warm breath against her skin and sighed in relief. Hesitantly, fearful of what she might discover beneath, she lowered the blanket from his chest to examine the wound at his shoulder.

It didn't appear nearly as bad as she'd expected—Ben's was worse, in fact. Still, judging by the stain upon his shirt, he, too, had bled quite a lot. Taking in the wide expanse of his chest, she peered up at Christian, unwittingly comparing the two. Christian gave her a narrow-eyed look, and her cheeks heated. She glanced quickly away, though Lord help her, she could scarce keep her thoughts from straying where they should not, even now.

She felt suffocated with him so near.

She examined Jean Paul's wound, completely at a loss as to what to do next. It appeared as though Quincy had ministered to him, as well, and she was silently grateful to the old man, for she truly doubted she could have done the unpleasant task herself. The awful truth was that Jessie wasn't even certain she'd have known how to remove the thing in the first place—nor did she have the strength of stomach for it. The very sight of so much blood made her dizzy and sick. She wasn't precisely experienced in this sort of thing, after all. She peered up at Christian in exasperation, silently asking him what he wished of her, because she didn't know what to do.

"He regained consciousness a short time ago," Ben revealed, "for only an instant."

Peering over her shoulder at her cousin, Jessie nodded and turned to place a hand to Jean Paul's forehead. "He's quite warm," she added softly. "I-I'm not certain what to do . . .

when I was ill, my maid Hildie would sponge
me with cool water. It seemed to help—at least
I think it did."

"Just do what you can for him."

The tone of Christian's voice, the gravity
with which he spoke, gave Jessie the impression that he'd come as close to begging as he
was able. She peered up at him.

"That's all I ask of you."

Their gazes locked, held, and Jessie fought
the urge to throw her arms about him, comfort
him. There was so much pain evident in his
deep blue eyes. "Christian . . . I—" Truly, she
wanted to help—despite everything—but she
just *didn't* know how. She shook her head, not
in negation, but in regret. And then anger
flooded her once more, that he should put her
in such a horrible predicament. She averted
her gaze. "You should have abducted a physician in my stead! God's truth, I know *nothing*
of healing!"

"You don't understand," Christian murmured low into her ear, and despite the gravity of the situation before them, a chill swept
down her spine as his warm breath stirred her
hair. "I—" His voice caught. "I had no choice,
Jess."

Jessie shivered. "Why not?" she asked,
swallowing. She peered up at him. "Your fa—
Jean Paul," she amended hastily, furiously,
glancing briefly about before speaking again.
"He could die without a physician's care—I
don't understand why you would risk that!
Why?"

His blue eyes glinted strangely.

"Because," he snapped. His jaw worked, and then suddenly his expression hardened. "Dammit, I simply cannot! Do what you can, or get the hell out of the way!"

Jessie worried her lower lip, torn between the desire to rail at him and the need to aid Ben and Jean Paul. She pretended an interest in Jean Paul's frilly sleeve cuff, rubbing it absently between her fingertips. Lord help her, but outrage nearly won out. She dared not meet his gaze, lest he see the awful pain he'd once more managed to inflict upon her. She held her tongue, resigning finally to do all that she could, though it seemed insane not to procure medical aid from a knowledgeable physician. There was so much to lose.

"I'm certain you'll at least do what you can for Ben," he said, and his tone was almost an accusation.

Jessie met Ben's sympathetic brown eyes over her shoulder. Her cousin seemed angered by Christian's disregard of her, yet he said nothing. Out of deference? Loyalty? What?

Rising abruptly, Christian peered down at her, his fists clenched at his sides. He closed his eyes, and when he reopened them, his expression was shuttered; only his eyes revealed his pain. "Please, Jess . . ."

He couldn't know what he was asking of her—what if she failed? She nodded, placing a hand to Jean Paul's chest, taking comfort in his smooth, even breathing.

Silence seemed to permeate the small cabin,

and then suddenly Christian turned and walked away, his footsteps a hollow echo upon the planking.

How could he put her in such a dreadful position? How could he drag Ben into his sordid affairs—and aye, she was certain the blame for everything, *everything* that had transpired this night, fell to none other than Christian. Gritting her teeth, she set about the task of removing Jean Paul's bloodied shirt.

"You love him don't you, coz?"

Jessie shot Ben a wrathful glare. He was watching her intently, his knowing gaze as penetrating as Christian's.

"As I love walking barefoot through snow," she replied. But even as she spoke the words, her heart ached with the lie; she feared she *did* love the rotten knave.

Quincy reentered the room, lugging in a small black kettle filled with water and a handful of rags. The kettle, he set down before her, sloshing water onto the floor; the rags, he dropped beside her. "That's it, mum."

"Thank you," she said woodenly.

The old man sighed wearily and stooped to speak softly to her. "I've seen worse, mum. He's just all out from my removing the slug, is all. Ye watch an' see iffen he don't wake up soon." He winked conspiratorially. "Now . . . his lordship, on the other hand . . ." His gaze locked with hers. " 'Tis *he* who needs you, Miss Jessie."

Jessie averted her gaze. "Thank you," she murmured, flustered. For the first time, she thought to wonder how he knew her name. *How could he possibly think Christian needed her?* She listened to the protest of his bones as he stood with a groan. She waited for his footsteps to fade as he left her, and then she set out to do the best she was able, using the scalding water to cleanse both Ben's and Jean Paul's injuries. She ripped up the rags into small strips and bandaged their wounds, and later, once Ben had dozed and the water had cooled, she used it to sponge Jean Paul.

Only when her eyes began to droop did she leave off, curling beside Ben upon the floor. She lay there, with her head pillowed upon his chest, listening to the smooth, even rhythm of his breathing, and fell asleep just so.

Chapter 17

C hristian didn't quite expect the sight that greeted him as he entered the cabin—should have, perhaps, but didn't. Yet, it didn't surprise him either. It *did* make his gut turn to see Jessie curled so familiarly beside her cousin upon the floor.

God's teeth, at least she was still wearing her cloak, he told himself, though it had ridden up her leg along with her gown, exposing her for God's and just about anyone's eyes. He strode purposely toward them, muttering curses as he stooped to cover her with her cloak.

Unable to sleep, he'd come several times during the night; each time he'd found her awake, holding her damnable cousin's hand, or gently sponging Jean Paul's brow. And so he'd remained hidden in the shadows, observing unheeded, not trusting himself to remain in the same room with her. After a while, he'd not been able to bear even that, and he'd withdrawn to the solitude of his own cabin. Now he had to wonder over the wisdom of his decision.

'Twas obvious the woman was a dim-witted fool to be lying so near a half-nude, half-conscious man—cousin or no! What the devil was wrong with her? Didn't she realize what she could do to a man with naught more than her presence? Christian might have been dead as a doornail and would have still scented her beside him; hers was a siren's perfume that called to his male senses more keenly than he cared to admit.

God's bones, she'd nursed her cousin so tenderly that he'd found himself wishing it were he lying there wounded instead . . . with her soft hand stroking his so lovingly. What ailed him that he would crave her touch so interminably? Even to such a degree?

Why had he felt compelled to seek her out last night, when somewhere within, he had to have known she couldn't help him.

Because he'd needed her.

Very simply, he needed her, and the admission tormented him.

Stirring at last, Jean Paul groaned, and Christian turned as his father opened weary blue eyes to the morning light. Behind him, Jessie roused at once; he was painfully aware of her every move, every gesture and sound. She hurried to Jean Paul's side, ignoring him—or mayhap she did not see him—turning the full impact of her stunning emerald gaze upon his father instead.

"*Mon Dieu . . . un ange,*" Jean Paul murmured weakly. He blinked at Jessie, his eyes glassy with fever. "I am gone to heaven, *ma petite chérie*, yes?"

"You've been ill," Jessie whispered, smiling sweetly down at him. She touched his brow and Christian shuddered. He found himself envying his father, as well; he couldn't help himself.

"I thought you were on your deathbed, old man."

Jean Paul turned to face him. "I'm much too stubborn to die, you realize."

Christian flashed him a grin.

"And who is this divine *ange*, Hawk?"

Jean Paul seized Jessie's hand, squeezing it. She snatched it away at once, so startled was she by the name he'd spoken.

Christian stiffened.

As she turned slowly toward him, he saw that her expression was one of shock and horror, and he braced himself for her anger.

"Nay!" she whispered, her face twisting. "It cannot be!" Her gaze reverted to Jean Paul. Jean Paul wore a guarded expression now, his eyes shifting uneasily from her to Christian and then to Ben, who was now awake, watching. Jessie met Ben's gaze then, her eyes searching his face for confirmation. And then her eyes narrowed as her gaze returned to Christian. She glared at him. "What did you call him?" she asked Jean Paul, though her gaze never wavered from Christian's.

"Not a bloody damned thing!" Christian thundered. Shoving away from the doorframe, he eyed Jean Paul wrathfully.

Jessie stood. "Well! No need to repeat yourself, sirrah," she said with a glower for Jean Paul. "I believe I heard well enough the first time!" Her gaze met Christian's. "Hawk!" she spat, as though the word were an oath. "I cannot believe I have been so dull-witted!" She spun about, going to the port window to gaze out into the harbor. "Good God, I should have known!" she whispered furiously, casting a wounded glance back at them.

For a long instant she was silent, and Christian hung his head back and closed his eyes.

She turned to the window.

Before her, the ocean was a blanket of molten silver beneath the cloudy heavens; Charlestown no more than a blur on the misty horizon—as were her emotions, for she couldn't seem to feel them. "And Ben?" Jessie asked. "How long have you known?"

"From the first. I'm not sorry for it, coz."

For a long moment, Jessie couldn't bring herself to face them, much less respond to Ben's confession. How well she understood, for she herself had tried in vain to feel regret for all that had passed between her and Christian.

Hawk.

The loathsome appellation twisted her heart, filled her with confusion and anger.

Fear. Another lie. She shook her head, the ache in her heart growing tangible now. How very, very, very stupid she'd been. She let her forehead strike against the pane and gave a wounded little laugh. She spun to face them abruptly.

"Of course you wouldn't be, Ben," she yielded bitterly. "He has a certain cunning about him, does he not?" She eyed Christian coldly. "The ability to twist a person's mind until that person sees him as all that is noble and good!" She laughed derisively, though it was directed more at herself—for her stupidity and blind devotion. She gave a small cry of despair and said, "What a travesty of a man you are, *Hawk*! I—" Her voice broke. "God help me—I despise you!" Herself, as well! What an undeniable fool she was, for even now she wanted to fling herself into his arms, beg him to love her. God's truth, if he only halfheartedly denied everything, she would believe in him even now . . . because fool that she was, she wanted to trust in him still . . . wanted to love him still.

She couldn't help herself.

Christian's eyes glittered cruelly, piercing her heart.

Her brows collided, the ache in her heart nearly strangling her. "Amos was right," she spat, wanting to hurt him as he'd hurt her, "you are the lowest of low! A filthy, rotten scoundrel!" Blinded by unwanted tears, Jessie bolted past him, wrapping her cloak more securely about her as she fled the cabin.

He caught her in the corridor, seizing her by the arm and wrenching her about, dragging her in the opposite direction from which she'd intended to go. "Release me!" she demanded, struggling against him.

"I don't think so, my love; you're in no condition to go anywhere."

"Unhand me!" she hissed, struggling in vain against his merciless grip.

Kicking open the door at the end of the passage, he dragged her within the cabin.

To Jessie's shock, this room was immense, disorienting her momentarily. Beautifully furnished, it came complete with window dressings and exquisite paintings. The curtains were drawn over what appeared to be an enormous window, keeping all trace of sunlight from the room and leaving them bathed in shadows. The bed itself was a massive canopied platform, ornately carved with beautiful rice blooms and steps beside it. Dark blue silks, nearly black, cascaded from the canopy, fluttering wildly as he slammed the door behind them.

His face a mask of fury, he led her toward the monstrous bed, thrusting her down; the mattress was soft, cushioning her fall. She settled deep within it, parting her lips for a scream. He held his hand up abruptly, silencing her, for she thought he meant to strike her. He didn't; he merely stood, glaring instead.

"Damn you," he warned, "I don't want to hear another bloody word from you!" Towering over her as he was, he suddenly appeared nothing like the man she'd come to love in England. She saw him in that instant for what he was: a ruthless outlaw against the Crown. How could she not have known before? All the signs ... only she had been too blind and too stupid to recognize them all. His hair, his dress, his manner—everything about him!

Wide-eyed, Jessie scooted backward across the bed, glaring wrathfully at him, her anger making her bold, despite her fear. "Of course not," she taunted, "*Hawk!* Heaven forbid that you should hear the truth about yourself. Lord knows, I should have listened to my brother! God's truth, even Lord St. John would have been a better man to love than you! I loathe you—God, I loathe you!"

"Do you?" His expression turned suddenly colder. His eyes glittering, he bent over the bed and said, "Do you truly, *ma pauvre petite*?" He reached out, snatching the cloak from her body. Jessie gasped as he hurled it across the room. Without warning, he caught her by the leg, jerking her down to the end of the bed, and then he leaned over her fully, trapping her between his arms, beneath him. He hovered above her, his breath ragged with anger, and his body taut. Panicked by the savage look in his eyes, she tried to wriggle free; he descended upon her at once, pinning her beneath his weight.

He caught her by the neck, his fingers tangling in her hair, his eyes glittering coldly as he tilted her face to meet his smoldering gaze.

"Do you truly despise me?" he asked softly, menacingly. He didn't wait for her to respond; his lips descended swiftly—hot, branding, stifling in their intensity. Lord help her, but she couldn't breathe—she thought she'd suffocate, his kiss was so unrelenting.

Her fingers grasped wildly at his back, closing about his queue. Tugging desperately, she tried to draw him away, twist free of his kiss, if only to catch her breath, but the uncompromising hand at the back of her neck prevented it. He squeezed her nape and she released his hair. She was well and duly trapped, yet even as she acknowledged the fact, she was suddenly so very desperate to hold him close to her.

It was like nothing Jessie had ever experienced. Gone was the gentle coercion Christian had exercised before. His lips were hard and punishing as they moved over hers, yet intoxicating nevertheless. She whimpered as his tongue masterfully pillaged her mouth. She struggled to rid herself of the warm, silky intrusion in her mouth, but his kiss only deepened in response.

He groaned, suddenly softening in his response to her as his other hand sought her breast. She was startled by the gentleness of his fingers as they caressed her. Her heart leapt, and she fought her treacherous body as it reacted to his touch. Gasping at the incredible sensations his shocking touch aroused, she tried to will herself to breathe. Her heartbeat quickened and her breath became more labored still.

She was mortified that he could affect her so, even as angry as she was, but she couldn't help it, she sank into the mattress, reaching out to clutch him to her, returning his caresses; her fingers stroked his back.

Good God . . . she couldn't help herself . . .

He jerked away suddenly, his look satisfied, yet furious still . . . so very furious. Jessie's breath came in labored gasps as she stared numbly up at him.

"Now," he said through clenched teeth, "tell me again how much you despise me, Jessie."

Jessie was struck dumb, unable to think clearly, much less open her mouth to speak. Her hand went to her throat as she gasped for breath.

"I didn't think so," he said smugly, and spun on his heels, leaving her so dazed that she had to wonder what it was he'd even said. Always he had to have the last word! When it finally dawned on her what he'd said to her, her cheeks flamed in anger. "Blackguard!" she screamed. "I do loathe you! I do!" She reached back and seized the first thing she encountered—a pillow—hurling it at his back. It bounced off him to the floor, and he halted in midstride.

His hand clenching at his sides, he addressed her with controlled deliberation. "I suggest you get some rest, lest you desire more of what I've to offer." He turned to face her then, his blue eyes glinting dangerously, letting her see the evidence of his arousal.

Her eyes widened.

"I see we understand one another," he said sharply, pivoting once more. "I'll send McCarney to Charlestown for your possessions in the meantime." He opened the door and stepped out.

"Nay—wait, please!" He hesitated in closing the door, and Jessie scrambled from the bed after him. "Ben . . ." He turned to face her, and his anger seemed to flare at the mention of her cousin. She forced herself to speak, stepping forward, clutching her gown together. "B-Ben and I shall go with him," she suggested, her eyes pleading. "Please . . . he needs a physician."

"You're a fool, Jess!" he swore softly. "He cannot go back!"

"Nay, nay, listen to me . . . I shall simply explain—"

"Christ!" he exploded. "You still don't understand, do you?" He gave her an incredulous look. "What will you explain, Jessamine?"

Her heart leapt. "I'll think of something . . . surely . . . something . . ." Her voice sounded weak and defeated even to her own ears.

He shook his head. "I've news for you, love . . . After last night, they would as soon hang him as listen to explanations." His eyes narrowed. "Is that what you want for your *beloved* cousin? To see him hang?"

Jessie shook her head, angry tears of frustration stinging her eyes.

"I didn't think so," he snarled. "Now, get some sleep! You'll bloody well need it!"

Jessie nodded in resignation and sat upon the bed, her eyes misting. God help her, she absolutely refused to weep before him. Again he turned to leave. "Wait," she pleaded still, more softly this time. "Wh-What will you tell Ben's father?"

"What would you have me tell him?"

"The truth," she appealed, her green eyes brimming with tears. "Perhaps he can help?"

He shook his head, his expression softening somewhat. "I doubt it," he told her. "But if 'tis your wish, then aye, I shall tell him."

"Do you not think my cousin deserves to know of his son's condition?" she returned, her outrage returning tenfold. "What if Ben were to die?"

"I've seen worse injuries," Christian informed her curtly. "I rather doubt he'll expire any time soon—but aye, you've a point, and as I said, I shall tell him. Now, get some sleep; 'tis been a long night." He left then, slamming the door after him.

When Jessie awoke, she was startled to find her trunks littering the cabin floor. Lord, she must have slept like the dead, for she'd not so much as heard anyone enter. At second glance, it appeared as though Christian had brought every last article she owned, and she wondered irately why he would have done so.

Surely she wouldn't be away so long—couldn't bear to be!

In one corner of the cabin, there was a large cheval glass that had not been there previously. Under normal circumstances she might have recognized the gesture as thoughtful, but she refused to be grateful to the likes of Hawk—damnable Prince of Smugglers! *Traitor to the Crown*. Her face screwed, for she loved a man she should not even like. Again she wondered how she could have been so witless that she hadn't known. She ran a hand through her tousled hair, lifting it out of her face, and then rose with a weary sigh.

Her green silk dress lay sprawled over one of her trunks. It was more than obvious that Christian had taken the liberty of rifling through her belongings—well, she wasn't about to dress to please the wretched mongrel, and so she ignored it. Searching indignantly through the largest of her trunks, noting with some relief that he'd neglected to bring her petticoats, she found the most unbecoming gown she owned—a blue one, almost the shade of his eyes. She frowned at the comparison, then irately tossed the gown aside. Again she searched, smiling with satisfaction as she spotted another more suitable one.

It took Jessie little time to dress. She braided her hair into one thick braid, and with a quick glimpse into the cheval glass, decided she looked unappealing enough. God's truth, she couldn't bear any more of his heated glances—

nor, for that matter, any more of his *kisses*. The last had nearly undone her.

Opening the door, she drew in a breath and stepped out of the cabin, making her way to the room where Ben and Jean Paul slept. The door was closed, but Ben and Jean Paul were awake, bickering ceaselessly with one another like cantankerous old men.

"Damnation, Jean Paul," she heard Ben grumble, "he needn't have brought her into this."

"Non," came Jean Paul's curt reply, "but he did what he thought was best. You cannot fault him for trying to help us." Neither could Jessie for that matter, and some of her anger left her with that realization.

"He knew not where else to turn—nor could he have known we would fare so well."

"Good God, man! You might have fared well enough, but I? I cannot even rise upon these useless limbs of mine!"

Jessie's heart twisted painfully at his disclosure, and she closed her eyes, placing her cheek against the door.

"Oui, mon fils, but you will given time."

There was a strained silence between them, and she thought to use it to her advantage, to make her presence known, but even as she made to open the door, Jean Paul spoke again. "You think I do not know what makes you so angry, but I do. You love her, do you not?"

Jessie held her breath for his reply, but there was none.

"I thought so," Jean Paul answered low, almost too low for her to hear. "In that case . . . allow me to point out to you a fact that you are doubtless already aware of. She's your kinswoman; 'tis unseemly you should feel so much for her."

"We're distant cousins."

"So distant?"

Another long interval of silence before Ben gave his grudging reply. "Damn you, Jean Paul, you're getting on my nerves—shut up, already!"

Having heard enough, Jessie knocked faintly upon the door, somewhat shaken. " 'Tis me," she called out, trying to sound blithe.

There was a long, impenetrable silence, then Jean Paul's voice rang out clearly. "Come in, come in, *ma petite*! Come in!"

She opened the door to find Jean Paul at the port window, facing her, looking drawn, but well enough.

Ben, on the other hand, sat upon his pallet, propped against the wall, his expression grim. The coverlet had been hastily tossed over his limbs, and his shirt was agape. In his hand he held a long, slim piece of oak, and he pretended to study the length of it, ignoring her.

Jessie's first thought was that Jean Paul should not have risen so soon. But then, unable to help herself, she quickly returned her gaze to Ben. She'd never seen a man unclad before, and couldn't help but stare. She found herself wondering if that were the way Christian looked without his shirt. They were sim-

ilar in build, after all. As though suddenly
realizing the direction of her gaze, Ben clasped
his shirt together, turning a pale shade of crimson as he concealed himself from her scrutiny.
Chagrined by her brazenness, Jessie managed
a hasty apology, and before either of them
could protest her leaving, she turned and left
them, closing the door swiftly behind her.

Going in search of Christian, for she fully
intended to demand he take her home, she
made her way above deck, only to discover it
bustling with activity. The one detail in particular that caught her immediate notice was that
the mainsail was being hoisted. As understanding dawned, it took mere seconds for her
anger to resurface.

Christian, the cur, stood upon the foredeck,
his legs set imposingly apart as he overlooked
the preparations for sail, barking orders to his
men. Enraged, she marched toward him, fists
clenched. "Just what do you think you're doing? And why have you brought so many of
my belongings aboard this—this *smuggler's
den* of yours? I do not intend to stay!"

His eyes glinted with amusement. For a
long moment it seemed he wouldn't reply at
all, and then when he did, his tone mocked
her. "It seems to be obvious, m'mselle, I am
readying the ship for sail." He eyed her gown
and lifted the corners of his mouth. "As for
your belongings," he told her somewhat scath-
ingly, "I believe you'll find that you need
them"—his brow rose—"unless, of course,
you prefer to wear your nightwear instead."

"Oh yes! Yes, of course," she replied in an acid tone. "I love to parade about in my nightgown! More than that, even, I love to be abducted in the middle of the night and brought against my will to a den of thieves! Indeed I do!" God help her, she wanted to slap the self-satisfied smirk from his face.

He gave her a quelling look, narrowed his eyes, then glanced away as though to remind her that his men were listening, as well. "Watch your tongue," he warned. "I'd loathe to have to—"

"Cut it out?" she demanded indignantly. "Famous! Smuggler, traitor, ravisher of innocents—and butcher now, too! You would, wouldn't you?"

"Kiss you?" he murmured low. His lips curved slightly, taunting her. "What do you think, *mon amour*?" His smiled deepened, though it never reached his eyes. "Wouldn't I?"

Jessie shuddered at his veiled warning. "Nay!" she said quickly. "I-I meant that you would cut out my tongue!"

"Don't tempt me," he said drolly, lifting a brow, and cocking his head.

"You! You are—despicable! I insist you take me back to Charlestown at once! Now! You don't need me here! Nor do I wish to remain."

"Nay."

"Nay?" she repeated incredulously.

He nodded. "I believe 'tis what I said."

"But you cannot keep me here!"

"Can I not?" Once again he cocked his head and lifted his brow in challenge.

"Nay, you cannot!" she countered, bristling. "I can do no more for Ben—or Jean Paul—than anyone else aboard this accursed ship—and I will *not* remain to be abused by you!"

Christian eyed her sharply. "M'mselle, I've not so much as lifted a finger against you, but I warn you, I'm sorely tempted this moment to put you over my knee and paddle that delightfully tempting derriere of yours, audience or nay." He lifted his chin, indicating the scrutiny of his men. By now, all had suspended their chores in order to watch them with unconcealed interest.

Jessie followed his gaze, mortified to have been threatened in such an intimate manner before so many watchful pairs of eyes—and ears! "Oh!" she gasped. "You just bloody well try!"

He crossed his arms over his chest. "Threats, m'mselle?" He actually laughed then.

Jessie narrowed her eyes at him. "I'm not completely at your mercy, you realize," she reminded him, chafing at his arrogance. "Ben remains belowdecks." In an angry whisper, she confided, "I would need but tell him what you did to me back in your cabin, and he would surely find cause enough to call you out!" In truth, it was the very last thing Jessie intended for her cousin to do—particularly in his present state—but it seemed the only thing with which to threaten the incorrigible beast.

Christian never blinked an eye at her dire proclamation, but said quite amiably, "That would be a rather unfortunate mistake on his part." Though his tone was casual, his eyes seemed to bore through her with brilliant intensity. And then he said soberly, "If you care at all for his life . . . you'll do no such thing. Ben's a good man—a bit green about the edges perhaps, but even so, I'd like to see him live long enough to get over loving you. You see, my love, he doesn't realize it yet, but you're unequivocally the worst thing that could ever have happened to him."

Jessie's eyes widened at his cruel words.

"Aye," he said low. "Don't tell me you didn't know." His arms crossed, his legs set arrogantly apart, he challenged her to deny it. She couldn't—not with what she'd heard below—and her face heated under his scrutiny. He turned from her long enough to order his men back to work, and he was revealed to her fully in that moment, for he was within his element at last, feral and magnificent. Despite herself, the sight of him stole her breath away; his features hard and hawklike, and with his dark, unbound hair flowing, he *was* the Hawk. With his snug black breeches and loose white shirt billowing in the breeze, he'd never appeared more ominous than he did at the moment. Evidently his men thought so as well, for without him having said a word, all eyes turned from them at once.

Satisfied that their conversation would no longer be overheard, he returned his gaze to her. "In future," he told her, "I would suggest you refrain from bedeviling Ben—trust me, love, a man can only take so much."

There was nothing of the man she'd thought she'd known in him now, nothing. She truly didn't know him. Had she ever? she wondered bitterly. "How dare you speak to me so?"

"Had he been himself last night," he continued coldly, ignoring her angry objection, "and not beset with fever and pain, you'd no longer be virgin—I assure you, cousin or no. Or," he suggested, his tone fierce, "perhaps *that* isn't a concern any longer." He narrowed his eyes, and asked softly, "Is it, Jessamine?"

Jessie's face flushed a bright crimson. "Oh! You! You *are* truly despicable! *That* is certainly none of your concern—though I assure you my cousin is a gentleman through and through, unlike you!"

"Really," he replied evenly, giving her a ruthless smile, but he'd managed to discover what he'd needed to know, and the truth was that he was well pleased with the answer.

Christian had to suppress the urge to grin outright. Ben hadn't touched her, he was certain of it, and neither had anyone else for that matter; she wore a virgin's blush.

"I really must insist you take me back to Charlestown!"

Christian shook his head, sighing. "Nay, Jess. The fact is that your cousin already bandied word that you and Ben have sailed for England." He grinned at her then, unable to suppress his glee. "It seems you've developed a nasty case of homesickness. As you see . . . I cannot allow you to go back, for in doing so you'd raise suspicions, and I will not permit you to do that, my love. After all, 'tis my father's life you would endanger, as well."

Christian could see the fierce determination leave her features, though it was immediately replaced by resentment. *Was his company so disagreeable to her? Did she truly loathe him so much?* He couldn't allow himself to believe it, for if he did, a part of him would shrivel and die. He thought to put the issue of her leaving at rest once and for all, and he yielded, "We'll be gone only as long as necessary, and if you endeavor to stay out of the way, 'twill pass all the easier for you. Rest assured, Jessie, that I'm no more thrilled for your company than you are for mine."

Her expression became mutinous suddenly, her green eyes reflecting the depths of her animosity, buffeting him as surely as though she'd struck his cheek with her palm. "I—well—and—truly—despise—you!"

His jaw grew taut, and his chest tightened, but he managed a nod. "Despise me all you wish," he allowed, "only stay the hell out of my sight." He felt little satisfaction when she stiffened as though she'd been cuffed, and less when she turned and stalked away. He forced himself to let her go, telling himself that her anger was a welcome barrier between them.

Without it, he was lost.

Chapter 18

Sweating from his labors, Christian made his way back to his cabin. He'd not intended for the *Mistral* to set sail again so soon, and so there had been a number of things he'd had to see to before leaving Charlestown harbor. It had been a near miraculous feat to resupply his ship in the coarse of a day, without earning suspicion, and he wouldn't have been able to accomplish the task at all without the generous help he'd received from the men of the Wilkes club. Ben was obviously well thought of among them, for they'd rallied together without thought for their own safety, procuring supplies and hauling them aboard.

His intent now was simply to sail down the coast to the West Indies, collect a payload, then return to Charlestown, arriving in the dead of night. Fortunately, because it was hurricane season, they wouldn't be the only ones departing the harbor, and his only true concern was that he was sailing directly into hurricane territory, but there was nothing to be done for it. He'd have to take his chances.

And then there was the matter of their return . . . They would be back long before the harbor became congested once more, and because Jessie and Ben were to have sailed for England, he'd need to steal them down the Ashley to Shadow Moss as quietly and covertly as possible.

He chuckled suddenly, for it would likely mean muzzling Jessie until they arrived at his plantation house—impudent wench that she was. And then again, he considered, Shadow Moss was nowhere near to completion, and Jessie would likely squawk all the louder when she discovered the fact—most females would, he didn't doubt—so perhaps he would consider leaving her gagged until Ben healed . . .

He turned the knob to his cabin door, gave a little shove, and then again to be certain before slamming his fist upon it. Locked! Damn it all! "Jessamine! Open the blasted door!"

The deafening crack startled Jessie, rousing her at once, though she remained disoriented, having awakened to foreign surroundings. It took her a full moment to regain her faculties. The room swayed gently and swells of water could be heard smacking the side of the ship. They were no doubt at sea by now.

"Jessamine!"

Recognizing Christian's thunderous voice, Jessie smiled triumphantly and stretched lazily, refusing to be cowed merely by the sound of his voice. Raking her hair from her face with her fingers, she rose and went to the door as quietly as she was able, smiling at her ingenuity. She'd used Christian's very own sea chests against him, piling them against the door, and then further braced them with her own hefty trunks. It had taken much time and toil to accomplish the masterwork, but now she was certain the only door to the cabin was truly impenetrable. To her mind, it was a fine job . . . and this was precisely the moment she'd been awaiting. She fully intended to savor it.

Using the bottommost trunk as a step, she carefully climbed the stack to place her ear against the oak door. Christian pounded the door unexpectedly, ringing her ears with the unholy vibration, and Jessie leapt away, nearly tumbling from her carefully laid mountain to the floor.

"Damn you, Jess! I demand you open this door! I'm not in the mood for games," he warned.

She gave him no response.

"Jessamine? Do you hear me? I desire my bed!"

God forgive her, but she couldn't resist baiting him. "I suggest you seek it elsewhere, then," she told him flippantly, "for I'll not be giving this one up! Nor will I share!" And that was that, she swore to herself, slapping her hands in a definitive manner, smiling with self-satisfaction.

"The devil you say, woman! 'Tis my cabin you would have me give up, and I'll not do so," he apprised her.

"Oh, but you will," she demurred sweetly, "for I doubt I shall ever allow you entrance. I did not ask to be brought aboard this *thieves' den*, and because you seem to have little regard for my wishes, nor will I for yours, *my* nefarious Prince of Smugglers— *Lord Christian, hah!* What a farce!"

Her words brought a smile to Christian's lips.

It was the *my* that settled him so quickly. His grin was smug as he disclosed, "Perhaps you don't realize, as yet, but you'll need come out of that cabin sooner or later, love. You'll need to eat sometime, and when you do—"

"Camp by the door then," she suggested. "Though I fear you'll have quite a long wait. Your cabin boy—Peter, I believe is his name—was quite accommodating, you see."

Christian shook his head, disbelieving his ears.

"I simply told the dear boy that I was feeling under the weather," Jessie told him, "and that I preferred to take my meals in my cabin. He understood perfectly and gave me enough provisions to last, well . . . a few days at least." She giggled suddenly, and added, laughter in her tone, "How very tired of waiting you shall grow!"

Christian was no longer amused; the thought of waiting days for his bed was wholly unpalatable. "Damn you!" he bellowed. "You little hoyden!" Losing his patience all over again, he slammed his boot against the door. She had it bolted from within, he was certain, but it seemed too solid a barrier to be simply barred. It was as though she'd placed something before it . . . His brows furrowed. What the devil could she have moved to bar it with? he wondered. Most everything was nailed firmly to the floor in protection against the movement of the sea. And damn her, for she sounded so very self-satisfied; it rankled to the bone.

Releasing the full magnitude of his temper, he agitated the doorknob, nearly detaching it in his fury, and shook the cabin door so violently that Jessie had to wonder whether her barricade would even hold against him—yet hold, it did, even if the trunks seemed somewhat the worse for wear.

Another string of vile curses stung the air, and then utter silence fell between them.

Had he given up at last? Jessie doubted it; somehow she had the distinct impression *Hawk*, odious Prince of Smugglers, never simply gave up.

But then . . . where had he gone to suddenly? It was entirely too quiet on the other side of the door.

More important . . . what did he plan?

When there was no more sound from behind the door, Jessie had to assume victory. Yet it had come too easily . . .

Her brow furrowed. Unsure of what to do next, she paced the cabin floor, clasping her hands at her back to stop them from quaking. After a long interval, when there was still no sign of him forthcoming, she decided to pour herself a goblet of Christian's fine Madeira to calm herself. God's truth, but her nerves had never been more frazzled than they were this instant, and were becoming more so by the second.

Finishing it quickly, she gave a choked little cough. God knew, all she needed now was to drown herself in his good wine— probably stolen or smuggled! she reflected resentfully. With a ragged sigh, she poured herself another brimming goblet full and then wandered to the cheval glass. The woman staring back at her was haggard looking; hair mussed from slumber, and faint shadows darkening the hollows beneath her eyes. And the neck of her gown choked her, strangled her breath. She drew at the neckline irritably, and gave a derisive little laugh, for the gown had surely had its desired effect above deck; Christian had not so much as glanced at her untowardly. He was quite obviously unaffected by her.

He didn't care.

He'd never cared.

Aye, his threats had been lecherous, but there had been no heat to them, no feeling. No intent. God, what was wrong with her? Surely she wasn't thinking . . . that she wanted . . .

She shook her head vehemently, and took another sip, refusing to continue her present vein of thought.

Stay out of his way indeed.

So she had won this round, after all. *Against whom?* a little voice niggled. She raised her goblet in silent acclaim, clinking it gently to the silver mirror—against herself, it would seem, for if she could be honest . . . 'twas not Christian she feared at all . . . but her own wicked yearnings.

Standing before him there upon the foredeck, she had found herself wishing he would silence her raving with his soul-weakening kisses—that he would take her into his arms and tell her he loved her, beg her forgiveness. God help her, she had baited him, wanting only that he would lift her up into his arms and sweep her back to his cabin—she shuddered—in truth, back to that day beneath the elm tree . . .

How long could he possibly be kept at bay?

She glanced back at the door . . . It was not made of iron, after all. If he truly wished to come after her . . . She shook her head, for then again . . . he was quite obviously not trying overly hard. Perhaps he would leave her be, after all . . .

With a very unladylike snort, she lifted her goblet and quaffed down the rest of her wine, then set the crystal gently down upon a small table beside the looking glass. With a sigh, she unbuttoned the topmost button of her gown, and then the next, and the next, sighing wistfully.

She stared at her image, trying to see herself as he might, and then irritably turned from the mirror. She wandered to the drapery-covered window with the intent of drawing it open to the fading daylight, and then it dawned on her suddenly that she'd forgotten to procure flints with which to light the lanterns tonight. She sincerely hoped she could find some within the cabin itself, for she had no desire to remain in total darkness. Shuddering at the thought, she tugged open the blasphemously dark window coverings, and gasped aloud at what lay beneath.

The most beautiful stained-glass window she had ever beheld stood there in all its grandeur before her—three full-length panels! The left and right were wholly painted in colorful biblical scenes, but it was the double-wide center pane that caught her attention and held it fast.

There in the middle of the depiction stood a grand apple tree, its limbs outstretched, forming a beautiful green shelter. Beneath it lay the figure of Eve, her dark hair unbound and spread gloriously beneath her like a carpet of black silk. In her proffered hand, she held a burning ruby apple, offering it up to ... Adam?

The resemblance between the figure of Adam in the depiction and Christian was striking—and good Lord, he was nude as the day he was born! So was Eve for that matter, beckoning to Adam with the apple like some seductress straight from a preacher's fire-and-brimstone sermon. Her green eyes were brilliant, haunting in their intensity.

Her gaze was drawn upward. The sky of the depiction was clear glass, a masterpiece, utilizing the blue of the true sky as its color—if it was dark outside, the painting would be as somber as midnight; if it was bright and sunny, Adam and Eve's world would be as blue as sapphires; and if the weather was foul, then it would draw them both into the stormy tempest. This moment, it was faded a blue-gray, with orange and pink hues streaking as far as the eye could behold. The sun in the horizon was rapidly sinking from view, plummeting into the murky darkness of the sea.

Jessie's gaze reverted to the nude form of Adam, and she swallowed convulsively as her eyes settled upon that very male part of his anatomy. Such an odd, odd member ... and so very, very ... erect. She scrunched her nose. And then suddenly, her eyes widened as she recalled a certain something she'd said to Christian.

It boggles the mind to consider why men were

not born with horns or other weapons on their person. Do you not agree, my lord? Her heart leapt at the recollection.

Are you quite certain of that fact? he'd asked her.

She couldn't have known. Her eyes narrowed in outrage and her lips trembled with misery. The cad, he'd been mocking her, even then . . . How he must have laughed at her naïveté—how he must have rejoiced in her stupidity!

She was a fool.

She was still a fool.

Unable to keep herself from it, she reached out for him, her breath becoming labored and her body stirring wickedly, heating with the Madeira . . . and something else; as she smoothed her fingers over Adam's full body. She stopped abruptly at his groin—couldn't help herself, brazen as it was—feeling with wonder the almost indiscernible raised lines where one color met another. She was awestruck by the artfulness of the glass, by the beauty of the man depicted. Shuddering with the desire that burst to life within her, she caressed the cold glass before her . . . her heart thundering . . .

Her eyes closed, and her head fell back, remembering . . .

Christian's heart began to hammer.

From his precarious perch just outside the window, he felt the bold caress as though it were on his own body. Heat surged through his veins, its potency just short of heart-stopping.

Christ, how he wanted her, ached and burned for her. His body shuddered at the sight she presented, head back and her face flushed with desire, her bodice undone and exposing her throat. Making certain his feet were secure within the toehold he'd fashioned within the rope, he shifted so the knot he was perched upon wouldn't cut quite so sharply into his groin.

How many times had he dreamed of that caress? So soft and innocent, and yet lustful too. Whatever else she was, the woman was passionate—that much he had to give her. The wistful look on her face made him burn all the more fiercely. He tried to ignore her. While she was otherwise occupied with Adam, he used it to his advantage, peering in at the door through the distorted glass. Damnation, but he couldn't begin to imagine what she'd barred it with.

He muttered an oath when his eyes finally focused upon the objects before the door. There were what appeared to be five trunks stacked before it, not one, not two, but five. His own two, which were by far the largest, were doubled at the bottom, and three of hers, one large, two small, sat directly above them, braced against the door. How the devil had she managed it?

He knew the very instant she spotted him, for she suddenly leapt away from the glass, shrieking. She fell back upon the floor. Now that she was aware of his presence, he swung into plain view. He peered through the clear glass into the cabin, knocked on the window and smiled.

Jessie seemed to recover quickly enough, scrambling to her feet at once. She stood staring, that hideous gown of hers gaping at the neckline, and he had the sudden urge to shatter his precious stained-glass window— to hell with the cost of it—throw her upon the bed and climb atop her, lift up her skirts without preamble and rut like a blood-maddened bull. He was that badly in need. That provoked. He willed her to open the door, so that he could have McCarney and Tibbs haul him up—so he could go to her and slake his insane need for her, and only her. In all the many months he'd been away from her, he'd not touched a woman. None of them had been Jessie.

"God," he croaked, his voice hoarse with restraint, and something more as he recalled her cozy familiarity with her damnable cousin. "Jessie . . . open the door . . ."

Spurred to life by his request, Jessie suddenly tugged the drapery closed. "Really!" she shouted. "Sleep there upon your bloody rope, for all I care! Or loop it about your neck," she added flippantly. "I care not which!"

"Jessie! Open the goddamned door!" Now that he knew what was before it, he could quite possibly open it himself, for he'd noted that a few of the trunks were already tilting precariously, but Jessie had placed them there and Jessie would remove them, he vowed.

Having barred his smug face from view, Jessie went to his massive dark-curtained bed and plopped herself down upon it, trying desperately to ignore him—good Lord, he had caught her fondling his window! Her face heated with mortification.

Such a deep hush prevailed from beyond the curtains that she found herself feeling uneasy as she surveyed the room in its unholy darkness. Why was everything so ... so black? she wondered irately. His bed, more suited to a sultan, was curtained in dark midnight blue silks. A beautifully carved armoire in dark wood graced the wall by the door, and a table with wicked claws for legs hunched in the middle of the cabin, its fearful talons gripping the bare wood floor. There were paintings of indescribable value and beauty, bookcases built into the wall with dozens of leather-bound volumes housed within them. And then of course, there were the stained-glass windows ...

"You'd think the man was a prince!" she muttered. But then, he was, wasn't he? He was Prince of Smugglers. She laughed without mirth, cursing herself for a silly hysterical fool. Her gaze reverting to the curtain, she decided it was much too still for her peace of mind, and she rose to peek behind it ... to be certain he was gone.

He was still there, smiling knowingly, taunting her, his teeth flashing in mockery. His brow lifted diabolically.

"Oh! You! I hope the rope snaps and you plummet headlong into the ocean and drown, you cur!" Yanking the curtain shut again, Jessie fumed. But his voice when next he spoke seemed unsettled, and she experienced a twinge of guilt for her hateful words.

"Dammit, Jess!" Then more frantically, "Jessie! I'm slipping . . . dammit . . . Jess!"

Arms crossed stubbornly, Jessie refused to reopen the drapes, refused to believe him. It was a ruse, she was certain. He was a cad! a cur! a lecher! And he sounded no more distressed than a gluttonous toad at home upon his lily pad.

Yet even as she endeavored to convince herself, there came a cacophonous thud against the side of the ship, followed by an awful, endless abrasive sound that concluded with an ominous splash far, far below. Jessie's heart lurched, and she snatched open the draperies with trembling hands.

Lord, what if he had fallen?

The rope dangled dismally before her eyes, swinging ever so slightly, evidence that he'd been there—but was no more. He was nowhere within sight.

Oh, God—dear God. He *had* fallen. Hadn't anyone seen? She glanced up, pressing her nose to the tinted glass, spying no one above—not that she could see a blessed thing through the colored glass! Frantically her gaze slid down again, to the fathomless ocean. She could see very little through the greens and blues and reds of the stained glass . . . and yet . . . and yet . . . she could have sworn that the water rippled away from a foaming center.

'Twas all her fault! Not daring to waste even a single precious second, she went to the door and began clearing it of obstacles at once.

"Someone! Anyone!" she shouted hysterically. "Please, Christian—Hawk!" she screamed. Lord, what to call the accursed man? "Your captain!" she decided finally. "He's fallen overboard! Someone, please—help!"

Thank heavens that her own trunks were easy enough to remove, but the other two, his two, were another matter entirely. They were as heavy as sin! Squatting upon the floor, she planted her feet squarely and gave a mighty heave. It moved a little, though at this rate, she thought that by the time she removed the last of the sea chests and made her away above deck to summon help, Christian would be long gone—dead—and at her hands, no less!

Good Lord, she was a murderess! Tears stung her eyes. The very thought of never seeing him again made her heart suddenly ache. The possibility chilled her, left her bereft.

Giving the trunk one last desperate heave,

she shoved it out of the way, and with a groan she tackled the largest of them all, the one that was buttressed so securely against the door, the one that had taken her a lifetime to set into place.

"Dear God," Jessie prayed aloud, "please don't let him die—don't let him die—please!" Her face turned scarlet with her efforts and still the trunk would not budge.

"Someone, please—oh, please, please, help!" she cried out, despairing ever to be free of the cabin. She was desperate to aid Christian. The armoire she'd admired earlier was within reach, and she happened to brace her feet upon it in her despair. Finding anchorage there, she shoved with every last bit of her might. Nailed down as it was, the armoire gave her the much-needed reinforcement and the confounded chest inched slowly but surely away from the door. Her face flushed and her brow beaded from her exertions, she gave the chest a final shove, sliding it just barely out of the way, and then she stood hurriedly, unbolting the door.

Her mouth fell agape as she opened the door.

"What took you so long?"

In one swift, agile motion, Christian shoved away from the wall that faced her, smiling devilishly. Much too belatedly, she tried to slam the door in his too wicked, too handsome face. His hand swept out to hold it ajar.

"My, but you do seem distressed," he said

much too calmly. "Tell me . . . where are you off to in such a frantic rush, my love?" The gleam in his cobalt eyes told Jessie that he truly didn't wish or need an answer to that particular question, and she didn't offer him one.

His jaw working angrily, he suddenly shoved the door further open, causing her to lose her balance for the tiniest fraction of an instant. One boot on, one conspicuously missing, he came into the room, stalking her as a lion would its prey. Jessie backed slowly away from him, fearing him suddenly.

"Y-You tricked me!"

"*You* locked me out of my cabin," he returned smoothly, his glittering blue eyes never leaving her own.

"B-But you t-told me to . . ." He shook his head slowly in negation and her voice suddenly failed her.

"I told you to stay out of my sight, not to lock me away from my bed." He grinned then, but it was an ominous, mocking grin, not the least bit reassuring.

"Wh-What were you doing out there anyway?" she asked defensively.

"Why, I was looking to see what you'd barred the door with, of course," he told her. "But tell me . . . what were *you* doing at the window?" He smiled that wicked, knowing smile of his.

Jessie ignored the impertinent question, though her cheeks flamed. She fanned herself reflexively, unaware that she did. "How did you get back up?'' Her treacherous knees began to wobble. Nor was he wet, she noticed, frowning.

Slowly, ruthlessly, he backed her toward the bed. "How else do you think, Jessamine? At my signal, my men hauled me up."

"B-But I heard you fall," she stammered, her legs buckling as the bed came up behind her unexpectedly.

Christian watched with ill-concealed amusement as she fell back upon it.

"I swear it—I shall scream!"

"And who do you think shall come?" he taunted, his voice little more than a whisper. "Your hobbling cousin? I very much doubt it, Jess. At any rate, you deserve a good lashing, and 'twas he who first suggested it, *ma belle*."

"But you wouldn't dare!"

Christian's eyes gleamed with the devil's own light. "Wouldn't I?" he said, his jaw clenching.

"N-Nay! Y-You'd not dare!" she stammered, and truly hoped it was so. The look in his eyes, however, confirmed otherwise. He *would*, indeed, dare, and thoroughly enjoy it besides!

"I wish to God you had fallen!" Where she found the strength and courage to do so, she would never know, but she flew at him in that instant, her hands pummeling his chest. "I heard you fall!" she cried. "I know I did! Why didn't you? Why didn't you?"

Christian caught her hands with a single

sweep of his own, stilling them against his chest. She felt his heart beating fiercely beneath her fingertips.

"Ah, *ma pauvre petite,*" he said huskily, "what a dreadful shame for you . . . Alas, but 'twas only my good boot you heard plummetin' into the sea." He nodded, his eyes glinting with arrogance. "Aye, my love, you *did* note I was lacking one, did you not?" He patronized her. Her eyes shot him with cold contempt and he added, "Aye, I see that you have. Tell me, m'mselle . . . should I take the price of them out on your pretty little derriere?" He reached back as though to make good his threat, swatting her backside.

Jessie shrieked indignantly and began to struggle anew, twisting her arms to be free of the prison of his grip. In one swift motion, he lifted her and thrust her down upon the bed. He straddled her then, taking his sweet time so as to prove to her how very defenseless she was against him, that she would bend to his will even against her own.

He bent low over her, to look into her eyes, his own eyes gleaming ruthlessly, and she swallowed convulsively, never feeling more vulnerable than she did at the moment. And then his lips came nearer still, until she could feel the heat radiating from them, beckoning . . . and Lord help her, she wanted him to press his lips to her mouth, mold them to her own. Even as angry as she was with him, she found herself wistfully remembering the way his velvety tongue had felt within her mouth, so warm, so insistent, and her breath quickened.

She wanted to taste his fierce hunger... again... and again... and again... never to stop. The sweetest ache began again to unfurl within the depth of her body, reaching deep into her soul, tautening the peaks of her breasts and making them ache for his touch.

If only he could touch his lips to them once more, tenderly now. If only...

She flushed crimson at her wanton thoughts.

But then, in that bittersweet instant, he shifted and came closer, brushing his lips against hers so very gently, too gently, almost as though that brief contact were part of his warning.

"I could have sworn," he whispered, "that I'd told you once already... 'twould go all the easier for you did you simply stay out of my way. Do so... and you shall save us both much trouble... Do not... and you shall pay dearly... I swear it. My patience is at its end—doubt it not."

Her mind dazed with his nearness and his whispered threats, she returned, "Really, m'lord..." She lifted a brow, mocking his imperious gesture. "What more can you take from me that you've not already?"

He laughed then, the sound ruthless, his breath searing the tender flesh of her lips. "More," he swore, the threat no more than a whisper, "more, my naive little princess...

so very, very much more." With that, he released her abruptly, lifting himself from the bed.

He sat on the edge, ignoring her, lifting his one booted foot to his knee to remove the shoe, and still Jessie dared not move. His boot slipped off, and he tossed it unceremoniously across the room, where it landed with a wrathful thud.

He rose from the bed abruptly and went to pour himself a snifter of brandy, tossing the contents down and pouring himself another. Eyeing the bottle of Madeira that sat beside it, he lifted it, assessing the lack, and said, his back to her, "Well, well . . . as long as we are at it, then." He lifted a clean goblet and poured her another glass of Madeira, bringing it to her and pressing it into her hands.

Then, with his own glass in hand, he strode to, and sprawled backward into, his blue damask throne of a chair. He sat there, ignoring her for the longest time as he finished his brandy. She sipped nervously of her Madeira, watching him all the while, as the sun continued its descent, leaving them finally bathed in little more than dusky shadows.

"You *will* light the lanterns?" she asked after a long, strained silence.

"Nay, I'll not." His gaze met and held hers across the shadows. He shook his head. "I came to sleep . . . yet here I find myself sitting instead, wondering just what it is I should do with you."

Jessie sat numbly, not knowing what to say, unable to move, unable even to tear her gaze away from his much too stunning face. In the growing darkness, his features took on a sinister cast; his eyes seemed to glow by the light of the moon, and a shiver traveled her spine. Dread settled in the pit of her stomach. What *would* he do? she found herself wondering—but to her shame, not without exhaling a shattering breath of anticipation.

"You plan to share my bed with me?" his husky voice inquired after a moment.

"O-Of course not!" she cried indignantly, but she was mortified to feel the flutter, the thrill, that raced through her body like wildfire.

"Then get out of it," he advised her. *"Now."*

The last was said so softly that she barely heard the command.

"I swear that you are no gentleman!" Yet having said that, she gaped, fascinated by his sleek grace as he proceeded to unbutton his shirt cuffs.

Though his features were now hidden deep in shadow, she could have sworn he smiled at that insult, his teeth flashing white. Taking a nervous sip of her wine, she swallowed it with a tortured, strangled gasp, and continued to sit, hopelessly entranced, watching shamelessly as he then started upon the buttons at his throat. She was utterly helpless to tear her gaze away from his ritual performance.

Belatedly recalling her own gaping dress, she clasped it together, holding it fast, cutting off her breath as her flesh burned under his scrutiny. But Lord help her, she really couldn't care that she couldn't breathe just now, could only be thankful for the darkness of the cabin to conceal her brazenness.

And her desire.

He stood then, his body little more than a dark silhouette before her, and she was spurred into life finally, clinking her goblet down quickly upon the small table by the bedside.

"I believe I've given you fair enough warning," he said low, unbuttoning his breeches and shrugging out of them. Her heart leapt as they slithered to the floor and he stepped out of them, magnificently naked.

Like Adam.

She froze, again staring as though transfixed, her gaze leaving him only to revert to the window, to the silhouette of Adam glowing faintly there by the light of the moon, before returning to Christian, but Christian stood too deeply in shadow and she could see nothing of him.

Chapter 19

"**I**'ll not ask you again," he swore, and then his shadow descended.

Jessie leapt from the bed, scurrying away. She listened intently to the rustling of the sheets as he snuggled between them, nude, she knew, and the thought made her shiver, though she could see absolutely nothing as his body slipped into the crisp coolness of the sheets. She knew they were cool, even as she knew his body was hot, even as was her own. She burned as though with fever.

Once he was settled, he tossed her a blanket. It fell at her bare feet. She stooped to retrieve it, holding it close to her as she stared into the darkness of the curtained bed.

"And where will I sleep?" Her voice trembled slightly. Lord, she loathed herself for that weakness.

He grunted, as though annoyed by her

question, and said, "Wherever you wish . . . In the bed, if you please." And then he added, "If you dare . . ."

It was a challenge, a gauntlet cast at her feet, but one Jessie had no intention of accepting, or even acknowledging. She didn't dare, for she'd be lost if she did.

"I-I shall sleep on the floor, then."

"If 'tis your wish."

"Oh! I do so wish!" she assured him, her voice laced with bitterness. What manner of man was he to allow her, a gentle-born woman, to sleep on the floor—on the deck of a ship, no less, to roll with the ocean's waves! God, how could she have ever thought him a gentleman? And again, she had the despairing thought that she was the worst kind of fool, for she was a fool in love.

And he was a devil and a knave, the lowest of low!

Resigning herself to a night of discomfort, she settled upon the floor, drawing the blanket to her chin to keep away the chill of the night. To her chagrin, she found the one blanket was not proof against the cold. And then again, perhaps the chill came from within? And then, too, it was dark . . . and she could hear him breathing, smoothly, evenly, peacefully.

And then slower still—the cad! How dare he sleep!

In that miserable moment, Jessie despised him immensely. Cursing him, she shifted, trying in vain to find comfort on the hard, cold floor.

He snored.

"Famous!" she muttered to herself. "God, but I loathe the man—aye, I swear that I do!"

He made some curious sound, and then it seemed his entire body jerked, as though to catapult him into blissful slumber.

Jessie couldn't bear it—that he could sleep so peacefully when she was so very miserable.

"Christian?" she whispered. There was no reply. Louder this time, she hissed, "Hawk?" Still no response.

She waited a moment, and then shouted, "Are you sleeping?"

He grunted, and responded finally, "*Not anymore.* What the devil do you want *now*, Jessie?"

"I need a pillow," she said petulantly.

"I have only the one."

"Might I use it, then?"

"God's teeth, woman! Nay, you may not use it—*I am using it!*"

Jessie gritted her teeth.

"But you may share it," he conceded irritably.

"Share it? With you? Thank you, but nay. Is there another cabin I might make use of, then?"

"Nay."

"Another bed?"

"*Jess.*"

"Another cot? Another world?" she mumbled beneath her breath.

Some choked sound escaped him, as though he would laugh but refused to allow himself the concession. When he spoke again, his whisper sounded for all its caressing softness an irate command.

"Go to sleep, Jessamine. Tomorrow will be a long day."

Indeed, Christian amended silently, a long voyage, for it was going to prove wholly impossible to share the same cabin with her while keeping his sanity.

It was impossible to sleep with her scent filling his nostrils, arousing his senses. Yet there was truly no place else he would have her go.

Certainly not with that damnable *cousin* of hers—and there *was* no place else.

"I do so loathe you!" she informed him with great feeling.

"And the sentiment is mutual," he returned dispassionately. "Now, be a wise little wench and go to sleep. Or I swear, you'll come to regret it."

"You don't understand," she cried softly. "I cannot sleep in the same room with you! 'Tis unseemly . . . and . . . and—"

"To bloody hell with what's proper, Jessie! 'Tis a man's ship," he apprised her, his voice strained, "and there is no other place for you to sleep but here . . . in my cabin—where you will be safe," he added almost reluctantly, for he wasn't truly certain she was safe with him either.

"Why couldn't you have thought of that before you abducted me?"

He sighed. "As I've already told you, there

was no time to consider. Look at it from my view. It was my belief that two men lay dying, and I knew not where to turn for help ... Being that one of them was your *beloved cousin* ... I rather hoped you might feel somewhat inclined to aid them. Perhaps I was wrong?"

There was a long moment of silence, and then she admitted finally, her voice quivering faintly, "You were not."

The pitiful sound of it did not escape him, and Christian's sigh slashed through the darkness. "If 'tis your virtue you fear for," he relented, "then you should leave off the worrying, *mon amour*. I've absolutely no wish to touch you at all," he lied, his lip curling with self-contempt at the blatant falsehood. Even now, he stood ready. Yet, even despite that fact, he played the noble for her, ever the righteous gentleman. He cursed her fiercely beneath his breath, for making him want to be something he was not.

"Even so," he interjected, "I swear that if you do not let me be, Jessie, I'll assume you wish to divert me, and I might find that I do, indeed, desire a certain *diversion*, after all—if you take my meaning?"

He heard her sharp intake of breath, and the helpless whimper that escaped her, and he felt her pain, and despised himself for his weakness to her.

Neither of them spoke.

After a long moment, Christian grudgingly tossed her his pillow.

It landed with a soft whooshing sound atop her head. Jessie snatched it quickly, burying her face into it, soaking it with tears.

"Thank you!" she sobbed, swearing to herself that she loathed him still, and despising herself for the lie. After a time, his husky snores filled the cabin, and hours later, still unable to sleep, Jessie lay shifting uncomfortably in the darkness.

She stood finally, clutching Christian's pillow to her breast, and approached the dark pit that was his bed. She stared at his moonlit features for a long moment, gathering her courage. God, he wore a scowl even in his sleep. He was a fiend—so why *did* she love him so? Why?

She was cold.

And she was desperately miserable.

And *he* had the bed.

Lord, but he was rude and ill bred not to have offered her the bed!

Mustering her courage once and for all, she lifted the coverlet carefully and slipped within, making certain to stay as far from him as possible.

The beast never stirred.

He was sound asleep, she acknowledged resentfully. And he had fallen so very easily. How, when her own body lay burning so fiercely, kindled merely by his presence? It was as though the very air were filled with him, making her yearn . . . She shouldn't feel such a wanton longing for his kisses . . . and more. Only, when she tried not to recall that day beneath the elm tree ... her body seemed to have a will all its own, demolishing her resolve.

"*I never did betray you,*" she whispered softly into the pillow beside him. She rocked herself consolingly, gently, so as not to wake him. How could he have believed she would?

Oh, God, how could he sleep?

He really didn't want her.

He didn't care. A tear slipped through her lashes.

The moon's glow illuminated the stained glass with an uncanny light. Eve's eyes seemed lucid, melancholy almost, and so very damning, for those eyes were the mirror to her own soul.

She was lost to him, and he didn't trust her, and he didn't love her ... and he didn't even seem to want her.

The tears she'd been fighting so long spilled from her eyes, coursed shamelessly down her cheeks.

"I did not betray you," she swore again, her whisper soft and full of pain. " *'Twas you, Christian, who betrayed me!*" She gazed longingly at the exquisitely depicted figure of Adam, his face unreadable, his eyes as blue and fathomless as the sea.

"I did not tell my brother—he knew already." Though she knew he slept, she felt compelled to go on, "It was your brother, Philip, who told my father. Not I," she swore softly. "Amos told me so later." She continued to rock herself, eased by it, and she wept softly.

"But *you* . . ."

The single word was filled with over-whelming grief.

"You came to seduce me—and you let him—" She choked away a broken sob. "Oh, God! You let my brother *pay you* to wreck my heart and my life! How could you? Aye, you came to make me love you . . . and to tear my soul to tiny, wretched shreds—and God curse me, for I let you!" She turned away from him to lie upon her side in a dev-astated heap, unable even to accept his pres-ence next to her upon the bed, for she wanted nothing more than to turn in to his arms and be comforted by him.

She was weak . . . oh, so weak.

" 'Tis my fault . . . I let you hurt me," she whispered. "And I despise you!" she swore. And then her sobs came full force and she muffled them with the feather pillow that bore his musky male scent, allowing her an-ger to become a balm for her pain. "I loathe you."

As though he'd heard her somewhere deep in his slumber and meant to comfort her, Christian's weight shifted. His arm reached out and wrapped about her waist. Jessie stiff-ened, thinking she'd inadvertently awakened him, but he made some sleepy sound before snuggling closer to her. His breath was as smooth and even as before, and she knew then that he slept on, that he'd never awakened at all. In his dreams, he probably thought her some tavern wench warming his bed!

Still, in the darkness, just this once . . . Jessie dared to be comforted by his embrace—no matter whether he mistook her for another.

Just this once, she swore to herself. No one need know.

Tomorrow she would be fine. She would make certain of that, for never could she reveal to him just how much he'd hurt her with his lies and his deceit.

Nor could she bear that he know how very much she loved him . . .

Still.

The sun broke, transforming Adam and Eve's world into a brilliant picturesque display. As she stretched sleepily, Jessie's gaze followed the path of the morning sunbeam to where it performed a kaleidoscopic parade upon the wood floor.

With a start, she remembered just where it was she'd fallen asleep—more important, with whom—and whirled about to stare at the empty space beside her.

He was gone.

She moved onto his side of the bed, closing her eyes against the cool sheets, savoring the lingering scent of him.

She had dreamt of him . . . his warmth, his hand upon her breast . . . drawing down the neckline of her gown. His kiss burning her flesh, trailing down, down . . . leaving a fire burning in its wake . . . She burned still . . .

She opened her eyes in self-disgust. Good Lord, but she should be ashamed for thinking such wanton thoughts. Hating herself for them, she arose and dressed for the day, pulling out the first thing her fingers encountered from her trunk. Her brow furrowing with resolve, she determined to do as he had bade her.

God curse him, she fully intended to stay out of his way.

Chapter 20

It took very little effort on her part, for it became apparent that Christian had no care to see her, at all.

Truth to tell, it was amazing how vast the ship suddenly seemed, despite that she shared his cabin each night. He came only when he was certain she slept . . . and then, on the third night, he didn't come at all. She learned from Ben the next morning that *Hawk* had begun to share their cabin.

"He's in a foul temper," Ben told her as she came upon him. He sat, whittling the crude piece of oak Jessie had found him clutching that first morn. It was beginning, despite Ben's amateur strokes, to take on the shape of a walking cane.

"Who?" she asked much too innocently.

Taking a moment's pause from his sculpting, Ben peered down at her, his brown eyes troubled. "You know very well to whom I refer." He nodded in Christian's direction, nonetheless.

Jessie didn't bother to turn. She knew *he* was there. She needn't look to know he was watching them.

"Tell me," she said, changing the topic, "how is your leg? Does it pain you still?"

"Here and there," he confessed somewhat reluctantly. His features softened as he gazed down at her. " 'Tis healing, though, and I'd not have you worrying over it, sweet coz."

Jessie averted her gaze, unable to bear seeing his pain. He wore one pant leg split up the side so that she wouldn't be exposed to his nudity while attending him, for despite her lack of medical knowledge, there was no one else to do so. Jean Paul, too, was healing well enough. And though he suffered a lingering fever, it had been mild enough that he'd not bothered to take himself back to bed. Only the paleness of his complexion gave any evidence to his illness, for the man was as out-of-hand as the rest of the crew, stubborn too, for he refused to be coddled or cared for. Ben, on the other hand, seemed content enough to accept what little aid Jessie could give.

"You need your bandages changed. I brought these." Dropping the bundle of rags from her arms into Ben's lap, she sank to her knees to better inspect his thigh. The bandages were free of body fluids for the first time—a good sign, she thought, though she truly couldn't be certain. With a heartfelt sigh, she began to unravel the soiled wrappings.

"You shredded one of your gowns for these?"

Jessie peered up at him to see that he was toying with a bit of lace that still clung to a strip of it, obviously having been overlooked in her haste. He removed it carefully, mindful not to tear it in the process, while Jessie busied herself with his leg. "It was old," she assured him, "it was nothing."

Freeing it at last, he held it between his fingers, stroking it meditatively. "I've never seen the likes o' this mood of his, Jessie, and I've known the man an eternity."

Jessie tugged off a section of his bandage much too quickly and cast him an irate glare.

"Ayeee! Gad, Jess, be easy with me!" Resisting the urge to shield his wound from further aggression, he gritted his teeth, allowing her to continue. He said through clenched teeth, "Tell me, coz, what is it you said to him to turn his mood so foul?"

"And what makes you think 'tis me?" Jessie peered up at him with narrowed eyes.

Ben shrugged.

"Nothing he didn't deserve," she assured him. "And *you*! You haven't been alive an eternity!"

But *he* had! Jessie thought, glancing briefly toward the ship's wheel, for he was the devil's own!

"Not an eternity, mayhap, but long enough to know . . ."

With Ben's bandages finally unraveled, Jessie glanced up into her cousin's handsome face. He smiled down at her, though it was a cheerless smile, and it made her heart ache terribly.

Catching her hand at his knee, he stroked the back of it with his thumb. Jessie could merely stare as he caressed her, feeling uncomfortable with it, yet not quite able to withdraw her hand.

Her expression anguished, she lifted her face to his, and their gazes met and held.

"Sweet Jess," Ben murmured. "How I could love you . . . if only . . ." She flushed, averting her gaze, and he said, "How depraved I must sound to you, wanting you as I do—but I cannot help it! I've tried," he swore, "and I just cannot!"

"Ben . . ."

"Hush," he demanded. "Listen to me, sweet coz. I do know you can never be mine, though it pains me . . ." He placed her hand to his heart. "I can only hope that someday . . . *someday*," he repeated solemnly, "though I doubt it very much, I shall find another as kind and beautiful as you. Until then, know my heart belongs to you, and only to you."

Jessie shook her head, her heart twisting at his disclosure. "Ben . . . please . . ."

He placed his fingers to her lips, shushing her. "Listen to me, please, because I must say this. I swear I'll not speak of it again, not to anyone. Know I love you, Jess, and know I'll always be there for you, no matter the circum-

stances. I pledge that to you here and now."
He groaned suddenly, the sound tormented.
"God's teeth! I feel such a fierce loyalty to
Hawk, for he once saved my arse from the gibbet. You see . . . I risked my father's ship on a
venture—a worthy venture, though it matters
not a whit now, for the outcome remains the
same." He shook his head regretfully. "Hawk
came to my rescue. He didn't have to, but he
did." He shrugged. "Had he not, well then . . .
my father would have lost his ship in the Indies, and I . . ." He chuckled without mirth. "I
daresay, I would be as lifeless as this wooden
cane in my hand."

Placing the staff he spoke of down upon the
deck, he reached out, taking her by the arms,
drawing her closer, yet gently, as though to
gain her full attention.

"Even so . . . hear me well . . . Does Hawk so
much as touch you in the wrong manner, does
he hurt you . . . then he'll answer to me. And
yet . . . I know in my heart you'll not need me,
because Hawk is a good man. I know only too
well that he is . . . and so . . . you truthfully
have no need of me at all." An anguished look
crossed his features. And then, as though he
could not help himself, he brought her closer
still, his lips not far from her own as he spoke
to her. "Oh, God . . . Jessie . . ." He groaned. "I
might ask only one thing of you . . . I dream of
you so oft, sweet coz—much too oft! I would
have you put an end to these dreams. I cannot
. . . Mayhap if you would kiss me, just once . . .
your soft, sweet lips to my own . . . just once.

I shall not ask it of you again—I swear it on my honor!"

"Ben!" she choked out, panicking, and tried to withdraw from his embrace. He held her fast and came nearer still, urging her with his compelling gaze to assent.

"Please, Jess . . ." He sounded as tortured as a man could possibly sound.

Jessie's eyes closed and she swallowed convulsively, knowing in her heart that she could not deny him this once. She nodded, and heard his moan of relief as he pulled her exuberantly into his embrace, touching his lips tenderly to hers at first, tentatively, as though he were afraid she would bolt. His kiss was achingly sweet . . . and she should have felt something . . . anything, for he was nearly as masterful with his lips as Christian, yet she could feel nothing. She was numb. Her heart was dull and heavy for she was cursed to love another.

After a long-suffering moment, he tore himself away. "Christ," he concluded, scowling fiercely. "I believe that might have been a first-rate mistake." He winked at her halfheartedly. "Tell me, Jess, can you never . . ." He paused then, seeming to rethink his words, and said instead, shaking his head, "Never mind. You love *him* and there is nothing to be done for that. You cannot give full measure . . . and I can take no less . . . Only know that I shall always—"

"How very moving."

Jessie whirled about to spy Christian looking down upon them from the upper deck, his expression dark and stormy, his stance threatening, and his dark hair whipping with the breeze. His blue eyes shot her with contempt.

"'Tis not what it appears, Hawk," Ben swore at once, his tone repentant, if only slightly irritated. "She was ..." His gaze reverted to Jessie, but he could not bank the look of intense yearning that was there for her to see, then suddenly he did, and he looked again at Christian, slightly more composed. "I stole a kiss from her," he yielded, "and she had not the heart to refuse me."

"How very charitable of her." Christian cast her a ferocious glare before turning and stalking away.

"I'm sorry."

Jessie shook her head. "It matters not ... He couldn't possibly loathe me more than he does already."

Christian felt rage like never before, though he'd be damned if he'd fault Ben for it. It was Jessie he blamed. Curse her faithless hide! He'd listened with bated breath to her soul-stirring confession a few nights past and had felt her pain.

The biggest part of him had been elated at the possibility of her innocence; still, he'd not been quite able to bring himself to believe her. For all he knew, she'd performed the dramatics for his benefit alone, knowing he was awake and listening. And yet, though he'd not dared believe in her, the need to hold her had been irrepressible, and he'd reached out to comfort her even against his will.

How could he have thought to believe her?

For the last days, and nights, while he'd lain next to her, he'd respectfully let her be, while he'd grappled with his heart and his conscience, coming so close to trusting in her . . . so close . . . He'd not gone to her last night because he hadn't trusted himself.

And now . . .

Had he been even remotely near them, he might have torn Ben limb from limb. God's truth, he felt like doing so even now. With a curt nod, he urged his first mate away from the wheel, taking charge of it himself, his expression furious. Black-haired, bushy-browed Tibbs gave up his post immediately, eyeing him warily as he scurried away.

Damn. He didn't want to believe her, not now—particularly not now. But her pitiful wails had resounded with truth, tearing his own heart into tortured shreds. But she was lost to him, for it was apparent she loved another . . . *that she despised him as much as she claimed.*

He recalled Ben's blissful expression as his lips had touched upon Jessie's, and his chest constricted painfully. Christ, he had come to such foolish conclusions all those months ago in England, and now he would pay for it. He couldn't stand the thought of her with Ben. Couldn't bear the thought of Ben's hands upon her, his lips worshiping her. He closed his eyes for an instant, feeling dizzy with anger and regret. He'd never loathed himself more than he did at the moment, for he'd had her once, and he'd lost her.

How could he have been so witless?

How could she be so faithless? So fickle?

She was a treacherous bitch—even if she had not been the one to betray his confidences. She'd played him false with her inconsistent emotions—damned female turncoat!

But then, she was never yours to love in the first place, he reminded himself bitterly. *She was never yours to begin with . . .*

Nor could she ever love the man who had caused the death of her father . . .

And he was that man.

The remainder of the journey passed uneventfully.

It took just over two weeks to reach their destination, a small, picturesque island as bright and vibrant as the lush background of stained glass with which it competed. Jessie remained within the cabin the entire day they were docked. They departed early the next morn, stopping at yet another port two days hence. There they spent merely a few hours, and were gone again by noon.

If she thought Christian had avoided her before, he certainly did so now. She saw him only fleetingly, when she happened to search him out. God only knows why she should do such a thing, but sometimes before she could stop herself, she would find herself seeking just a glimpse of him.

So many times she'd been tempted to go to him, to speak with him, but Christian would need only glare at her with that devil's fire in his eyes and her courage would immediately falter. And then she would scurry back to her cabin.

God's truth, were it not for Ben's and Jean Paul's company, she would have died of the doldrums along with her broken heart.

They were half a day from Charlestown when a knock sounded upon her cabin door— Christian's cabin door, though he had so generously abandoned it for her. How gracious of him, she thought bitterly. "Come in," she said, knowing instinctively it was not Christian, for he never would have bothered to knock upon his own door.

The cabin door opened at once and Jean Paul came sauntering in, his expression grim. He took a seat at the claw-footed table without invitation. In so very many ways he was like his son, Jessie mused, but she liked him anyway. She felt sorry for him, in truth, that he should be so close to his only son and have no knowledge of their relationship. He'd told her once already that he'd never married and had never had children. *How could he not know?*

Once seated, Jean Paul looked at her pensively. Screwing his lips, he gazed at her as though he would speak but was unsure of how to proceed.

"What is it? Ben?"

"*Non, non, mon ange*, not Ben. Fear not, for he is well. His leg seems to be healing and he

walks well enough with his cane—although,"
he yielded with a regretful shake of his head,
"I very much fear he shall be left with a limp
for the remainder of his days. And yet he's
quite fortunate, for the leg bone did not shatter, and it well could have."

Jessie shuddered at that ghastly thought.

"*Oui*, demoiselle, I have seen it before." He
raised a brow. "But enough of Ben—'tis my
son I've come to discuss with you just now."

Jessie's eyes widened and her jaw fell. She
closed her mouth abruptly, for she had no idea
what to say in response. "You know?"

His face contorted. "I take it Hawk has confided in you, then, for you seem to know precisely what it is I'm speaking of." He nodded,
seeming pleased with the discovery. "But
then, of course, he would have," he addressed
himself. He sighed. "So much makes sense to
me now." He chuckled softly, the sound so
oddly familiar that it sent a chill down Jessie's
spine. "I take it you think I did not know?"
He clucked his tongue, casting Jessie a reproachful glance. "But I ask you, *ma petite*,
how could I not? A man would have to be
blind—nay, there can be no mistaking it,
Hawk is my son."

Jessie's shock was evident in her expression.
"I—" She shook her head in stunned disbelief.
"He has no idea that you know," she told him
after a moment.

"Aye," Jean Paul confirmed, "and that is my
own fault, I fear, for I made his sweet *maman*
swear to me that she would never tell him . . .

and then, when I thought he knew, I pretended ignorance, as well. I just could not seem to meet his eyes when he spoke of her, for then he would know, *chérie*, that I love her still."

"But . . . I don't understand . . ."

"I was not certain until now that he knew, you see. But if my son has confided in you, then he knows. And still . . . I must allow Hawk to decide to accept me. I would not betray his mother by speaking of it first. Until the day he discovers it, I am content simply to have Hawk as my friend. Tell me, how blessed can a man hope to be? I cannot give him my name, but my son has my friendship, and that is so much more. How many fathers can say as much? *Non, non,* fear not, *mon ange,* I am perfectly content with my lot—but enough of this! I came because I must know for certain . . . do you love him . . . do you love my son?"

"He's a rude, contemptible boor!" Jessie told him with conviction, taking the seat across from him.

Jean Paul watched her with probing blue eyes, as though to see through her words. He chuckled softly. "Yes, I know, but do you *love* him, *chérie*? That was the question."

"Nay!" Jessie said much too quickly. She shook her head emphatically. Perhaps a bit too zealously, for something in Jean Paul's expression told her that he did not believe her.

Suddenly Jean Paul slapped his hand down upon the table. "I see," he said, smiling slyly.

He nibbled at the side of his mouth for a moment as he stared at her. "Very well then." He nodded, rising from his chair, obviously through with his interrogation of her, brief as it was. "Yes, I do think I know what must be done then, demoiselle. And you are quite certain you do not love him?"

Misunderstanding his question, Jessie shook her head, and then realizing what she was saying, nodded at once with a certainty she didn't quite feel.

Jean Paul chuckled, giving her a conspiratorial wink, and Jessie had the most awful premonition as he turned to leave, yet before she could question him about it, he was gone. She spent the rest of the afternoon worrying over Jean Paul's strange visit, wondering at his cryptic remarks.

That night, however, her curiosity came to an end when the door to the cabin burst open and slammed shut behind Christian.

The room was pitch black, the lanterns having been snuffed for the night, but Jessie knew it was he. Her skin prickled, and gooseflesh erupted.

"Why isn't the door bolted?"

Jessie didn't have time to reply to his question before he spoke again, this time his tone somewhat less angry, though ominous still.

"That whoreson cousin of yours!" he muttered irately, his words slightly slurred. "And that damned Jean Paul! Those two are enough to tax even a dead man's soul! I swear before God, woman, did I remain one more instant in that bloody cabin with those two bickering idiots for company, I would like to have shot them both!"

He turned to her, searching the darkness as though to be certain he was not talking to himself, for Jessie had yet to give him indication she was awake. She knew the moment his eyes adjusted to the darkness and he saw her, for his scowl immediately disappeared. His features softened, illuminated by the light from the window, and the strange tenderness evident in his gaze gave lie to the brutality of his words. "Say one word against my presence, and you shall find yourself overboard in a twinkling!" Having said that, he lapsed into a strained silence as he proceeded to tug off his boots. They fell to the floor, each with a thud. Without preamble, he began removing his breeches, then deciding against it, left them on, but unclasped. His shirt, which was already gaping, he removed quickly. Jessie thanked God for the shadows that concealed—to hide not *him*, but the flush that even now was burning through her body.

And then he asked, more softly this time, as he wadded his shirt and hurled it to the floor, "Why in bloody blue blazes wasn't the door bolted, Jessie?" Jessie tried, but couldn't find her voice to speak. "You were perhaps expecting someone?" He stood there, awaiting her reply, and when it was not forthcoming he demanded, "Scoot over."

Apparently Jessie didn't move quickly enough for him, for he very nearly lay upon her as he plopped himself down next to her upon the bed. She did scoot away then—at once—to the far, far side of the bed.

Christian gave her a cynical little laugh. "Can't bear to touch me, love? Damn, but you are a deceiving little prude. *Pardonnez-moi*," he said scornfully, "but I'll bloody well not sleep on the floor for you, so you might as well bear my presence as best you can and simply go to sleep."

With that, he promptly snatched the pillow from under her head. Jessie's cheek hit the bed with a soft thud as he then proceeded to pound the pillow with his clenched fist, as though to remove all trace of her presence from it. She didn't bother protesting. It wouldn't have done any good. The man was an insensitive oaf!

"*Bon nuit*," he whispered "Pleasant dreams, *mon amour*!"

Tears filled her eyes, and she cursed herself, for it seemed with him, she was always weeping over something. Lord, how she despised him! She tried to stifle her sobs, but they seemed to find a way of their own, forcing themselves through her throat in pitiful little whimpers.

Christian heard her and fury gripped him.

"Christ! What have you to weep over now, woman!" With a snarl of disgust, he reached out for her, snatching her into his arms, hating his body's reaction to her even as he did so. She screeched and tried desperately to move away, but he was too strong. Her back to him, he wrapped his arms about her, holding her close, imprisoning her within then. And no sooner was she within his embrace than he felt himself pulse and swell against her luscious little bottom. He closed his eyes, grimacing, trying to ignore the reality of her within his arms ... after so long ... trying to ignore his raging desire for her.

It had been so bloody long.

He held her tighter, closer, but her wails only increased, and so did his need, for she was squirming without mercy against him. He breathed in deeply, filling his lungs, commanding restraint of himself, but her hair smelled so very sweet ... like lilacs and fresh sea air combined; the two shouldn't have mingled so exquisitely, but they did.

Unable to stop himself, he pressed his lips to the back of her head. He was quickly losing himself, losing his will. He moved to her neck, feeling the strands of her silky hair brush between his heated lips, and he took a deep breath, never releasing it, for he could have sworn she trembled within his arms. It took very little, just that simple gesture to remind him of the passion she'd once shown him. Her sobs ceased at once and she froze, bringing a measure of sanity to his fogged senses. Perhaps she feared him instead?

He exhaled finally and breathed in deeply the scent of her. Christ, she smelled so devilishly good. He'd consumed an entire bottle of whiskey tonight, straight from the flask like a mindless drunkard, before coming to her in hopes that he would be numbed to her presence beside him. What was it about her that made him buckle to such weaknesses? Maxwell Haukinge had been a bloody sot—his brother Philip as well—and he loathed them for their condescending arrogance and their flaws, yet here he was, no better than they, in truth.

His breathing quickened and he groaned, holding her closer as he tried to regain his reason. She was no good for him, he argued. He was no good for her. But it was no use, the noble gentleman had fled, probably cowering in some dark corner, terrified of the beast within his soul.

It was about time, he thought grimly.

It felt damned good to have himself back.

His hands unlocked and roamed her body at will, her breasts, her belly, her thighs, and then slid between them, committing the feel of her to his memory.

He wouldn't be denied, not this time, he swore . . . not this time . . .

Christian turned her so that she faced him in the darkness. His hand went to her face and he caressed her lips, her soft cheek, moving down to her chin, slowly, taking his leisure. *She let him.* Holding her delicate chin between his thumb and forefinger, he stroked it with his thumb as he lifted her shadowed face for his kiss.

She didn't resist him, and victory, sweet and potent, swept through his veins in that instant—along with it, a hunger more compelling than the physical, a yearning so deep and fierce that his mind went blank of all thought save for that of the woman in his arms. When his lips met hers at last, he found them trembling sweetly for him, and he couldn't help himself, his fevered tongue thrust within, tasting and taking with a delirium he'd never experienced before.

In that moment, as their tongues met and sparred, he found the sweetest taste of paradise, discovered a glimpse of heaven and beyond . . . and knew instinctively it was a place he would never see . . . save through her.

God, he wanted her so much . . . so bloody much . . .

And this time, he was not going to stop.

God Himself couldn't keep him this time. He'd waited far too long already—honor be damned! Conscience be damned! If he should burn in hell the rest of eternity for this night, then it was a penance he would eagerly pay.

And curse her, for she responded much too wantonly to his every thrust, his every touch, moaning and undulating for him so wildly, in such sweet abandon. Aye . . . she was fiery heat in his arms, and he reveled in the reality that she desired him, as well.

Christian felt her body shudder at his touch, heard the passionate little whimpers she made, and saw himself suddenly tearing the bodice of her gown in his fierce need to taste her, to suckle the sweet buds, not recognizing himself or his actions anymore.

At the instant, he felt as savage and ruthless as he was reputed to be.

Jessie whimpered, though not from pain or fear, but from a longing so great, she could scarce comprehend it, much less deny it. Her sanity was swept away, and she could only feel—couldn't think, only feel . . .

"Christian . . ." She moaned. "Please . . ."

She wanted to plead with him never to stop, but her voice failed her, and she closed her eyes to savor his touch instead. "Please . . ."

"Nay," he growled, "I cannot—God curse me, but I cannot! I want to see you, Jessamine . . . all of you . . . kiss you all over . . . everywhere . . . ah, Christ," he hissed, leaving her lips and touching his burning mouth to her throat. "I've waited so long, Jess . . ."

Arching for his lips, Jessie moaned. It felt so blessed good to be kissed and loved by him . . . but then, he didn't love her, she had to remind herself. And still . . . if she would be condemned for this weakness all the rest of her lifetime, then let it be so, for she could not deny him—nay, she could not deny herself! When his warm lips closed over and suckled at her breast, she thought she would die from the intense pleasure it gave her. "Please . . ."

"Please what?" His breath was hot against her flesh as he moved lower still, tasting her as he ripped the gown further from her body, reducing it to little more than tattered rags . . . like her will.

"This, Jessie?" he asked softly, touching his lips to her body in that most private place.

"Yes," she hissed, undulating and twisting with the sheer pleasure of it. "Yes . . ." She moaned, her eyes closing tightly as she cherished his loving. She wanted to remember forever every detail of this night, every sensation he roused within her. The passion in his hands; the way he touched her as though he adored her. "Yes," she murmured, her body responding with tiny little shudders.

"Jessamine," he whispered hoarsely, sliding up, bending low over her and burying his face within her hair. "I'm not going to stop this time . . ."

His whispery breath was velvety soft and blazing hot against her ear.

Christian lifted himself above her, waiting for her to reopen her eyes before continuing, wanting to know that she'd understood him clearly, wanting her to understand that it was to him she gave herself . . . not Ben.

She lifted her dark lashes at last, relief and anguish both evident there in the brilliant green of her eyes. They seemed to glow in the darkness, beckon him on . . .

She watched without moving as he tugged down his breeches, shrugging them off.

Her gaze met his and his lips turned ever so softly as her eyes lowered to that very erect male part of him. Her gaze flew once again to his.

He made some sound, part chuckle, part groan, at her reaction, for through the years Christian had lain with many women, all with diverse personalities, each with varying degrees of experience, but never had he been privy to such an expression as that Jessie gave him now. It was obvious to him that she'd never seen a man unclad before, and that knowledge gave him pleasure like no mating ever could have.

"Wh-What are you d-doing?"

"Making love to you," he answered huskily, leaving no doubt as to his intent, and then his hands were moving across her once more with an urgency he could no longer restrain. Not gently at all, he jerked the last threads of her gown from her body, revealing her completely to his scrutiny.

"My God . . ." He swallowed with difficulty. "You are so beautiful . . . more than I'd imagined . . ."

Jessie's heart squeezed at his words. Suddenly she couldn't breathe, couldn't think, only feel . . . His hands moved over her, searing her flesh, and then he cupped her breasts with his warm palms, kneading them gently beneath his expert fingers, as he bent to kiss her once more, his tongue delving deeply, possessively.

In the next instant his mouth left her lips to replace his hands at her breast, suckling her like a babe at his mother's bosom, and Jessie discovered some heretofore unknown connection between that part of her and the *other*.

And then he knelt above her once more.

Heat flared in the innermost reaches of her body as she felt his hand slide like molten fire between her legs. She moaned as one large finger thrust within her body, exploring the depths of her, and in response her legs lifted of their own accord. His body shuddered violently in answer to her instinctive invitation. Seeming to have found what he sought, he tensed over her, staring at her through the darkness as though he were overwhelmed by his discovery. Jessie could not tell his expression for the shadows, but his hand arrested there in the very depths of her. Then, all at once, she felt his finger stroking deep within her as his body quivered once more.

In an instant, he withdrew, covering her, his weight pressing her into the bed, and all the while he continued to adore her flesh, with his hands and his lips and his tongue. He was a man driven, it seemed. His arms slid behind her knees, and then it seemed he was parting her, separating her legs, lifting her. She obliged, wrapping her legs about his hips.

And then suddenly she felt it, the delicious pressure as he eased that part of himself within her, impaling her. Moaning, Jessie instinctively lifted against him, accepting him even as her body refused him entrance.

Cursing, Christian withdrew just a little, but the incredible tightness was his undoing. It seemed he'd waited for this moment a bloody lifetime.

A lifetime too long.

Crying out hoarsely, he lost control, surging down against her, tearing her maiden's flesh in one fell swoop.

The fierceness of their joining drowned Jessie's pleasure with such unbelievable pain that she instinctively recoiled with the shock of it. "Christian!" she cried as he began to thrust wildly. "Christian! Oh God!" But he would not stop. His movements were swift and hard and his handsome face contorted as though in pain.

Jessie fought him, trying to dislodge him, yet even as she resisted, he rode her more fiercely still, as though her maneuvers, in fact, urged him on. And then she felt the heat again, and understood completely this deep joining of the flesh, for he'd somehow touched her all the way to her womb . . . and it seemed to ease the bittersweet ache so deep within her.

He filled her completely, her body, her heart, her soul.

His hands moved to her buttocks, lifting her slightly, as though to raise her more evenly for his thrusts, holding her immobile as he pumped savagely, furiously, within. Jessie tried to give back full measure, but he was too strong and too quick, and his thrusts too unbearably sweet, and then he stopped, crying out savagely, casting his head back to reveal the taut cords of his neck. He held her so tightly that she thought he would crush her as his body shook, violent spasms wracking his entire form. After an eternity, he fell listlessly atop her, though he supported the majority of his weight upon his arms. His cheek was to her bosom, his breath ragged and spent.

She wanted to demand that he continue, for

she'd been on the brink of something wonderful, something exquisite, but the muscles of his jaw tautened against her breast, and he whispered fiercely, gravely, "*Pardonnez-moi . . . pardonnez-moi . . .* forgive me, but I could not stop . . ."

And then the warmth and the need were suddenly gone, replaced by an anguish and disappointment so great that Jessie could scarcely bear it. Her heart hammering without mercy, and anger surging through her veins, she shoved him from atop her. He went willingly enough, giving a low, tormented growl as he turned from her to face the door.

Frustrated, and too furious to care that he was angry once again, Jessie turned her back to him, facing the blasphemous window. As she stared out at the inky black sky and pale moon above the oak tree, ignoring the figures beneath, she felt more bereft than ever.

Chapter 21

The rap upon the door awoke her at once—or so Jessie thought, for when she opened her eyes she saw through the shadows that Christian had already reached it and was turning the knob. She wondered then if he'd slept at all.

Frantically she searched out the discarded sheet to cover her nakedness. Scarcely had she found it and shielded herself when the door opened. The light from a single lantern spilled into the cabin. It was McCarney. A frisson passed down Jessie's spine as the man spoke.

"I've come tae tell ye, Hawk, as ye asked me to, that we've arrived at the mouth o' the Ashley. We've come in as silently as the mist, as ye said we should—none ha'e seen us, I'm certain."

Christian nodded. "Lower the boat, then . . . We'll be there in ten minutes."

"Aye, sir, will do."

When McCarney would have peered into the cabin, Christian slammed the door in his face. Turning to the bed, he saw that Jessie was sitting, facing him, the sheets pressed protectively to her bosom. His head pounded fiercely—his conscience worse. Unable to face her, he turned from her, seeking out his breeches in the darkness, not bothering to light a lantern.

The less light, the better, for they were not so far from land that they might not be discovered yet.

"Get up and get dressed."

"I don't understand . . . 'Tis the middle of the night," she protested.

"Just do it," he directed. *"Or I shall do it for you."*

She moved hesitantly from the bed, drawing the coverlet away, and came away with a torn fragment of her gown within her hand. Her face contorted, and his heart twisted. "Why must we go about in the dead of the night, when only thieves and rogues prowl about? I cannot bear to be part of such depravity!"

Christian had no need of light to know that she was weeping now. He could hear the sorrow plainly in her voice, and he had the sudden urge to go to her, but then she spoke again and her anger kept him at bay.

"How can you do treason against the Crown, Christian? And my cousin—my God! I cannot fathom what would make Ben follow—"

"The likes of me?" The implication was clear. "Can you not?" Hearing only her grief for Ben's sake, he taunted, "Poor, poor Ben. And so you believe I've corrupted him?"

Jessie turned away, unable to face him, but it was an unnecessary gesture, for the room was too dark to see more than shadows. "I don't know what to believe anymore."

"Well then, allow me to enlighten you, *mon amour* . . ."

Fastening his breeches, he came closer, until he could see her face more clearly—pallid in the light of the moon. "Like me, Ben is appalled by the lack of justice in the colonies. But I cannot begin—nor have I the time or inclination—to give you all the arguments for what I do. I make no apologies for what I am, Jessamine."

And yet, giving lie to his words, he sat beside her upon the bed. Prying the tattered gown she held from her hand, he stroked it meditatively between his own fingers, looking down upon it with genuine regret. "I'm sorry, Jessie . . . This should never have happened between us."

He peered up at her then, dropping the tatter of her clothing in favor of a strand of her hair, rubbing it wistfully between his fingertips. Her eyes were such a brilliant green, luminous with unshed tears. For a long instant their gazes held, and he felt himself transported in time, to a sweeter moment he'd found beneath an old elm tree. He'd loved her even then, he realized, for she'd made him yearn to be that man she saw in him. *Only that man didn't exist.* He almost looked away then, so much sorrow and regret did he feel . . . and still . . .

Ah, but Christ . . . even now, he felt the need to explain himself to her when never before had he even thought to doubt his motives, or himself. He tried to conceive of a way to explain . . . some way to make her comprehend. Recalling a certain conversation they'd had once, so very long ago, he said, "Do you remember, Jessie . . . once, some time ago, we discussed at length Adelard of Bath's questions on nature?"

She nodded and Christian lifted her chin gently with a finger, searching her eyes through the shadows. "What did he speak of? Being guided by reason? Of authority as a halter?" As he spoke, he never lifted his gaze from her shadowed face. " 'For what else should authority be called but a halter?' " he recounted, his tone soft but impassioned as he spoke. She closed her eyes, refusing to see him, but he continued nonetheless, " 'Indeed, just as brute beasts are led by any kind of halter, and know neither where nor how they are led, and only follow the rope by which they are held, so the authority of your writers leads into danger not a few who have been seized and bound by animal credulity. For they do not know that reason has been given to each person, so that with it as the first judge he may distinguish between the true and the false. And whosoever does not know or neglects reason,' " he finished, " 'should deservedly be considered blind.' Is that not what he wrote, Jess?" A tear slipped through her lashes, silent and wretched, and it tugged at his heart.

She opened her eyes to him then.

"Well, I am not blind!" he told her with feeling, gripping her jaw a little harder to gain her full attention, though not hard enough to hurt her. "Nor am I an animal to be led blindly by a halter to my grave! I am a man, Jessie, and only a man, but with a heart and mind that tell me things are not as they should be. I merely do my part to change what I cannot abide—and I am not alone! Our number is great . . . Your cousin is only one of many, so do not fault him, nor myself, if you would, until you know and understand our grievances."

She gripped his wrist firmly. "Then tell me," she pleaded. "Explain them to me . . . Make me understand, because I do not!"

He let his hand drop from her face, but still she did not release his wrist. "I've not the time just now, but aye, I shall . . . and soon . . . just not now."

Freeing himself from her grasp, Christian rose to stand before her. Jessie averted her gaze, staring at her hands. She clasped and unclasped them, holding them fast in her lap.

Christian shook his head, his jaw working. He couldn't be weak, knew he couldn't be weak, but he was. "Dress yourself. We are awaited and the hour grows late. Morning comes swiftly, and I would see you safe at Shadow Moss before the first light."

She turned her face upward in question, her brows furrowing softly. "Shadow Moss?" She shook her head, uncomprehending.

"My home, Jessamine; 'tis where you'll stay until such time as Ben heals . . . and then you'll return to your cousin Robert."

"Oh." Her gaze skidded away.

He studied the shadowed contours of her face a long moment, but there was no emotion discernible there, and he turned from her finally, going to the door, opening it. His hand on the knob, his back to her, he told her, "I shall await you above deck."

Only silence answered him, but he knew she would come, and he left, closing the door softly behind him.

The double-storied plantation house was clearly visible from the Ashley. Its white-washed brick facade reflected the moonlight, making it glow, a silent beacon to those who would navigate the foggy river. Enormous white columns buttressed the stately portico. It was a magnificent house, Jessie admitted to herself as she stood before the massive oak front door, stunningly so, but it seemed oddly unbalanced. In the darkness she couldn't quite discern why.

No sooner had Christian opened the front door when he again seized hold of her arm, guiding her within. She would have protested save that she was rendered speechless upon

entering the house. Nothing could have prepared her for the sight within. Certainly not
the perfectly constructed classical architecture
of its exterior.

The entrance hall was in a lamentable state
at best. At least five hastily constructed scaf-
folds occupied the room. The ceilings and
floors completely lacked decorative molding,
and the walls were unsightly, bare of everything save for the gaslit lanterns that now gave
the room light. There was not a single stick of
furniture within the room.

Jessie could scarce hide her stupefaction.
She peered up at Christian with furrowed
brows and saw that he was watching her intently, as though he anticipated her reaction
and was bracing himself for the worst.

" 'Tis under construction," Ben told her
when he saw the look that passed between
them.

She lifted a brow. "So I've gathered." She
cast Ben an amused glance. Did he think she
could not tell? Splotches of white paint gar-
nished the wall that faced them, and wood
pieces of all sizes and shapes littered the bare
wood floor. This, she thought, was likely
where Christian had procured the oak for Ben
to fashion his walking cane from, and it struck
her then that he should have been so attentive
to such a small detail, and then again, one so
grand. She swallowed, secretly moved that he
should be so thoughtful of Ben. And she
couldn't help but recall the cheval glass he'd
brought to her aboard the *Mistral*; she never

had thanked him, nor had he ever mentioned it.

Her gaze returned to Ben, for it seemed to her he did, indeed, walk with a slight limp, though his leg was much improved. She watched her cousin hobble before them, trying to clear away the clutter from their path, and her heart felt burdened for him.

Christian left her to aid Ben, and no one spoke another word as they attempted to wade through the chaos of his home. Again to her surprise, Jessie was led up the spiral staircase to a fully furnished chamber decorated in much the same manner as the cabin she'd occupied upon the *Mistral*. Here, however, there were no stained-glass windows. Instead, there were six full-length panes, one set of them being a double door that led to what she assumed was a balcony.

She went to it, unlocking it and opening the doors. Leaving the lantern behind, upon a table, she stepped out into the black night, taking a deep, calming breath, for it had not escaped her just *where* Christian had brought her. For a long moment she merely stood, staring into the darkness, unsure of what to say or feel. He came up behind her, his footfalls soft and almost inaudible; she sensed more than heard him.

"I take it this is the master's chamber?" she said after a moment.

"It is."

"And where am I to sleep?" she dared to

ask, her tone dauntless, though she wasn't quite brave enough to look at him as yet.

"Here, of course," he said firmly. "As was the case upon the ship, there is no other place but here. As Ben said, the house is still under construction—only the kitchens are complete as yet, the dining room, my office, and the entrance hall. Upstairs, there is this room, and one other, and Jean Paul and Ben will utilize the other. You *shall* sleep here."

"And where will you sleep?" She braced herself for his answer. "Here?" she persisted, turning to face him. She shook her head. "If so, Christian, I'll not stay with you! In case you've forgotten, you've already ruined my life once—I'll not let you do so again!"

Christian sighed regretfully. " 'Tis a bit too late for that, don't you think?"

Her vision blurred at his insinuation. "You are heartless!" she choked out, refusing to cry.

"The truth is, Jessie, that you have no choice." He sighed deeply, shaking his head. "You cannot leave Shadow Moss, as you well know. Everyone believes you've sailed to England with Ben. If you go back now, then you're going to raise suspicions, not to mention the fact that your reputation would surely be in tatters then. After all, there were no other women aboard the *Mistral*."

"Aye!" she hissed, her lips trembling in her fury. "Though what difference does it make if I go now, or wait until Ben heals? Either way my reputation will be ruined—and 'tis all your fault!" Her face twisted with grief. "Why couldn't you have simply let me be? Why? You didn't need me."

Christian averted his gaze, his jaw working. "It seemed the thing to do at the time. I thought Ben and Jean Paul were injured more seriously than they were." He met her eyes once more, his own sparkling with some emotion Jessie couldn't quite decipher. He shuttered it quickly, masking it with sarcasm. "Aren't you pleased I was wrong?"

Jessie shook her head, unable to speak, and he cast his head backward staring into the sky, closing his eyes.

"I'm sorry," he said without opening his eyes. The rigid planes of his face were so taut, he seemed carved of stone. "I wish . . ." He shuddered and said slowly, *"I wish I'd left you alone, but I did not.* What we've done cannot be undone, much as I wish it." His eyes flew open, piercing her with their blue intensity. "And now . . . much as I loathe to . . . I must insist you stay."

"And will you build a gaol for me?"

His tone was unyielding. "Nay, Jessamine, but you will, indeed, remain here. The only way back to Charlestown is by boat—my boat," he pointed out coldly, "and everyone already knows you are to stay as my guest, willing or nay. You might make the best of it. After last eve," he added cruelly, "what have you left to lose?"

Jessie gasped in shock and outrage. Her palm cracked furiously against his shadowed jaw. "How dare you say such a thing to me?"

He caught her wrist as she retreated. His jaw taut, he clenched his teeth, rubbing his face with his free hand. His eyes flashed with anger. "Because," he said, his eyes narrowing, " 'tis the bloody damned truth!"

Jessie tried again to slap him with her free hand, but he caught that wrist too, encircling it with fingers of steel. "*Once,*" he allowed, "but never again, *mon amour.*" His whisper was frightening in its violent intensity. Had he shouted, Jessie doubted his words would have been more ominous. "*Never think to strike me again.*"

Their gazes clashed, warring—Jessie refused to cow before him this time—and then he suddenly released her, pivoted about on his boot heels, and left her upon the balcony.

Chapter 22

Only when she heard the door slam behind him did Jessie reenter the room.

He'd left the lantern beside the bed. By the light of it, she removed her cloak and slippers. She was so weary by the time she put out the lamp and climbed into the bed that her lids seemed heavy as lead.

She'd gotten so little sleep during the night, for it seemed the moment she'd managed to close her eyes, they'd been awakened again by McCarney's knock. She didn't like the man—could scarce bear his presence. There was something about him ... something she couldn't quite place—aside from the fact that he was violent when he had no cause to be. Before she could contemplate it further, she drifted to sleep.

When she awoke hours later, she was alone, sunshine filtering through the windows; dust motes danced in their brilliance. She turned to peer at the far side of the bed, and reached out to touch the cold sheets. As far as she could tell, he'd not slept there. Nor had he come to her. And then she spied her trunks against the far wall. Had he brought them? Or had he sent them, instead, unable to bear the sight of her?

God's truth, she didn't want to think about him. Rising at once, she washed her face in the small basin of water that had been supplied for her, then dressed, spying the green silk gown that was once again spread out over a chair. *So . . . he'd come after all.*

And then had left her alone.

As she'd asked him to.

It was evident he favored that particular gown, but Jessie couldn't quite bring herself to wear it for him. Instead, she chose a soft lavender-dyed calico with white lace peeking out at the bodice. Without her petticoats, this particular gown was far too large, but it couldn't be helped. It didn't matter; what need for such propriety now? She brought her hair away from her face, securing it low upon her nape with a strip of lavender ribbon. And then, feeling an overwhelming craving for fresh air, she went in search of it.

In the broad light of day, 'twas perfectly discernible why the house seemed unbalanced, for the right wing, for some odd reason, was still under construction. The brick walls were complete, but in place of the roof, only the framework stood, like a wooden skeleton against the greenery behind and above it.

The extensive lawn boasted only overgrown weeds and felled trees, and then closer to the riverbank, golden-tipped marsh grass swayed with the breeze. The dodder grass seemed to grow as far as the eye could see. Lord, she missed England suddenly. Nay, not her brother or his wife, for they had made her life intolerable before banishing her to this god-forsaken place, but she missed the comfort to be found in her family's ancestral home, the sprawling, manicured gardens in which she so often took refuge. There was no order to this place, no order at all, and it made her feel strangely out of sorts.

Finally, finding repose amid a small cluster of trees, upon a half-buried, half-rotten log near the marsh's edge, she sat and, for the first time since her banishment, allowed herself to grieve for all that was lost in her life. She had lost everything, and it was all his fault—Christian, or Hawk, or whatever the devil his name was! This instant she loathed him, despised him for every shred of her lost dignity. He'd taken her greatest possession without a single word of love, or even comfort. Her eyes blurred with tears she refused to shed. How could she have allowed it?

A flock of seagulls swooped silently toward the water in the distance, all of them flying out of formation. She watched them, curiously mesmerized by their graceful, airy dance. One sailed just above the surface of the water, so close that it seemed its flapping wings were skimming the water's edge, and yet never did it so much as immerse a talon into the river. One bird led the flock above the trees, and the three behind made the ascent as though it were a dance they'd choreographed and rehearsed. In their wake, a small fish vaulted into the air. So quickly did it do so that by the time she turned in its direction, all that was left to show of its hasty retreat was a small circle of ripples that filtered its way past the waterlogged marsh grass and ultimately faded into nothingness.

For a long while, Jessie sat in that nothingness, hearing nothing, seeing nothing. When suddenly she heard Christian's voice calling her, so close, she started, and nearly panicked. God's truth, but she had no wish to see the lying cur just now! Searching about desperately, she spotted the low limb upon an enormous oak behind her, and made her way quickly toward it. The trunk itself must have measured at least twenty feet in circumference, and massive, weepy limbs stretched groundward, grazing the leafy ground as though their groaning weight were somehow too much for the poor oak to bear. Its majestic stature reminded her of a protective old grandfather, arms outstretched and bending earthward to pluck even the tiniest of insects from the perils of the forest floor. Just now, 'twas she in need of shielding.

Starting at the lowest point, shoving the hem of her gown between her teeth, she scrambled upward upon the thick limb until she was perched safely out of sight. She was probably behaving foolishly, she knew, but she couldn't bear to face Christian this moment. Sheltered here, she didn't have to worry about it. Nope, she thought somewhat flippantly, and almost giggled at the absurdity of the situation. She would simply wait until he was gone and then hurry to the house; surely there was someplace in his accursed mausoleum where she could find sanctuary?

It was only another moment before Christian found his way to the decaying old log she'd been sitting upon only an instant before. As though by instinct, he stopped there, gazing out over the expanse of river, shading his eyes with a hand. Then, as though sensing her presence, he turned, and Jessie held her breath as he scanned the area. Cursing him under her breath, she watched his movements.

Good Lord, but even now he was much too handsome for her peace of mind. His hair caught the glow of afternoon sun, making it seem lighter than it actually was. He stood there a long instant and his profile mesmerized her, with his thick, lightly whiskered jaw, and those deep-set blue eyes that could liquefy her limbs with scarce a glance.

"Jessie!"

She bit into her lip, refusing to answer.

"Jessamine!"

Jessie remained perfectly still, unwilling to be discovered now in such an absurd place . . . unwilling to be caught spying, for spying, she was, whether she liked to admit it or nay. She sat there without moving, watching him search the area as he shouted her name at the top of his lungs, and the inanity of the situation struck her all at once. Good Lord, what was she worried about? Christian would never think to search a tree for her, and here she was, hanging like a chimpanzee directly above his head!

"Dammit!" he muttered irately to himself, coming closer. "Where the devil has she gone?"

He never even bothered to look up, and when he walked to the lower end of the very limb she was perched upon and then sat, arms crossed and deep in thought, she was suddenly giddy with the hilarity of it all. They were sitting upon the very same tree limb, yet he could have remained there an eternity and never thought to search up here for her. She couldn't help it. For the first time in days, she felt like laughing hysterically. Lord, what if she started to cackle and fell out? Never could she bear that! Suddenly a vision of him as he'd looked when Mrs. Brown had toppled him from the fence assailed her. She tried desperately not to giggle, but her laughter burst forth.

As though unsure his ears had heard correctly, Christian slowly turned his head up, and the surprised look upon his face made Jessie giggle all the harder.

"What the devil are you doing up there?"

She couldn't help herself, she started to laugh without restraint. She held on tightly to a small tree limb for support and resisted the urge to clutch her aching sides as she shrieked with laughter.

"Get down here!"

Overcome with glee, Jessie shook her head, refusing him, even as another bout of laughter overcame her.

"Whatever possessed you to climb up there?" His brows cocked. "Come down from there, Jess, before you fall."

Biting her lip to keep from shrieking once more, Jessie shook her head again. "Nay," she refused, choking on her giggles.

"For Christ's sake, if you won't come down," he advised her, "I shall be forced to come up after you." Even as he issued the warning, he was making his way up the oak branch. Yet when he reached the spot where she sat, he merely hauled himself onto the limb beside her, instead of dragging her down as she'd expected him to do.

"You had everyone worried."

She sobered at that.

"I didn't mean to," she admitted, still smiling, though her eyes remained melancholy. "I simply needed to be alone."

"You couldn't do that safely within?"

Jessie choked on her reply. "Safe . . . within?"

He misunderstood her.

"I'm sorry for the disorder."

That *wasn't* what she'd been referring to, but she asked, "How can you live like that?"

"Actually, I haven't been." He yielded a lazy grin that sobered her completely. That smile had been her downfall once upon a time. But not this time, she swore—not if she could help it. She would not allow herself to melt like a giddy schoolgirl falling under his devil's spell.

"It was my intent to stay in Charlestown during the construction," he explained, reaching out and plucking a leaf. He stared at her. "Circumstances, of course, have dictated otherwise."

She nodded knowingly. "If you've been inconvenienced," she informed him at once, "then 'tis your own fault."

Christian's jaw tautened, but he said nothing in response to her accusation.

The silence between them grew awkward, but he found himself unwilling to abandon their unlikely refuge so soon. Nor could he end this bittersweet diversion as yet.

There were traces of tears in her eyes and upon her cheeks, but he attributed them to her laughter, and ignored the flash of guilt that stabbed at him.

Nor could he deny the fear that had gripped him when he'd found her gone. "Jessie," he began, his words carefully weighed so as not to frighten her. "Do me the dubious favor of not leaving the house again—not without apprising someone of your whereabouts, whether it be Jean Paul . . . or even Ben," he ceded reluctantly, raking his thumbnail over the spine of a leaf. He gazed at her with narrowed eyes as though to see into her thoughts, then sighed heavily. "So I'll know . . . where to find you, if . . . if I need you."

She averted her gaze. "What if I've no wish to be found?"

"Just give me your word," he demanded, overlooking her flippant response. He tossed the leaf before him. "We've had reason to be concerned over gators here," he lied, looking away. " 'Tis for your own well-being I ask this of you." He turned again to face her. " 'Tis true," he insisted, seeing her wide-eyed expression. "We've a few animals missing with no sign of a carcass to be found. I should loathe that fate to be yours."

A shiver passed down Jessie's spine, but whether it was over his grisly disclosure, or the way he was gazing at her so solicitously, she could not discern. "And what makes you think 'tis a gator?"

His eyes held hers, unblinking. "For one . . . 'tis their way to haul their prey back to their nest and dispose of it there, thus no carcass would be found."

Jessie made a disgusted face. "How gruesome!" she declared, tearing her gaze away. "They are the vilest of creatures."

He smiled ruefully. "I rather thought you believed I was the vilest of creatures?"

"Yes, well . . . it seems you have a rival, after all, my lord." She cocked a brow at him, unable to reassure him, though she was tempted. "Tell me," she said on a sigh, glancing away, then back, somehow more composed, "are they always so vicious?"

He shook his head, his eyes alight with some unnamed emotion.

Christian's heart began to pound, for it had not escaped him that she'd managed to call him "my lord."

"Of usual," he said, clearing his throat, "they keep very much to themselves."

"Really? Why not now?"

"Mayhap because their hunting ground has been overrun—because there are too many, possibly. I dunno. Of usual, they are rather docile creatures." He smiled, thoroughly amused over the way her brow rose at his disclosure.

" 'Tis true," he asserted, his smile deepening when she cocked her head as though considering. "In fact, I once stood so close to a gator as to be nearly standing upon its snout." He chuckled softly at the memory, shaking his head in wonder. "It did nothing . . . nothing at all. In fact, the lazy beast did not so much as stir from the spot where it lay sunning. However," he continued on a dire note, "those to be found here upon the Ashley seem more vicious than those found inland. They seem to prefer fresh water, and 'tis my guess that if they are found in these salt rivers, such as the Ashley or the Cooper, it is because they are hungry and foraging."

Shivering, she told him, "I believe I've heard quite enough, my lord. I shall suffer nightmares as it is." She turned her gaze away, seeming suddenly bored by his presence.

"Perhaps 'tis not the most pleasant subject, but 'tis for that very reason you should not wander about unescorted." He couldn't bear it if anything were to happen to her.

Jessie turned to frown at him. "If 'tis such an awful place, then why did you choose to come here, my lord? I thought you were so enamored of Rose Park."

Gazing into her eyes, he again marveled that they never lost their power to captivate him, to reach into his soul. He could never admit to her how he'd felt that day after leaving her at Westmoor—that he'd felt nothing but revulsion for anything that reminded him of her. And Rose Park reminded him of her more than he would have thought possible. He'd envisioned fathering their children there . . . in the bedchamber he would have eagerly shared with her. He could almost picture her there now, as he'd so often imagined her . . . lying thoroughly loved within his bed—their bed— her dark curls tousled and softly framing her face . . . a child's voice calling to them from the hall . . . little feet scurrying to greet them . . . and Jessie . . . scrambling to repair herself in order to face their . . . son? daughter?

His tone carefully devoid of emotion, Christian told her, "I'd as soon not discuss Rose Park. Enough to say I sold the estate months ago. Shadow Moss is my home now."

Could she love him?

Aye, she had given herself to him last night, but lust was one thing and love another entirely.

When Christian looked at her once more, his expression was solemn, his eyes questioning, and Jessie longed to ask him what he was thinking. But she had gone that route once before, and that had been her first mistake. He'd made her care so very much, and then he'd ripped her heart out from her breast. She didn't want to know anything more about him. Didn't want to care.

They were probably all lies anyhow.

She found herself staring at his lips, remembering how they'd felt upon her body, and her heart lurched.

"Jessamine," he whispered. "If you don't stop gazing at my mouth just so . . . as though you would devour my lips . . . I might have to kiss you senseless, love."

Startled by his words, Jessie dragged her gaze from his mouth to his laughing eyes, and her face flushed crimson. "I—I wasn't staring at your lips!"

Was it so obvious she yearned for his kisses? Could he read in her eyes that she wanted him to touch her again? to make her feel alive once more? Her head reeled at the possibility, and she felt a tiny thrill at the memory of his love-making, bitter as it might have been.

His answering grin infuriated her. "I see . . . and you weren't wishing that I might lean forward . . . like this," he asked her. His hand slid behind her neck, though instead of drawing her toward him, he only supported her as he came the distance to her. She didn't resist him, couldn't, so dazed was she by his boldness

and his nearness. "And you weren't wishing
that I would touch them ever so softly to
yours . . ." His lips brushed hotly against her
own. Jessie closed her eyes, helpless to answer.
"Like this?"

Jessie was dizzy with wanting him, but she
opened her mouth to deny it still. Her negation came out a wistful sigh that made him
groan in response. Her body became suddenly
liquid, her limbs lethargic and heavy. She felt
as though she would die from the sheer pleasure he was offering her. Her belly fluttered
nervously as his breath mingled with hers and
she caught the scent of sweet brandy.

Their lips separated briefly, yet long enough
that Christian was able to take in her blissful
expression, and he reveled in it. His mouth
touched upon hers once more, tentatively at
first, then moving urgently as he suckled her
lower lip before raining more kisses upon her
delicate chin, moving down ever so slowly to
the heated flesh of her throat.

Lord, Jessie thought, his kiss was searing
her clear unto her soul! Had she no pride?
Had she no will?

"Jessie . . ." He groaned. "You taste so very
sweet, my love."

His words felt like delightful caresses to her
ears, sending shivers of anticipation down her
spine. Desire swept boldly through her, making every inch of her body sensitive to his
nearness. Heaven help her, but if the truth be
known, she hoped he would never stop. Even
against her will, she had dreamed of this,

ached for this, wished for it—even at the high cost of her dignity.

God save her, he'd given her the sweetest taste of heaven, and it was not such an easy thing to forget.

Cupping her face within his hands, he turned her cheek, kissing it hungrily as he nibbled her face and whispered softly against her throat, "Come back to the house with me, Jess . . . Let me love every inch of you as I yearn to." A shiver coursed through her.

It was a long moment before her mind registered his words. But when finally it did, she felt much as though she'd been slapped and then called a whore. He did not love her, she knew that well enough. Did he think she would lie with any man who asked it of her any time it was asked of her? Surely he did, if he thought for one moment that she would allow him to touch her again after all that had passed between them!

Anger filled her breast, and she reared back and shoved him, hard. Somehow, he managed to remain rooted to the tree limb, and it made her all the angrier. It would have served him well to break his neck, or leg—better yet, his pride. Curse the man! "You mean to ask me if I would lie with you, do you not? You cur! Unless you mean love, then do not speak of it, my lord! Say what you mean instead!"

As though he were privy to her thoughts and was now taunting her, Christian suddenly grinned, a slow, lazy grin.

Eyeing him wrathfully, Jessie scooted

around him and down the stout limb, and in
her haste nearly tumbled to the ground. When
she was far enough away that he was no
longer a threat, she turned and screamed, "I
loathe you, Hawk, you bloody whoreson!" But
his expression remained smug and it reignited
her temper. So infuriated that she could barely
contain her pent-up emotion, she shrieked, "I
loathe you, loathe you, loathe you!" And
wished fervently that she were near enough to
scratch his accursed eyes out. And then she
turned and marched away.

Smiling still, Christian never moved from
his perch within the ancient tree, only
watched, chuckling softly. "I'll just bet you
do," he replied glibly, rubbing his jaw pensively as he watched the saucy sway of her
hips.

His curiosity was more than appeased.

Chapter 23

If it was the last thing Jessie did, she was going to find her way back to Charlestown! She was not—absolutely not—about to remain in this crude hollow even one more instant! In the short time she'd been out of the room, someone had managed to unpack her trunks.

Angrily she now searched the bureaus for her personal items, and when she found them tucked neatly away into Christian's wardrobe, she snatched them out at once, stomping across the room and shoving them wrathfully back into the trunk in which they belonged. She would *not* remain near that man for even one more accursed moment! Not if she could help it!

She didn't bother to turn as the door opened, knowing very well that Christian was the only one who would dare enter while she was within without knocking. She was ready for him now, she swore. If he came near her, if he dared to touch her, if he so much as dared utter a word, she knew just what to say to the man, besides, of course, *I loathe you, loathe you, loathe you*. Good Lord! What was wrong with her that she would lose even her ability to speak coherently when in his presence?

She was startled speechless when it was Quincy who spoke from behind her instead.

"Anythin' else I can do fer ye, mum?"

She turned abruptly, her eyes wide with surprise, though she recovered enough to fix the old man with a wrathful glare. If her eyes had been pistols, Quincy would have tumbled lifeless to the oak floor. "Did—you—do—this?" she ground out fiercely, each word sharper and more hostile than the last. She waved a handful of her clothing at him, and the old man nodded warily, backing away a pace.

"Well! *I* never gave you permission to unpack my belongings, now did I? And 'tis because I do not—I repeat, *do not!*—intend to stay!"

Cramming the green silk dress Christian had chosen for her earlier and a pair of matching slippers into the largest trunk, she slammed it shut and fastened the tarnished brass clasp.

"Now, Jessamine," Christian appealed as he sauntered into the room at last. "There is absolutely no cause for you to be taking your frustrations out upon poor Quince. He did only what I requested he do." She spun about to face him, ready to do battle.

Nodding discreetly to Quincy, Christian commanded the old man to leave.

"Now," he directed, "unpack your trunks. You're not going anywhere."

"You can't keep me here!" she shouted madly. "And I won't stay!"

"And you *loathe me, loathe me, loathe me.* So I've heard." He laughed then, the mirthful sound infuriating. "Unpack your things, Jessamine," he said again, still chuckling.

"I will not!" She turned and slammed the lid down definitively. Her breathing labored and her heart hammering, she stood an instant, weighing her options as she stared blankly at her trunks. Truly, there were no options available to her, for how would she go back? She gritted her teeth in outrage. God curse him, but she certainly didn't have to share the cad's bed, now did she? Nay! She didn't! Seizing the side handle of the smallest trunk, she jerked it into movement. With some effort, she pulled it toward the door.

Christian leaned against the doorframe, watching her with unconcealed interest, eyeing her as though she were some novel curiosity. Not until she'd moved the trunk into the hall did he speak.

"Would you care to tell me what you're doing?"

"Picking gooseberries, can't you see!" He chuckled, and she said, "I'm not sharing your filthy bed!"

Brows raised, Christian glanced at the newly made bed, his gaze returning to her. "Actually," he countered, grinning, " 'tis a perfectly clean bed."

Jessie had made little progress back into the room since moving the one trunk into the hall, and he thought it might be because she'd managed to trap her skirt beneath the unwieldy baggage. With some difficulty, he resisted the urge to aid her, and the greater urge to laugh.

Unable to keep himself from it, he chuckled softly when Jessie finally discovered her skirt pinned and uttered an almost inaudible groan of mortification. He might have asked her if she needed his help, but he rather doubted she would accept it. Besides, he was thoroughly amused watching her struggles at the moment.

"You might at least tell me where you intend to go," he said much too jovially.

She gave him a very unladylike snort, a deadly glare, and turned again to the stubborn trunk upon the bed, shoving it with all her might. She said nothing until she'd passed him by, and was in the hall.

" 'Tis none of your concern where I intend to sleep!"

Christian's smile faded and his gut twisted as she halted beside the only other door along the corridor. His tone warning her, he asked, "Surely not with Ben, my love."

Her gaze flew to his angry blue eyes. "Oh! You would think such a despicable thing, wouldn't you? Nay!" she shrieked. "Not with Ben! And not with you, for certain!"

She had the bloody trunk halfway to the stairs now, and shaking his head, Christian wondered just how she expected to carry the thing below. "You do recall," he told her presently, "that there are no available rooms beyond this wing . . . unless, of course, you count the entrance hall."

"I shall take my chances, my lord. Surely I would prefer to sleep outside—in the rain," she added with a cutting smile, "to your delightful company!"

No matter that he'd braced himself against her anger, her stinging words, expertly flung, cut him to the quick. "Suit yourself, then."

He muttered an inaudible curse and then turned his back on her hapless struggles, reentering his room and slamming the door so hard that it shook the walls.

Later that night, Jessie was forced to admit the truth of the matter: Christian had been right, and he *had* warned her, so she had not even the solace of blaming him for her misery.

There had, in fact, been no other rooms available for her use. Only the one wing was complete. Belowstairs there was the dining hall and Christian's study, both of them without doors or even curtains on the wretched windows. Anyone could have peered within.

The other wing, the one she now occupied, remained only partially constructed, but at least this room was windowless, because the windows were as yet boarded up. Here, at least, no one could spy her—unless, of course, the person somehow managed to climb atop the high brick walls. She shuddered at the thought.

A strong, sturdy, lockable door separated this one wing from the rest of the house. The only problem, however, was that it locked from the other side, probably to keep out prowlers, judging by the size of the bolt. She'd managed only to drag the one trunk out of *his* chamber, and it now sat flush against the door, barring it from any who would enter.

Striving for a comfortable position, she fidgeted upon the pallet she had made from scraps of wood in the hall and a lone blanket she'd borrowed, but try as she might, she couldn't find relief from the stone-hard bed she had made for herself—much less sleep!

Staring despondently through the skeletal roof, she spied the half-moon peeping through a muddy night. It seemed to be eyeing her sleepily. She sighed at her fancy and shivered. The night air was much too cool for comfort. Heaven help her, she wanted desperately to close her eyes and forget where she lay, but she could not. Oh, that man, he was insufferable!

Crickets trilled softly. An owl hooted in the distance. Jessie listened intently to those peaceful night sounds, the tender music of nature, and despite the chilly November air, she felt at last the inexorable lure of sleep. Exhausted by the trials of the day, she closed her eyes, but even as she did so, an ominous roar sounded in the near distance. Her eyes flew wide to see the skies suddenly burst with light.

"Oh, dear God . . . don't let it rain! Not now! Not tonight! please, please . . ." But He was not to hear her; a mere instant later, she felt the first tender droplets, carried all the way to her pallet by the rising wind. Staring incredulously at her hand, at the glistening moonlit raindrops, she felt suddenly like weeping.

She lay there for the longest time, wishing the rain away, telling herself that it was but a dream and that she would awaken snug and dry and safe in her cousin's home. "Oh, God," she sobbed, " 'tis a bloody nightmare!"

When the rain had thoroughly soaked her blanket, she moved onto the crude unfinished wood floor, into the far corner, but that spot was no better than the first, and she moved back to her pallet to lie there, resigned to her misery. Her eyes squeezed tightly shut as she remembered her pledge to Christian, that she would prefer the cold, bitter rain to his company. God was surely punishing her now for her cruel words.

And curse Christian, for he'd merely smirked at her before turning his back and leaving her in the corridor to fend with her trunks alone. By God, she would not go crawling to him now, even if it rained all blessed night, even if she sickened from it, even if she died of exposure. But she would not die! she told herself firmly. She would not!

She would live to regret this.

Chapter 24

In his chamber, Christian lay within his bed, listening to the rain pelt the roof. In his hand he held a near-empty flagon of whiskey. Bringing it to his lips, he gulped the last of it. Against his will, he found himself wondering just where Jessie had encamped for the night. He had fully intended to give her his bed, to sleep in the room across the hall, as he'd done the previous night, but her cutting words had angered him, and he'd let her go.

Damn her! A thousand times, damn her! How was it that she could rile him so? Tossing away the flagon, he closed his eyes, groaning. God's teeth, but she could drive a man to drink!

Ignoring the prick of his conscience along with the increasing patter of rain, he strove for sleep. By God, he should let her suffer out the night in misery. 'Twould serve her right. Perhaps tomorrow she would agree to take his bed without a bloody battle of wills. He smiled ruefully then, for he had to give her her due; she had mettle enough for an army of patriots.

A bolt of lightning lit the sky, illuminating his window with a bright, ghostly light, and seconds later came an ominous rumbling.

Lightning.

What if she'd stupidly ensconced herself within the unfinished wing? Stubborn wench—'twas likely exactly where she was, trying to prove a point, no doubt.

Cursing her beneath his breath, Christian rose from the bed, found his breeches, and tugged them on, buttoning the top button. With angry strides, he reached the door and threw it wide.

The corridor was dark, but he knew his way well enough by now. Thunder cracked once more, shaking the rafters, and he quickened his step. Taking the stairs two at a time, he made his way to the hall, but halfway down, lightning flashed, illuminating the entrance hall for the briefest second. And he froze, catching the silhouette of a man standing next to the temporary door to the unfinished wing. His eyes searched the impenetrable darkness. Another bolt of lightning came quickly on the heels of the first, and the figure was suddenly gone.

Had he imagined it, then?

He cursed the whiskey, then cursed himself for drinking it to dull his senses. Searching the shadows with keen eyes, he listened for any sound to alert him of danger. He could hear nothing, yet the hair on the back of his neck continued to prickle. After a long moment, he began a cautious descent down the winding staircase, his gut burning.

Reaching the hall without incident, he crossed the room and heaved a sigh of relief when he spied Quincy sprawled across the floor in front of the door. Stooping, he checked the old man's breathing; his chest rose and fell in the gentle rhythm of sleep. Could it have been Quincy he'd spied? He shook his head. More likely, there was no one about and 'twas simply his overwrought imagination. He loathed to, but he had to wake Quincy in order to open the door. He shook the old man's shoulders.

Quincy came awake with a start. "Who? What?" He squinted through the darkness. "M'lord!"

"Aye, Quince, 'tis me. Move now so I can open the door."

"Aye, m'lord, but she's barred it."

"Barred it?"

"With her trunk, I think."

Christian sighed, shaking his head in exasperation. "She's a damned stubborn wench."

"Aye and 'tis rainin'," Quincy added.

Christian grunted in answer, irritated beyond measure.

"She'll catch the devil of a chill," Quincy added plaintively. "Thought I'd climb to the rooftop meself and fix it where she wouldn't catch the rain, but these rickety old bones o' mine just wouldn't allow it, m'lord."

"I understand, Quince. Don't worry, she'll be fine once I get her out of that blasted wing. Now, get yourself back to bed afore you catch the ague yourself."

Stiffly Quincy rose from the floor, groaning his discomfort.

"Oh . . . and Quince," Christian called out, "my thanks to you for watching over her."

"'Twas nothin', m'lord. Slept better out here on the bare floor than I would've up there with those two bickering fools."

Christian chuckled. "That bad, eh?"

Quincy's voice now sounded from the stairway, his tone forlorn. "Aye, m'lord, 'tis that bad, it is." His footsteps stopped abruptly. "Ye certain ye won't be needin' me help, m'lord? I did tell ye the door was barred?"

"You did," Christian assured him. "G'night, Quince."

"Night, m'lord."

Jessie's shoulders trembled from the cold as the rain drummed its icy fingers upon the back of her head and body. Straining, she listened to the faint mumbling beyond the door and felt only a strange sense of relief at hearing Christian's voice there.

When the doorknob had jiggled softly only moments before, she'd been wholly terrified. Assuming it was Christian, she'd called out his name, but when he'd not replied, she'd become alarmed. Hearing his voice now, she decided he was not only a knave but he was rude as well!

The voices finally quieted and he again jiggled the knob. She didn't bother to rise as the door burst open and her trunk went skidding across the floor. Protecting her face from the rain, she huddled into a protective ball, turning away from the door. His footsteps thundered across the wet wood and halted beside her.

Towering over her, Christian told her, his words slightly slurred, "You're quite resourceful, my love, but 'tis asinine to make yourself ill merely to spite me."

Jessie remained silent, but the simple truth made her eyes sting. He knelt beside her, turning her gently toward him, and she closed her eyes. Against her will, tears spilled shamelessly onto her cold cheeks, scalding hot in comparison to the frigid rain that was now striking her full in the face.

Closing his eyes only for the briefest moment, Christian ignored the stirring of his heart. She seemed so very fragile lying there before him, her pale green eyes now open and bright with her tears. Moonlight spilled through the rafters, illuminating the sopping midnight strands of her hair. Damn, but she was soaked to the bone.

He felt entrapped by her gaze, unable to look away. Nor could he find his voice to speak just then. It was her eyes, he acknowledged. They seemed a beacon in the dim light of the room, drawing his gaze even as a moth was lured to the flame. The light of it was irresistible, and he felt suspiciously ablaze this moment. It was not at all an unpleasant sensation, nor was it unfamiliar to him, and he determined that this night might not end so unpleasantly, after all. Droplets of rain glistened upon her flesh, and he had the sudden urge to kiss every last one of them away. He was not about to argue with her, nor would he remain here and make himself ill simply because she lacked the bloody sense to come out of the rain.

Without a word, he swept his hands down to lift her into his arms. She didn't protest, nor did he bother to explain his intentions. He carried her silently from the room, somehow managing to draw the door closed behind them before sliding the bolt loudly into place.

Cradling her chilled body close to his thundering heart, he bore her through the entrance hall, his breathing labored as he swept her up the stairs to his chamber—though not from the burden of her weight, for she was light as the breath of spring ... and her scent more intoxicating than any liquor.

He set her upon her feet on the floor before his bed, uncertain whether to stay or go. Curse her, for even now, after all that had transpired between them, he found himself wanting to play the noble for her.

However ... he was anything but an honorable soul, and they both knew that fact well enough, so there was no reason for him to pretend any longer. He was what he was . . . and she was no longer a virgin besides.

The damage was done.

Lighting a candle to better see her, he placed it upon the nightstand. She was shivering. The pristine white gown she wore dripped with rain, bonded with her flesh, revealing dark nipples to his greedy eyes. "You're sopping wet," he whispered.

Jessie nodded, and her tears began anew.

Christian moved a finger to sweep her tears gently away, and Jessie couldn't find the words to protest as his hand reached for the tiny bow at her throat, then slipped down to the next one, and the next. She felt suffocated by uncertainty. She didn't loathe him, but how to keep herself from loving him?

Or was it far, far too late for that?

Boldly he slipped her gown from her shoulder, and all she could do was gape at him stupidly, her heart pounding madly. Christian wore no shirt at all, and the light curling hair upon his chest streaked lightly downward to vanish within his breeches. Her gaze slid up to meet his penetrating blue eyes once more. And neither of them moved.

Neither of them so much as blinked.

"You've been drinking," she said, as a flash of white light lit the room and flickered over his swarthy flesh. Her breath caught at the beauty of him, and a burst of anticipation snaked down her spine, shocking her.

"Aye," he murmured thickly, "what of it?"

Thunder struck somewhere near, resounding throughout the room.

Her voice catching, she whispered, "If you were a gentleman . . . you would leave . . . this moment . . ."

Christian's hand reached out to grasp her bare arm, in order to draw her toward him, and Jessie felt dazed by that mind-jarring contact. She whimpered, and her lips parted unconsciously for his kiss.

"I think we both know very well that I'm no gentleman," he said low. His hand then slid to her shoulder and he drew her slowly to him, groaning as the shock of her wet gown touched his bare chest.

Jessie's heart slammed against her breast. Christian seemed to revel in the feel of her, pressing her immediately closer and clasping her more firmly against him. His hand slipped down to boldly cup her bottom, urging her closer, kneading her flesh feverishly, making her tremble with longing. She felt utterly helpless, dizzy with desire, breathless with anticipation.

And dear God, so very, very much afraid.

Christian was afire, and the sopping wet material of Jessie's gown was soaking through his breeches. He longed to strip her naked and press her down into his soft bed, fall greedily upon her, ride her like the ruthless ruffian he was claimed to be. But he would not. He placed a hand to her waist, tugging gently at her rain-sodden gown. It slipped down just far enough to expose the creamy flesh of her breasts. He stood as though transfixed by the sight of her for the longest instant, and then his lips descended to her mouth.

His kiss was gentle, coaxing, just a tiny teasing peck, and then another, and another, until her face was finally upturned, her lips trembling, waiting eagerly for more, beseeching him, even. He needed no further urging, he kissed her thoroughly, exploring the depths of her mouth with his tongue.

Jessie's legs would have given way, but Christian held her steady as his lips trailed searing kisses along her throat . . . to her breasts. He suckled them each in turn, lavishing the soft but firm flesh with tender care.

Moaning with pleasure, Jessie felt as if she'd been transported to some place not of this world, where only the flesh mattered and the mind was incapable of coherent thought.

Dropping to his knees, Christian kissed her thighs through her wet gown. His hands clutching at her cool, wet bottom, he drew the V of her body close to quench his burning lips against the rain-soaked gown.

"Nay . . ." Her protest was a breathless gasp. She tried in vain to pull away, for he held her fast. "Mercy, Christian . . . Oh nay . . . please, nay . . ." Her voice trailed away to a helpless whimper. She was lost to him once again, but she didn't care, couldn't think to care. She quivered with pleasure as his lips worshiped her in places she'd never dreamed a man would want to taste.

"God's bones!" He groaned against the wet

gown. "You are so blessed sweet . . ." He buried his cheek against her, and murmured again, "So sweet . . ." He slid up her body then, rising, stroking her provocatively as he went. He urged her to the bed and lowered her gently down upon it, and then merely stood there, towering over her, gazing down upon her with those fathomless blue eyes, and Jessie felt paralyzed. She swallowed convulsively, but was unable to contain her startle as his hands then slid upward, across the bulge in his breeches, to the top button of his trousers, popping it quickly, impatiently. Then, as she watched, he simply shrugged out of them, never taking his eyes from her as he did.

Her breath caught at the sight of him.

Grinning, he brought one knee down beside her, and the bed sank beneath his weight; then came the other until he was sitting gently astride her, careful not to crush her beneath him. And she continued to stare, both frightened and incredulous, at that peculiar male appendage that confronted her once again, for she vividly recalled the pain he had given her the first time.

Jessie swallowed again as her gaze lifted to his in silent appeal. The candle positioned beside them left one side of his face deep in shadow and bathed the other in golden light, making him appear almost sinister. Lightning flickered for the briefest instant, illuminating his features fully.

One last bow held Jessie's gown together, and Christian reached for it, his blue eyes dancing with hypnotic fire. Very slowly, he peeled the rain-sodden garment from her body, then tossed it away. It landed with a wet thump upon the bare wood floor.

The fierce determination in his blue eyes sent a shiver down her spine. His lips curving with sensual promise, he lowered them to her body, and again his mouth covered her breast, suckling first one nipple, then the other, and all the while he peered up at her seductively, silently pledging to her things that, strangely, her body seemed to comprehend—and even more, seemed to revel in.

Moving with slow, easy finesse across her flesh, his hands affected her in ways she'd not thought possible. His fingers caressed her as though he would commit every inch of her to his memory, then slid beneath her, to rest between her shoulder blades, lifting her bodily to better taste of her. She quivered as his tongue swept across one nipple, then traced deliberate circles around it, before searching out the other.

She moaned deep in her throat, and Christian drew her closer still, nibbling at her throat languidly. Some tortured sound escaped him then, a hiss that sent gooseflesh racing across Jessie's skin.

Tears stung her eyes. How could she want this so desperately if she loathed him so much? "Oh, God . . . I—I d-don't understand what you d-do to me!"

Between bold, fiery kisses and shocking caresses, he whispered, " 'Tis not . . . so difficult . . . to comprehend . . . my love . . ."

Her heart cried out at his endearment. *But I am not your love.* "You . . . you don't love me," she whispered brokenly. "Nor do I you," she lied.

Her honesty wrenched his gut. "Nay, but I *want* you, and at the moment, *wanting* is quite enough, I assure you." But was it the truth? he wondered, even as his hands sought the sweet, tantalizing wetness between her thighs. He thrust a finger within her body, preparing her.

"Christian," she sobbed.

"Don't talk anymore, Jessamine! Don't say another bloody word!"

Lord help her, though his words pierced her heart as surely as a blade, she was powerless to resist him. She wanted this. She wanted this so much . . .

Taking his hand, she guided it boldly to her breast, and then reached out to tangle eager fingers into the crisp hair upon his chest.

Slipping one warm knee between her trembling thighs, he nudged them apart, and then fell upon her, pressing himself slowly into the very depths of her. She was at once swept into a maelstrom of feeling and emotion.

The heated place where their bodies had fused was now the only place she was fully aware of . . . there and her temple, where his whiskered jaw pressed against her face. His breath was ragged, and dear God, the explo-

sive joining of their bodies made her mad with
wanting.

Meeting his powerful thrusts with her own
eager ones, she allowed instinct to guide her
now. Their bodies met, the rhythm almost as
violent as the thunder and lightning ringing in
her ears.

Groaning with pleasure, Christian stroked
her body with his own, giving her ecstasy in
return. And when Jessie's culmination came
suddenly, shattering in its intensity, and she
cried out her release, he was shocked to his
core by her words.

"Oh, God—I love you!" she sobbed, and her
whispered declaration was followed with a
tormented moan of pleasure. Then again, as
though she could not quite help herself, she
murmured obliviously, "I love you . . . truly
love you . . ."

Christian's entire body convulsed violently
at her words, but he froze above her, the jolt
to his heart painful. She tilted her hips and
pressed against him, her body seeming to cry
out for more, and again his heart leapt against
his ribs.

"Who am I?" He withdrew slightly, and
then thrust forward, unable to keep himself
from it. The arms that supported his weight
trembled and threatened to give. Sweat
erupted upon his brow. His voice was
strained. "Speak my name—who is it you
love?" Her eyes were closed against him.

"You," she cried out, still undulating softly

beneath him. Tears slipped through her sooty lashes.

Thunder cracked, drowning out her voice, but he held her crushed to him as she sobbed, losing his control, even his reason. Still, he needed to hear his name upon her lips, and he dared not stir, not wanting to miss her declaration. Amazingly, despite that he had stilled himself within her, he watched as she came to another soul-consuming completion. The incredible look of bewildered passion upon her face was his undoing.

His hands swept down, seizing her buttocks, and he withdrew almost entirely, thrusting again, almost savagely, burying himself completely into her warmth. His body beset with spasms, he again held fast, needing her sweet words far more than his own release, afraid that she would give them and that he would miss them in the throes of his own white-hot climax.

"Who?" he demanded, losing what was left of his control. He withdrew slowly, torturously. "Say it, Jessie! Say it!"

Lightning erupted, its light brilliant white, but it was his oppressive need that blinded him to his surroundings. In the ensuing darkness, his ears strained to hear her words.

"You, Christian," she whispered, and his heart leapt with the booming sound of thunder. Reveling in his victory, he surged forth with such ferocity, such fervor, such glee, that he cried out almost as though in pain. And in

that soul-consuming instant, he poured more than his seed into her, he dared to give her everything—God, everything—including his soul.

Chapter 25

When the storm abated finally, Christian lay, reverently stroking her cheek with the back of his knuckles. He brushed the hair from her face. Through the balcony doors, he could see the sky brighten in the distance, but the sound of thunder never carried to his ears. He thought perhaps it was because his mind was still ringing with her confession. He listened closely, but could hear only her soft breath. She exhaled and it blew gently across the hairs of his arm, sending a delicious chill across his flesh, making him stir yet again. He ignored the insatiable hunger of his body for the yearnings of his heart.

Had he imagined her sweet profession of love?

Ah, Christ—he swallowed, battling the great sweep of emotion that threatened to crush his chest—he hoped not.

He wanted nothing more than to wake her now and ask her, but he knew she was exhausted and he had no wish for her to sicken from the rain. And then again, he wished she'd never waken, that they could stay thus forever. Because once the morning came, he would have to tell her everything.

Everything.

He wanted nothing more between them—not lies, not half-truths, nothing. Yet, for the first time in his life, he feared the truth. His heart rebelled at the thought of telling her his most damning secret, for it might very well destroy the love between them forever . . .

Even before it had begun.

He closed his eyes and fell asleep some time later, holding Jessie close . . . as though to be certain she'd not leave him whilst he slept.

God help him, he couldn't bear to be without her.

Morning light streamed through the balcony doors, falling short of the massive bed.

Jessie stirred, stretching lazily, smiling, and then, as she seemed to remember, heat stained her cheeks. She opened her eyes to find Christian gazing down into her face, his eyes searching.

"No need to feel ashamed," he assured her, noting the color that bloomed upon her cheeks. He brushed a dark strand of hair from her face, gently, tenderly, wanting nothing more than to ask her now, but he was, by his own admission, afeared of her answer. Perhaps her love words were nothing more than nonsense uttered during the heat of passion?

And then there was the lie between them.

He couldn't bring himself to speak the incriminating truth.

"You asked me once," he said, "why I chose to come here ... to make Shadow Moss my home instead of Rose Park. I'd like to show you today, if you wish?"

For a moment she said nothing, and then, "I'd like that very much." Her eyes shone suspiciously with moisture.

"First," he whispered, giving her his most engaging grin, "there is something else I would show you." If she would despise him ... he wanted this one last time ... this one last memory to carry him through.

One arm encircled her waist and he drew her close against him, kissing the tip of her nose, her cheek, her closed eyelids, and her brow with a fever that could not be denied. She was so beautiful, and the feel of her warm bare flesh beneath him made his heart pound and his breath strangle. He refused to let her feel regret—refused to feel any himself.

God's truth, this morning he had not the stamina for foreplay, and when he found her wet and ready for him, it nearly unmanned him where he lay. He needed only to undulate into her softness and she opened to him willingly, wrapping her legs about his hips and closing her eyes.

Sliding up, he entered her, and no sooner had he done so when she began to undulate softly of her own accord, instinctively, moaning beneath him. He held himself fast, letting her guide his strokes at first, but when her hands moved to his buttocks to urge him deeper into her sweet warmth, he at once lost his resolve.

Driving himself into her, he loved her as though there were no tomorrow, as though in truth this were their last joining. Her nails dug painfully into his flesh and he reached back to grasp her hands, unable to bear the sweetness of it, bringing them above her head and holding them fast against the headboard. With a mindless fervor he withdrew and thrust, sweat breaking upon his brow, and still he held his own release until he felt her quiver and moan beneath him. The sweet sound of her release wrenched away the last vestiges of his restraint and he went headlong into his own climax, crying out savagely.

The path that brought them to the stables was wide, with oaks lining both sides of it, their sweeping limbs arcing and meeting above them, forming a leafy underpass of sorts. It was fall, but the weather was so mild that the flora was still inclined to bloom.

" 'Tis beautiful," Jessie said with a sigh. "Truly beautiful!"

"Aye," he agreed, pride in his tone. "Rose Park cannot begin to compare, though I swear there was a time when I was blind to this splendor. No more. I can see now, quite clearly, that I was not meant to make my home in England. Come now, there is more I would show you." He took her firmly by the hand, releasing it only when they entered the stable itself.

A youth came forth from the shadows, a straw broom in hand. "My lord, you wish to ride?" he asked, his brown eyes flashing with obvious admiration.

"Aye, Peter, aye," Christian replied. "Fetch my mount, if you would, and then give my lady the finest mare to be had—the bay, I think."

"Very well, m'lord." When the fair-haired youth would have turned away, Christian stopped him with a gentle hand to his shoulder. "On second thought, she'll ride with me ... Leave off with the mare and simply fetch my own." Turning to Jessie, he said, "The area is still somewhat unknown to me and I would not endanger you."

Jessie nodded, though the thought of sitting so near him made her heart flutter wildly and her breath quicken painfully. Even now, in the full light of day, he affected her so.

Peter brought forth from the stall a great black beast with a white streak blazing down its forehead. It was a beautiful specimen of a horse with eyes set wide apart and an exquisitely formed muzzle. The lad prepared the mount while they waited, and then led it outside. Its blue-black coat shone brightly in the daylight. Jessie followed them out, and Christian lifted her upon the animal without a word, mounting behind her, bringing her close against him as he urged the steed into a slow canter.

Instead of taking her back through the tunnel of trees whence they'd come, he chose another path that led briefly through a dense thicket of pines.

They rode in silence, and after some time, came to a clearing, a meadow so green and lush that it seemed chimerical. In the center of the grove stood the gutted remains of a brick building.

She turned to him, her brow furrowing. "What is it?"

He kissed her temple, smiling slightly, but said nothing until they'd circled the ruins, halting abruptly at what appeared to be the front steps. " 'Tis the remains of someone's home, of course," he answered at last. "Whose, I cannot rightly know, but this land before us was the first site of Charlestown. 'Tis private property now, but have no fear, I know the holder." He winked at her then.

"Yours?"

He chuckled softly. "Nay ... at least not as yet, though it borders my own land and the proprietor is presently weighing my offer for purchase. If he sells to me, 'twill give me access to Old Town Creek as well as the Ashley."

"Does he live here still?" Her curiosity was piqued.

"Aye." He pointed out a direction. "His plantation lies beyond that small copse of trees."

Jessie nodded, but could see nothing.

Pointing out the river that glittered like diamonds on the horizon, he continued, "That was once known to us as St. George's Bay, named so by the Spaniards, for the Indians themselves did not name the waters. They called this land *Kayawah*—all of it—after their tribe." He hugged her as he spoke.

He kissed her neck affectionately and then his gaze lifted to the horizon. The tall grass grazed his boots, tickled the horse's belly. The breeze riffled through them, lifting her hair into his face. Before them, the remains of the house were only partially visible through the weeds. Most of the masonry lay in ruin. Weeds and moss worked at the rest of the structure. Before long, if not taken into hand, the wilderness would reduce it to little more than piles of mortar and stone.

" 'Tis a beautiful, wild country you behold, still in its birth," he mused aloud, "and I mean to be a part of it, Jessie."

Jessie turned to him, hearing the note of pride in his voice, and saw that his eyes were glittering strangely with his words.

Christian looked down into her face and smiled warmly, his harsh features softening into a wry grin as he scrutinized her. With his hair so dark and long, falling unbound behind him, Jessie thought he seemed as primitive as the very natives of whom he spoke.

" 'Tis an incredible feeling," he admitted, "to be involved in the shaping of this wilderness—an experience I might never have known had I clung so stubbornly to Rose Park and to England. And that, *mon amour*, is the truth of it. I fear I've grown to love this savage place, for it suits me better than any I've known."

"I can well believe it." Her tone held a smile.

Unable to keep himself from it, Christian lowered his head and touched his whiskered jaw to her cheek, savoring the feel of her within his arms. He closed his eyes, hugging her, remembering her fire, and felt again that stirring of his blood. If he lived an eternity, he doubted he would ever have his fill of her. She was as beautiful and unmanageable as the wilds before them.

He savored this moment with her. It was such blissful torment to hold her so close and not be able to love her as he yearned to do. It was just as well . . . for there was that which needed to be said between them, and he could not bear to delay the inevitable any longer.

Closing her eyes, Jessie leaned back against him. In his arms she felt so alive, so cherished, so loved. As she recalled what she'd said to him during their lovemaking, a small pang tugged at her heart, for he'd never returned her love words. True, he was kinder now, more attentive, but the fact remained that she loved alone. *Unrequited love.* And yet, so long as he would give her this incredible tenderness, she told herself she cared not whether he reciprocated ever.

So long as he held her thus always.

Christian's hand slipped down suddenly, pressing at her belly firmly as though he would draw her within himself somehow and never let her go. The moment was excruciating in its tenderness. Breathing deeply, he moved his hand up to rest just beneath her breast. And then, as though he could not help himself, his other hand came around her as well and slid down to the apex of her thighs, caressing her there softly, boldly, kindling her inner fires once more.

Jessie arched backward against him, moaning at the unexpected assault upon her senses, but he halted suddenly, inhaling a breath, shuddering as though only just recalling their surroundings. He stilled his hands, bringing them about her waist, locking them there to keep them from roaming, though his body remained taut.

"Jessie, love . . . I've something to tell you . . . though you might despise me for it."

Jolted by his declaration, Jessie turned to look at him. Though his lips were smiling slightly, his eyes held no mirth at all.

She smiled sweetly, teasing him. "Are you so certain I do not still?"

He stiffened, though his hands never left her middle, and his smile disappeared wholly. "Do you, Jessamine . . . loathe me?"

She shook her head slowly. "How could you think so, after all?"

He laughed then, the sound hollow, and shook his head. A chill traveled her spine. "How could I think so? 'Tis God's own truth, you only said so a hundred times," he reminded her.

"Aye ... but I did not mean it," she confessed, her eyes misting. "I truly did not mean it."

"Didn't you?"

"Nay, I could never!"

"Jessamine," he began again, his tone grave now. "Listen to me, love, and do not speak until I've finished ... 'Tis a difficult thing I must say."

She wanted to tell him that nothing could be so terrible as what they had already endured. "Christian—"

"Hush, my love, listen ... Know that I do not wish to lose you, *ma belle vie*. Yet there is that part of me that would have you know everything, for I wish no more deceit between us—not ever!"

Christian fought the almost irresistible urge to tell her that he loved her and then to plead with her not to detest him for what he was about to reveal, but he could not find a way past his accursed pride. If she despised him, then he wanted at least that small part of him left intact.

He sighed then. "It has to do with your father. You see ..." There was no gentle way to put it. The truth was damning and there was no way around it. "It may be my fault that your father killed himself." She stiffened before him suddenly, and he knew his fears had not been unfounded.

"Aye, I know that he did; 'tis no secret, love."

He forced Jessie to look at him then, turning her face gently to his. Her eyes were wide with shock ... and then revulsion, he thought, but she remained silent just as he'd asked, and so he knew nothing for certain of her thoughts.

"I impoverished him, Jessamine, thwarted him at every bend in the road, all in the name of vengeance. I drove him to his death," he admitted bluntly, regretting his retaliation in whole for Jessie's sake. The silence lengthened between them and her face lost all color.

"I see," she said finally, her tone devoid of emotion, her green eyes vacant and unseeing.

"Jessie ..."

"I don't think I wish to hear any more." She turned suddenly away from him, as though she could not bear to look upon him.

Her father's murderer.

"I ... am ... sorry," he said, his voice catching. His apology seeming inadequate.

Unable to prolong the torture, for her sake, he clicked the reins, urging his mount away from the glade.

Not another word was spoken between them.

Hours later, Jessie found herself pacing the length of the woven carpet that graced the master's chamber. Not even the distant muddle of voices from belowstairs distracted her from her deliberation. And her musing was interrupted only once, when Quincy came to deliver the trunk she'd left in the unfinished wing.

After a while, she wandered out onto the balcony and she watched, barely noticing a small boat paddling away from the pier. Briefly she wondered who it might have been. But in truth, she thought little more of it, for Christian's confession weighed heavily upon her heart. At last she came to the conclusion that Christian might have, in fact, been partly responsible for her father's death. Though still, the blame fell to her father, and her father alone, for it certainly was not as though they'd been left completely destitute. Nay, 'twas none other than Francis Stone's decision to end his miserable life—if, in fact, he had.

And she was certain now that he had. 'Twas that realization more than aught else that had kept her tongue tied all the way back. The truth was that her father had been a weak man, cold and mean on the exterior to conceal his feebleness within—she could see that now.

Having thought it over, she washed herself, splashing her face with the cool water for courage. Opening her trunk, she drew out the green silk dress Christian seemed so fond of and dressed carefully, brushing her hair, and in her haste, not even bothering to fix it properly. She left it down instead, the length of it reaching her hips. And then she sought out Christian.

He was nowhere to be found. The house was intensely quiet, as though forsaken of all life. At long last, on the way back to the master's room, she spied Quincy in the chamber across the corridor, the one her cousin and Jean Paul had used for their own. He started at seeing her, both of his brows lifting in surprise.

"Where is everyone?" Jessie asked without preamble. "I need to speak with Christian."

"They've gone."

"Gone?"

"Yes, mum, gone."

Jessie bristled at his uninformative response. "Where? I saw a boat leaving the dock, but I thought it might be some of the men returning to the *Mistral* and I thought nothing more of it." Worry furrowed her brow as she asked, "Is that where they've gone? Back to the *Mistral*?"

"Well," Quincy hedged. He looked heavenward, one eye closing slightly, as though to consider an answer, and Jessie knew to doubt his next words. He surprised her by speaking what sounded to be the truth. "They've gone to Charlestown," he confessed. "M'lord said I should stay here wit' ye and see to ye—didn't want to worry ye none."

Confused, Jessie said, "I don't understand. I should think he'd have wanted Ben to remain as well. After all, he and I were to have sailed for England together. He shouldn't risk being seen, should he?"

"Aye, mum," Quincy yielded, "but yer cousin wouldn't hear of it. He went and there was no keeping him from it. God's truth!"

Jessie sighed. "I see, and what, pray tell,

could have been so urgent as to draw him into such dangerous folly?" She didn't truly expect an answer because of the frown that appeared upon the old man's face, but to her surprise, she received one, despite Quincy's tortured expression. It was obvious he didn't want to say.

"Well, mum . . . y'see . . . 'tis the *Mistral*," he revealed. "While you were away this morn . . . news came that it was arrested last night. M'lord was summoned to appear before Daniel Moore straightaway."

Jessie felt suddenly ill. "My God! Whatever for? What on earth could he wish of Christian?"

Quincy's eyes held hers. "Well, you see, mum . . . the *Mistral*'s been accused of bearing unauthorized goods into Charlestown harbor. They said—"

"Absurd!" Jessie exclaimed. " 'Tis ridiculous—why?"

"Because, mum . . . we set anchor in the dead o' night, nor did we report to the customs house straightaway, that's why."

Jessie's head reeled as she recalled that they'd departed late in the night, as well. Then, too, they'd sailed into the Dutch West Indies, reportedly a smugglers' and pirates' haven. And they had, in fact, returned in the deepest hours of the night. Heaven help her, but all at once it came clear to her. How could she not have suspected before? Lord, she hadn't dreamed he would conduct his business while she was aboard. Even knowing who he was—*what he was*. Placing a hand to

her brow, Jessie leaned back against the doorframe, feeling weak of a sudden. The *Mistral*
. . . Dear God, she'd sailed all that time aboard
a smuggler's vessel—one carrying an illegal
cargo, no less! She felt sick with the shock of
it all.

Quincy advanced upon her suddenly. "Nay,
mum," he said, as though he'd read her
thoughts and meant to acquit his master of her
silent accusations.

Jessie backed away from him, out into the
corridor, as though to escape his knowing
gaze. Had everyone known, save her? Ben,
too? Aye, even as she asked herself that question, she knew it was so.

"M'lady," Quincy protested, " 'tis not what
it seems, at all! M'lord *did* sail into St. Chris-
topher to clear his cargo with the authorities,
and he has his papers to prove it!" He nodded
fervently. "Aye, he does, an' he's carryin' 'em
with him to see Daniel Moore—told me to tell
ye 'e'd be back before eventide. He didn't wish
to worry ye, is all."

Relief swept over Jessie like a flood tide, diz-
zying her. Her knees buckled slightly and her
eyes shimmered with tears. "Thank God!" she
whispered fiercely. "But what of Ben? Why
need he have gone? Why should he have
risked himself if Christian bears proof?"

Quincy shrugged. "There was no one to
stop 'im. Yer cousin is a fierce one, he is, and
loyal to m'lord, besides."

"I see. As you are?"

"Yes, mum."

She took a deep breath and asked, "How long have they been gone?"

"Little more'n an hour," he declared.

"Very well, then. Thank you, Quincy." Still somewhat dazed by his disclosure, Jessie left him staring after her and made her way down the corridor quickly, down the spiral steps to the entrance hall. She intended to await Christian at the docks, so anxious was she to see him. She hurried, though halfway down the steps she halted abruptly.

Chapter 26

"**W**ell, well," Leland said, sauntering forward.

Jessie was momentarily stunned by his unexpected appearance. "H-How did you manage to find me?"

"McCarney, of course. The man is a veritable font of information . . . quite helpful."

Jessie bristled at his smug tone. "Well, sirrah! Now that you've discovered what you came to, you should leave," she apprised him, straightening her spine. "Lord Christian should be down any moment," she bluffed. "I don't believe he would relish your presence unbidden in his home. Indeed, I should loathe to see you—"

"Please, Jessamine," he interposed, "spare me the duplicity. I know perfectly well where Haukinge has gone, as I also know you're alone in this"—he glanced about, waving a hand in disgust—"place." He took another step forward, removing his tricorne and clasping it to his chest.

Jessie was on the verge of informing him that she was, in fact, not alone, but something in his expression suggested she should hold her tongue. Quincy was no match for him, and she certainly didn't want the faithful servant to be hurt.

"How would you know such a thing?" she asked instead, stalling, knowing the answer before it was given. Instinct told her he was up to no good, but beyond that, she was at a loss. It would help if she knew what she was up against.

"McCarney," he disclosed, smiling a thin-lipped smile. "Actually, he made certain of the fact for me. Oh, and of course, I should thank my good friend Moore, as well, for 'twas his writ that McCarney delivered unto him."

Jessie shook her head in disbelief. "But why, my lord? Why would you do such a thing?"

His jaw turned taut and he answered her inquiry with one of his own. "The question is, I fear, where will you go once it is known that you've not gone to England as Robert claimed? Aye, I kept your dirty little secret once, m'dear, but I'll not do so again. It cost me my pride—dreadfully high price, that was." He shook his head musingly, thumping his tricorne as he spoke. "To become the object of pity, the laughingstock . . ." He cocked his head at her, his eyes gleaming strangely. "Do you realize they are all spinning tales that you spurned me?"

Jessie shook her head in denial, thinking him mad suddenly. "I hardly think you're any of those things, my lord. If so, then 'tis only in your own mind, for I've heard nothing to that effect at all."

"If only it were so," he demurred. "At any rate, I'll not under any circumstance be made to look the fool again—leastways not alone! Too many times before has your lover—aye, Jessamine spare me your words of denial— your lover succeeded in doing just so. I'll not allow you to do so, either—never again!" he swore, his anger rising. His dark eyes narrowed, and for an instant Jessie thought she could see the hurt he was feeling, and she felt for him.

"By God!" he bellowed suddenly, startling her enough that she retreated upward a step. "I would have thought better of you, Jessamine! Aye, to my mind 'tis mighty poor thanks you would give me for all that I have done for you!"

He shook his head, and Jessie remained silent, watching him warily as he approached her.

She hesitated to speak, but her curiosity won the best of her. "Why did you keep silent, then? If 'tis the truth that you speak, my lord, then you need only have revealed the facts, and it would have been me they would have scorned, instead. Why do you not simply tell them and be done?"

"Nay, m'dear," he said, smiling coldly. "Either way, I'd be the object of pity, for it would be said then that you desired another over me . . . even at the expense of your own ruination. I might have suffered that well enough had it been any other man but Christian Haukinge. You had to choose a man such as that!"

"I did not *choose* him! My father did. I can no more help that than I can commit who my heart should love!"

His shout reverberated through the hall. *"You chose him!"*

She was taken aback by his fury. "How can you say such a thing? My father chose him, not I."

"Your father repudiated the contract! *I gave him choices, damn it all!* And then the bastard went and cocked up his toes! All that money I lost, but I was willing to pay again, and 'twas *you* who chose him then, even against your brother's will!"

Jessie's expression was incredulous. "You paid my father to repudiate the contract? Didn't you?"

He gave her a self-satisfied smirk and replaced his tricorne to his head.

"Why, pray tell?" He didn't respond and she moved down a step in her fury to confront him. "This isn't about us at all, is it, my lord? This is about your hatred for Lord Christian. Why? Why should you despise him so?"

He ignored her question. "Of course, you might come back with me now," he proposed, "leave Shadow Moss...and return to Charlestown with me. If so, I should be more than willing to keep your confidence in such case." He eyed the empty hall meaningfully. "I daresay your life would be a sight better if you did. I can guarantee as much."

"Whyever would you wish me to, my lord? What good could come of it now?"

He guffawed at her, the sound bitter and hard. "Apart from the fact that I might get a decent little tumble now and again? Why, absolutely nothing, of course. Except that mayhap I need not lose face entirely."

Truly, Leland St. John was not an unattractive man, but at the moment the sight of him literally made Jessie ill. How could she have thought to feel sorry for him? Bile rose in her throat and her fingers tightened upon the bare wood rail. "My lord, you may go and tell people anything you so desire. There is nothing you can give me that is worth my becoming your wife."

He burst into laughter. "Wife!" he said, aghast. "Why, whoever said I wished you to become my wife, Jessamine dear?"

Jessie chafed at his words. "You were, in fact, courting me, my lord, only a short time ago. Does your memory fail you so? Surely you might ask anyone in Charlestown and they would be very pleased to refresh your memory."

Her dart had been expertly pitched, and his face suddenly became flushed, his eyes narrowing to angry slits. When he laughed again, it sent chills down her spine.

"Perhaps 'tis you who needs enlightening, my dear girl. Didn't you realize? The wife, you simply buy; 'tis the mistress you woo." He laughed then and Jessie cringed at the hateful sound of it.

"I'd as soon be drowned in the Ashley as to become your mistress, my lord!"

He shook his head, smiling still, though his lip suddenly curled contemptuously. "Very well . . . have it your way." He sounded bored now. He started away, and then stopped abruptly, turning once more. "Though perhaps I might still persuade you as yet . . . You didn't happen to wonder how Daniel Moore knew to arrest the *Mistral*, did you? Or why he would think to suspect Christian? Did you wonder if he knew of *Hawk*? Aye," he replied to his own question when her eyes widened. He rubbed his chin pensively. "I see that perhaps you have contemplated such things." He smiled benevolently. "Well, then, you might be interested in knowing that I also know about Ben. Tell me, how is his limp now? Does he fare well?"

Jessie's face paled.

"Improved, I hope." He lifted a brow. "I'd like to see him walk tall and proud to the gibbet, m'dear." He turned from her once more, leaving Jessie confused and speechless. "Oh," he said, turning to address her yet again. "And you will give my felicitations to *Hawk*, will you not? That is, if you ever happen to see him again." With a dirty little laugh, he turned and strode confidently to the door.

"Wait!" Jessie implored. She could not simply stand by and see Christian hanged—and Ben! She shuddered to think what punishment would be meted them both. "I'll go with you."

"I rather thought you would," he said with little surprise, and laughed hideously.

Despite the way things had been left between them, Christian found himself eager to return to Shadow Moss—to see Jessie.

While her silence had not been promising, he realized, neither was it hopeless, and bearing that in mind, he made his way quickly up the staircase, his footfalls echoing throughout.

"M'lord!" Quincy exclaimed, appearing in the landing above, his face contorting miserably. Christian halted in his step, sensing something was wrong.

" 'Tis Miss Jessie!"

Christian took a step upward, then another, staring expectantly at Quincy as he ascended the stairwell. The hair at his nape prickled.

"Lord St. John was here, my lord."

Christian's jaw grew taut and his eyes began to burn with fury.

"He took her with him, my lord."

Christian halted in his step. *"What the hell do you mean he took her with him?"*

"She didn't go willingly," he said, and then, as quickly as he was able, related all that he'd overheard.

"When?"

"Not long ago, m'lord—just before you came."

Before Quincy was finished speaking, Christian had turned and was bolting down the stairwell, racing for the docks.

"I hope you're not overly attached to him," Leland said, lifting an imperious brow as he rowed. "I cannot simply allow *him* to go free."

Cold prickles swept down Jessie's spine.

She knew precisely to whom he was referring, but asked nevertheless, "Him?"

His smile was forbearing. *"Hawk, of course."*

"But you swore you'd leave him be if I returned with you, my lord—you gave me your word! Would you break it now?"

"I know what I said, Jessamine . . . but 'tis out of my hands, you see, m'dear. Hawk is a traitor to the Crown and he'll hang for his crimes. 'Tis as simple as that—Moore would never set him free. Certainly not now that he has proof against him at last." He shrugged noncommittally. "Ben, on the other hand, is another matter . . ."

Jessie resisted the sudden uncontrollable urge to fly at him and thrust him overboard— lying, misbegotten cur that he was! She wanted to tell him that Christian had proof of his innocence—at least this time he did—but what if Leland had already named him as Hawk? She had to know. "Have you accused him as yet?"

"Not as yet," he admitted. "There was no one to come forward till now . . . not with

Hawk free to wreak his vengeance upon them. Now, of course, with him in gaol, it shouldn't take much to convince McCarney to step forward. He wants revenge, you see, because Hawk killed his brother. Still"—he smiled coldly—"you must take comfort in the fact that your dear cousin is free . . . for now," he added in cautioning tones. "Though perhaps he shan't be for long if you don't prove worthy of my troubles. Perhaps you should remember that," he taunted, his face flushing slightly. "Perhaps you should remember that *tonight*."

Jessie shuddered with revulsion. Panic burst through her, for in that instant she knew Ben would never be safe. Leland had lied to her. And Christian—she couldn't bear to stand aside and see him hanged. Well, she wasn't about to! She had to warn them. Her mind raced. But how?

She glanced around wildly, and to her surprise, she spotted a small boat approaching swiftly from behind them. Her heart leapt, for somehow she knew it was Christian. Her gaze reverted to Leland, and she wondered if he'd spied the skiff as well, but when he continued with his crowing, she decided he was too full of self-admiration to be aware of anything but his own voice as he spoke. If only she could catch him unawares . . . jump into the river . . . but her clothing would make it impossible to outswim him should he decide to come after her . . .

She worried her lip, for jumping seemed her

only option. She forced herself to inhale slowly and calm her ragged nerves.

One, two, three, four, she counted silently, trying desperately to quell her fears.

Five. Six. Seven.

Could she do this? Lord help her, it didn't seem to be working. She wasn't calm at all. In truth, she felt weak with fright. Would Christian reach her in time? Would Leland come after her?

Eight. Nine. Ten.

Perhaps there was no need to jump, after all, she reconsidered, for she had every faith in Christian. Hazarding another glance behind her, she drew in a deep breath and released it, for it seemed he would never close the distance. And then, her gaze reverting to Leland, she happened to spy the gleaming silver of his pistol beneath his frock coat, and she froze at the sight of it. God help her, she knew instinctively he would kill Christian if given the chance, his hate was so deep. It was there in his eyes. Christian would reach them, she was certain, but somehow . . . before then . . . she had to seize the weapon from Leland . . .

Recalling that night so long ago when Christian had been so concerned that she would tip the boat, she lit upon an idea. Not daring to spare the time to think it through properly, she stood abruptly and screamed like a shrew, hurling herself at Leland, scrambling toward him, feigning hysteria. "Oh, my Lord! Something . . . there's something in the boat!"

Snatching at his leg frantically, she attempted to stand.

The small boat tipped precariously, and Leland bellowed in fear, his face paling. "Nay! Jessamine, do not—be still! You'll topple the boat!" Jessie ignored him and threw herself at him once more, as though seized by panic. "Nay, but I cannot swim!" He threw up his hands to gain his balance. Catching him unawares, she suddenly snatched away his pistol, and Leland, comprehending too late her ploy, lunged at her to retrieve it. Heaven help her, but Jessie refused to give him the opportunity to murder Christian in cold blood! She tossed it within the water, but he seemed not to notice, for he continued to struggle. The boat rocked treacherously as she fought him with every ounce of strength she possessed.

Christian's heart lurched as he recognized Jessie's petrified screams. Rowing furiously, he turned to watch from his own skiff as she lunged at St. John, then toppled backward into the small boat with Leland grappling over her. For an instant his blood ran cold as he stared at their struggling forms behind him, and then suddenly their boat pitched violently and overturned, toppling them both into the river.

There was no time.

"No!" he exploded, rowing faster, losing precious seconds as he turned again to watch the boat drift away from the struggling pair. "Jessie! Noooo!" All he could think of was that by some sordid twist of fate, he would lose her now—and God help him, he could not bear it!

Sputtering and kicking wildly, Jessie tried to free herself from Leland's fatal grip. He wouldn't release her! Try as she might, she couldn't break free.

Dear God, she was going to die here!

She wasn't going to make it!

Her sodden skirts weighed her down... down... and with sudden inspiration, she took a deep breath, allowing herself to sink with them. Her ploy worked. Leland released her at once, catapulting desperately toward the rippling surface, freeing her.

Relief flooded her—short-lived, for as she tried to resurface, the impossibility of it struck her like a blow to her breast. She panicked. And still her skirts carried her down... down ... down...

Nay! She *was* going to die, and there was nothing she could do about it!

But nay—she refused to!

God help her, but she refused to die! Her breast ached terribly with her pent-up breath, but she remained composed enough to know that she needed to dispose of her sopping skirts. Tearing wildly at her garments, she struggled free of them. It seemed to take a life-time, but with that done, she shot back toward the surface, desperate for even a small breath of sweet, lifesaving air.

Yet the light was too far now! The air, too far! And her lungs felt near to bursting.

Breaking through the surface suddenly, she sucked in a desperate breath, but it was immediately stolen from her when Leland once again seized her by the shoulders, climbing atop her, pushing her down, struggling to remain aloft at her expense.

His words came back to her then. *Nay, Jessamine . . . I cannot swim.*

Oh, dear God! What cruel fate! She and Leland were going to die here together! She would breathe her last without ever having told Christian that she loved him first and foremost, that nothing else mattered as long as they were together, that she did not blame him for what he claimed to have done to her father. *Oh God, Christian, I love you . . . I love you so very much*, her heart cried out, but she couldn't speak the words, for her lungs were burning for air . . . and she was entombed in ice-cold water . . .

"Son of a bitch!" Christian roared. "Get off her, you bloody whoreson!"

Christ! He was so close now, so close—yet not nearly close enough! And then he spotted the gator, gliding swiftly through the water, converging upon its struggling prey, and he lost priceless seconds over the shock of the sight.

His blood pounding through his temples, he began to row more furiously still, shouting warnings, cursing the beast at the top of his lungs. Jessie and St. John were so involved in the effort to stay afloat that he doubted either

of them heard a word or sensed the danger.
His gut twisting, he realized there was no way
he could make it in time; but his heart would
not surrender. A strangled, keening sound escaped him as he rowed, hoping against hope,
watching with pent-up breath as the gator
sped in Jessie's direction.

God help him, he had the sudden urge to
stand and hurl the oar at the beast, but that
would be the worst thing he could do, he
knew, for if by chance the gator chose St. John
instead, he would need both oars to reach Jessie still.

"*Ah, God,*" he prayed aloud, casting his head
back as he rowed, "*she doesn't deserve to die! If
You've never listened to me before . . . please . . .
please . . . please . . . listen to me now.*"

Even as he spoke, the enormous beast sub-
merged, and Christian watched over his
shoulder, fear gripping him as never before.
An instant later, both Jessie's and St. John's
heads jerked beneath the surface, and then an
explosion of bubbles ripped the water as the
river churned violently against the deadly
struggle.

There was little blood, for the gator's kill
was a clean one. Clamping its jaws about its
victim, it thrashed over, and over, and over
again, beneath the water, until every last trace
of air emptied from the victim's lungs. Christian could little bear it were that fate Jessie's.

Neither St. John's nor Jessie's head resur-
faced, and Christian rowed toward them with
all his might, muttering angry curses at God,

at St. John, at Jessie for going with the bastard to begin with!

His relief was tangible as he spied Jessie's glistening locks rising from the silvery water, at last. Her face upturned, she gasped for air, and he nearly cried out for joy. Just then, another splash caught his attention and yet another gator slipped into the river. Christian swore he'd kill the son of a bitch if it touched even a hair on her head. He reached her as the beast approached the midway point in the river. Tossing the oars into the skiff, he hauled Jessie quickly aboard, and drew her into his arms.

Her hands clutched at him wildly as she sobbed, not quite mindful of her surroundings. She was like a dreamer in the throes of a nightmare, unable to wake. She was drowning still, clutching for life.

"Jessie!" he shouted, anger vying with relief. He held her so tightly that he wondered she did not cease to breathe. "Damn you! Why did you go with him? Why did you go?" He released his hold only slightly and shook her gently, his eyes stinging raw with tears he couldn't shed. Tears he didn't know how to shed. "Jess . . ." His voice broke. "Jessie . . . love . . . listen to me, you're safe. I have you now," he crooned, clutching her desperately.

She struggled a moment longer, and then as his words penetrated, she stopped abruptly and threw her arms about his neck and began to cry. Her hands slipping from his shoulders to clutch at his shirtfront, she set her wet face against his chest. She was soaking him to the bone, but he didn't give a bloody damn. She was alive, and he loved her—and God help him, he would strangle the life from her if she ever did something so witless again!

"That's it, love," he soothed, his voice choked with emotion. " 'Tis over now . . ."

"L-Leland!"

"He's gone, love," Christian told her, grimacing as he searched the river over the top of her head. There was no sign of St. John anywhere. As much as he loathed the man, he couldn't help but feel for him; he wouldn't have wished such an end for his worst enemy—and Leland, though far from being a saint, had never been his worst. He knew instinctively that a search would prove futile—and yet he would search, despite the incredible sense of justice he was feeling this moment. The bastard might have killed her.

"H-He w-wouldn't l-let me g-go! I couldn't b-breathe!" she wailed, and then her words were jumbled and incoherent as she hauled herself up and buried her wet lips against his neck. He sat there upon his knees, stroking her soggy mop of hair, pressing his lips to her forehead. Clasping her cold, damp body tightly against him, he thanked God and vowed never again to let her out of his sight.

Chapter 27

The cool breeze brought Jessie awake shivering.

The nightmares had been horrid and so very real, but when she opened her eyes, it was to find bright morning light streaming past her face. *Shadow Moss. Christian.* She was alone as far as she could tell, but she could sense his presence still . . . like a comforting heat in the chill of the room. His musky male scent lingered, and she knew he'd not been gone long.

In the peaceful morning surroundings, with the birds chirping merrily outside, she could almost believe it had all been no more than a gruesome dream, but her ruined gown, the one Christian had liked so well, sat drying upon a wooden chair in the sunlight, providing indisputable evidence. She shivered at the memory. And then she noticed the balcony door was left ajar, and she rose. Wrapping herself within the dressing gown Christian had left for her, she walked toward the open door.

She found him outside, gazing silently down upon the crush of new workers who were busy this morning laboring over the unfinished wing. Sensing her presence, he turned to her, a lit cheroot in hand.

"Jessie?"

Her eyes focused upon the smoking cigar, for she'd never seen him smoke before now, and yet when the odor reached her, she recognized the rich scent at once. It was part of him, part of his mystique and part of his person.

"Should you be up?"

"I'm fine," she replied. "Truly." The way he stared made her heart trip painfully, for he seemed so lost somehow, so sad. "How long have I slept?" Self-consciously she wrapped the robe more tightly about her.

His face was more deeply stubbled than usual this morn, giving his swarthy complexion an even darker shadow. Smoke-colored stains rimmed his deep blue eyes. He was carelessly dressed in snug black breeches and a white shirt that was properly buttoned while left untucked, and it appeared to Jessie as though he'd not slept in an age. Indeed, he seemed vanquished somehow, and yet never more hardened.

"Since yestereve," he disclosed, smiling slightly. He shrugged. "If you might call it sleep. You tossed and turned more'n a boulder down a mountainside."

"I was dreaming."

"Aye," Christian acknowledged, averting his gaze. He'd tried his damnedest to soothe her, but she'd begun to prattle . . . about him . . . about her father . . . Ben. He'd understood mere fragments; *had to go . . . hang you . . . Ben . . . father's murderer . . . Christian.* Yet those fragments had been more than enough. They twisted his gut. Even now.

"You stayed with me?"

"I wouldn't have left you," he said without turning. And he wouldn't have. He didn't wish to even now, but he *would* if 'twas her wish. He couldn't bear to hurt her any more than he had already.

"What came of your meeting with Daniel Moore? Quincy said you had papers . . ."

"I did. St. John's accusations were dismissed with the proof I brought before him. He had no grounds to hold me, or Ben either; no matter that he might have suspected us. Your cousin has gone back to the city, and I was returning to tell you that you were free to go, as well."

The moment of silence lengthened.

"Christian," she began, and he winced at the solemn tone of her voice. "There is something I wish to say to you—something I meant to say before you left for Charlestown . . ." He turned to face her, hurling the smoking cheroot upon the balcony floor. He tamped it down with his boot and mentally braced himself for her pain . . . her disdain.

"You see . . . I was looking for you when

Lord St. John—oh, God, this is so difficult!"
She shook her head, averting her gaze. "I've
no idea how to say this, so I shall simply do
so and be done with it."

Christian's chest constricted painfully.

Her gaze returned to him. "I refuse to allow
you to blame yourself for my father's death! If
in fact he . . ." She swallowed and hugged herself, holding his gaze with her lucid green
eyes. "If he ended his own life . . . then 'twas
his own decision to do so, his alone. That
would be his sin to bear, not yours, not mine,
not Amos's—though I very much doubt my
brother will ever be free of the guilt!"

Christian swallowed, shook his head. He
wanted to stop her before she said something
she would regret. "Jessie . . ." He took a shuddering breath, moved as he was by her gen-
erosity. "You need not absolve me . . . I am
what I am. I did what I did." He shook his
head. "Much as I wish it, I cannot, in truth, be
judged innocent."

"Please," she protested, holding up her
hand in objection. "I listened to you when you
confessed yourself to me. Now . . . please, do
me the like courtesy. Aye, 'tis the truth you
bear some responsibility, but even still, the
burden of his death falls solely upon my father. 'Twas not as though we were left completely destitute, after all," she reasoned.
"Nay, for my father had resources to draw
on—myself, for one—had it suited him to do
so. Amos certainly had no qualms over using
me," she added somewhat bitterly. "The truth

is that my father chose not to do so." She sighed heavily before continuing.

"It seems to me that when my brother Thomas died, a part of my father died as well. You see, he was of the mind that Thomas was the perfect one; Thomas was his hope; Thomas was the wise one; he was courageous and diligent. And yet . . . Amos was the one most like him. I never understood why my father seemed so displeased by him, nor why he thought him unsuited to the dukedom."

Christian's jaw clenched visibly. "And so you would have me believe he would end his life because he lost his best son, and thus give the dukedom all the sooner to his most unworthy? I find that hard to credit, Jessamine."

"So do I," she agreed. "But you didn't know him as I did, and I tell you true that when my eldest brother died, so, too, did my father's will to live. I saw the change in him from the very instant he was apprised of Thomas's death—not even my mother's passing affected him so."

"Still . . ."

"Nay! You did only what you felt you must, and the truth is that I might well have done the same given your circumstances. None of it matters anymore."

"The devil it doesn't."

Jessie stood there before him, her hands clasping and unclasping at her sides, angry tears glistening in her eyes. "What do you wish me to say? Do you wish to hear that I despise you, after all? Do you truly wish to know my hatred when you can know my love instead? Nay, but I can lie to myself no longer—nor to you! I cannot!" she cried with feeling. " 'Tis impossible! Sweet Lord—do not ask me to deny what I feel, because I cannot! *I love you, Christian,*" she told him, her eyes misting.

He stared at her a long moment, and then said, as though he'd not heard a word she'd spoken, "The unfinished wing . . ." His voice broke. He turned from her, staring down below, leaning against the railing as he watched the men work. "No sooner had it been constructed when it was destroyed by fire. Did you know that, Jess?"

Jessie blinked at his words, staring at his back as though he were mad. Her heart felt as though it were wrenching. How could he change the subject so completely, all but ignoring her declaration of love? "Fire?" she repeated. Good God, what did she care about that now? "I . . . I didn't know," she relented, discomposed now. "Th-There are no signs . . . The walls are not—Good Lord, Christian!" she cried, shaking her head at the absurdity of their conversation. "Whatever has this to do—"

"Originally," he interposed, without bothering even to glimpse over his shoulder at her, "my chamber was in that burned wing." He continued to watch the workmen below, and Jessie felt like flying at him and striking her fist upon his back, screaming like a madwoman.

She swallowed, closing her eyes. He didn't love her . . . couldn't . . . "Really?" she replied, and choked down a sob.

"I learned yesterday that it was burned apurpose. McCarney admitted to it." There was a moment of silence as Jessie weighed his words before he continued. "He was somewhat emboldened by my arrest, I assume. He confessed to starting the blaze while I slept in revenge for something I'd done to his brother. It was an accident Jessamine; flash fire. I didn't kill him, though I might as well have. I didn't stop it, either. He was no more than a boy. I should have put a halt to it at once. You see, he was afraid of the cannons, and I thought I was doing him a favor by allowing the crew to force him into firing a volley. He had to learn—he wanted to. God's truth, he *needed* to learn. But the men were more drunk than I realized; they misloaded the gun." He was silent a long moment. "I didn't realize McCarney still held me responsible, but I might have known, for it took me a long time to acquit myself."

He shook his head. " 'Tis been more than three months since the fire and I've had the bricks scrubbed. I'd had it in mind to leave them their natural color, you see, but they had to be whitewashed. It doesn't really look so bad as I thought it might." He turned to face her, his eyes gleaming strangely. "What do you think?"

She thought he must be daft! Her brows collided. "I'm sorry. 'Tis beautiful, Christian—did you not hear me?"

"Tell me, Jess," he broke in once more, smiling slightly now.

"Did you not hear me?" she demanded.

"Can you see yourself as mistress here?"

Jessie's temper rose. "Can I—" And then his question penetrated, and her jaw dropped. She clamped her mouth shut, not entirely certain she'd heard correctly. Gazing skeptically into his face, at his lopsided grin, she ceased to breathe entirely. She was terrified to voice the question, but forced herself. "Did you . . . did you just ask me to wed with you?"

He nodded, and her heart tripped. "Not for the first time, I fear. I only hope you'll reply more positively than did your brother." He smiled at her then.

Jessie was momentarily stunned by his disclosure. Her brows rose and her heart soared. "You asked Amos for my—"

"I did."

"He . . . he told me you had not! He said you'd come only because he'd paid you!"

"To begin with, it was so," he confessed, his tone soft and laden with guilt. "But after having met you, Jessie, nay." He shook his head. "In truth, I never intended to follow through with it . . . Curiosity, and curiosity alone, prompted me to accept when I wanted nothing more than to batter your brother's agent to a bloody nub instead. But you see, I never considered I would fall in love with you," he admitted, coming forward. He closed the distance between them. Jessie's heart lurched as he reached out to brush her hair back from her face. He cupped her chin, lifting it to his gaze. "Do you remember that I did not return for some time . . . and you wondered that I had gone?" His eyes glistened suspiciously. "The truth is that I never intended to see you again, only I was drawn back . . . even against my will—God, you were so beautiful . . . so very beautiful . . ." He bent his head to brush her lips with his own.

Jessie closed her eyes. "Christian," she murmured, and he kissed her again, gently, his tongue coaxing her lips, and delving within as he lifted her up into his arms. He carried her within his chamber. Jessie clung to him, her heart beating fiercely.

Halting before the bed, holding her possessively, he whispered against her hair, "Jessamine Stone, will you do me the honor of becoming my bride?"

Unable to speak, Jessie nodded, burying her face into his shirt, drenching it with her joyful tears.

"I love you," he swore. *"Always have, always will . . ."*

God only knew—how long had she waited to hear those words? How much grief had she suffered and caused for them? Her eyes were liquid with tears as she gazed up into his face. At last she was unafraid to face the truth, unafraid to give her love, and her heart swelled with joy unlike any she'd ever known. "And

I," she whispered fiercely, "have always, *al-ways*, loved you, too, my lord!"

He lifted a brow. *"Always?"*

She wrapped her arms about his neck and drew his face down to hers. "I love you, Christian . . . and yes," she murmured, *"always."*

"And?" He kissed her throat with promise.

For a moment Jessie couldn't speak, didn't understand what it was he was asking, and then she did at last, and sighed contentedly. "Yes, my lord, I can see myself as mistress here."

"Gators and all?"

Jessie shuddered. "Nay," she said with a wan smile and a trace of good humor, "those, you must send away!"

He grinned. "And if I cannot?"

She sighed. "Well, then . . . I suppose I shall have to learn to live with them, after all!"

"Ah," he said waggishly, "then you do love me!" His smile deepened and he chuckled with unbridled pleasure as he lowered her to the bed.

Epilogue

꧁◦◦꧂

"**J**essamine!"

Jessie laughed as she bolted across the bedroom. Her slender body thoroughly enshrouded within the sheets from their bed, she ignored her husband's lighthearted rebuke. He feigned a charge, but she dodged him easily enough, despite the fact that she tripped over the tail of her blanket. She had the distinct suspicion her husband was merely allowing her to escape him, for he might have overtaken her any number of times already. He dove suddenly, tackling the floor instead of her legs, and Jessie scrambled towards the bed, laughing, tripping over her white train and landing unceremoniously upon the bed.

She stood at once, shifting her weight from foot to foot as though to leap away, but Christian merely sat upon the floor, watching her, his eyes twinkling and his sensual lips curving with unconcealed pleasure. "Jessie, love, 'tis been months now . . . There is nothing you would hide from me that I've not already seen. Come," he coaxed, his voice turning husky. "Spare my bones the chase."

"Nay," she said with an impish smile, "you mistake me, for I've no wish to hide a'tall." To prove her point, she suddenly dropped the sheets from her body. They slid slowly down the length of her, and she sighed at the way her husband watched so hungrily. " 'Tis simply that I would have you listen to me . . . now . . . before neither of us can think clearly any longer."

He chuckled at her brazenness. "And so you would torture me that I might listen to you?" Jessie nodded, and he laughed outright. "How very cruel of you, you little vixen. Very well, I'm completely at your mercy. Still . . . I think I should make you a sweet little bargain, if you would." He rose, approached the bed cautiously, and perched upon the edge. When she remained, looking interested, he reached out to stroke her bare calf with his fingers.

Jessie's heartbeat quickened as he caressed her; his fingers moved slowly up her thigh. Trying not to forget herself with the pleasure his touch promised, she said breathlessly, "The bargain, husband?"

He flashed her a roguish grin and lifted a devilish brow. "Sit here upon my lap, so that I might pleasure you while you speak your mind."

She seemed skeptical, so he snatched her

into his arms, and cradled her within his lap.
His fingers skimmed her belly as he whispered
into her ear, "Now, speak to me, if you would
. . . if you can . . ."

"You take unfair advantage! I cannot think
when you are touching me so!"

He flashed her a satisfied smile. "If I torture
you, my lovely wife, then I torture myself all
the more, for I want nothing more this instant
than to lay you back upon this bed of ours and
love you madly. Are you certain you wish to
talk?" He raised his brows in question.

Jessie smiled coyly. "Alas," she replied,
sighing dramatically, "but we must, you see."
She hesitated a moment, and announced, "I
wish you to speak with Jean Paul *today*."

"God's bloody teeth! Not this again!" He
made to drop her.

"Nay! But he's your father!" she protested
at once, and he lifted her up. "I shall never
understand the two of you—both of you
aware the other knows, but neither willing to
admit the truth of the matter! Really! I simply
cannot comprehend such mulishness!"

"Can you not?" he asked with a crinkle at
the corners of his eyes. He sighed then. "Aye,
I *shall* speak to him, in due time. And 'tis you
who is the stubborn one, I fear, for bringing
this up yet again." He winked at her to soften
his rebuke, and murmured, smacking her
thigh, "Even so, *mon amour, je t'aime*."

Jessie waved a hand at him crossly, scarcely
missing the tip of his nose. "And I love you!
But there's no more time! I'd have my children

know their grandsire for who he is, and not merely as your captain. You must tell him!" She cocked her head at him then, narrowing her eyes. "Do you take my meaning?"

He froze. "Are you?" She nodded. "Now?"

She smiled. "I cannot believe you've failed to notice!"

"And I cannot believe you'd frolic with me so carelessly when you're carrying my child! Have you been ill?"

She lifted a brow, in much the same manner he liked to do, and asked pertly, "Do I seem ill to you?" He shook his head. "There is simply . . . shall we say . . . a roundness to me now that is quite difficult to overlook," she pointed out.

He laid her gently back upon their bed to better inspect her. "How imperceptive of me," he muttered with a frown. "I suppose I shall have to remedy that at once!" When his mouth suddenly lit upon her belly, Jessie squealed and tried to wriggle free of his embrace.

"You would look with your lips?" she asked, scandalized, laughing softly.

"Aye, my love, for I see very well with them, indeed . . ." He tried once more, and this time she arched backward for him, her eyes closing with unabashed pleasure.

She sighed. "Yes," she murmured in agreement, "you certainly do . . . Look again if you please . . ."

Later, in the drawing room, the argument continued. "You'll tell him now, won't you?"

"God's teeth, Jessamine! I said I would!"

She frowned at him. "You never call me Jessamine!"

He locked his hands behind his back and peered at her, eyeing her pointedly. "I do now."

"Why?"

"Why? Because you're an impudent little wench!"

"Aye, well, it cannot be helped! I should remind you that you've promised near a dozen times before and never have spoken to him yet!"

He grunted, turning from the window long enough to give his wife a thoroughly disgruntled glance. "I shall tonight," he promised, and turned to peer out the window once more to see that Ben and Jean Paul were approaching the house.

"Christ," he muttered. "Here they come— sit, Jessamine! And don't you speak another blessed word!"

Undaunted, Jessie sat upon the blue damask settee to await Jean Paul and her cousin's entrance, eager for the scene to come. Her gaze wandered while she waited. The house was complete at last, the rooms furnished, some sparsely, others richly. This room was particularly grand, the ceiling high, and from the center hung a great ironwork candelabra. Two spiral staircases led abovestairs, one to each wing. The floor was polished oak, with an immense woven carpet stretched across its length. By the hearth sat two gold damask chairs along with the settee Jessie now occupied. She oft imagined them, she and Christian, sitting here along with their children, enjoying a blazing fire in winter. Soon it would be so.

She sighed, for so much had transpired since that day upon the Ashley. Lord St. John's body had never been found, though the river had been dredged. She tried not to think of that much, for in truth, there was much to be thankful for in Leland's death. It was a dreadful end for any man, one that she wouldn't have wished upon anyone, but the fact remained that if Lord St. John had lived, Christian might have hung for the sins of Hawk. She couldn't have borne that.

With the changing tide, Daniel Moore had fled to England in fear of his life . . . and there were whispers of war in the air. She tried not to think of them either. Many had chosen to return to England—McCarney included—before the tide turned completely. Jessie sighed, watching her husband at the window, thrusting the dark thoughts aside. For the time being, Hawk did not exist, there was only Christian, husband to her, and father to their unborn child.

The door swung open and both Jean Paul and Ben entered, wiping their boots upon the threshold. Jessie frowned at them, and considered rebuking them for the mess they created between them, but she sat patiently instead, her gaze reverting to Christian. He stood watching her, scowling really, and she lifted a brow in question.

"I haven't done or said anything yet!" she apprised him. "Now, have I?"

"Faugh!" Jean Paul exclaimed as he came within. "Lies, all lies, I tell you!"

Jessamine shared a look with her husband and laughed softly. Some things had changed; some things remained the same. More oft than not, Ben and Jean Paul were at one another's throats.

"If you say so, old man," Ben yielded, "though I'm glad 'tis your own hide you risk, not mine!"

She smiled at that and said pertly, "Please! Do come in! Quickly! Quickly!"

"Jessamine," Christian warned, eyeing her sternly.

Jessie ignored him, smiling brightly. "My husband has something he wishes to say to Jean Paul before the two of you commence to butchering one another."

"Jessamine!" Christian said. *"Allow me, if you please!"*

She sat, but her smile remained and was contagious. Ben found himself grinning as he came to sit beside her. Taking her hand, he patted it affectionately.

Jean Paul stood, staring expectantly not more than two feet from his son. Christian, on the other hand, seemed to be pleading with her, or perhaps he was glaring at her and Ben. She couldn't tell. When she returned his regard with a saucy smile, he grimaced and turned to face his father.

" 'Tis my wife," he began sourly, his face

coloring slightly. He shifted uncomfortably. "I . . . she—" His voice faltered. "Damn it all, *I! I* would have you know . . ." He swallowed, turning to meet Jessie's gaze briefly before continuing. "I would have you know . . . that you . . . you are soon to become a grandfather," he finished scarcely loud enough for Jean Paul to hear.

It didn't matter; one might have heard a mouse walk in a room as silent as this one had become. He took a deep breath and lifted his chin, looking more like a little lost boy than Jessie knew he would have liked. "What think you of that, old man?"

Jessie's heart swelled with pride for him, but she held her breath, waiting for Jean Paul's reply.

Jean Paul turned to Jessie, seeming to understand that she was the one responsible for this long-awaited acknowledgment. His eyes glittered suspiciously. And then, in a sweeping moment that brought tears to her eyes, he turned to Christian and said, choking on his words, "You make me proud, son!" Further words failed him and he moved forward, daring to embrace Christian.

Tentatively at first, Christian returned the hug, unsure of what to do, what to say. His grimace held a wealth of emotions, Jessie knew. Even so, the arms embracing him were not so easy to refuse, and finally he was clasping his father with as much force as was offered. Jean Paul peeled himself away, patting

Christian's shoulder, seeming embarrassed now by his show of affection.

Unable to bear not being a part of the hug, Jessie laughed and hugged Ben beside her. Ben reacted rather startled at first, looking quickly to Christian, and then again to Jessie. After another instant, he returned her hug somewhat cautiously and bent to whisper in her ear. "Felicitations, sweet coz! I shall carry the news to Mother and Father. They shall be del—"

Suddenly there was a hand wedged between them. Startled by the abruptness of it, both Ben and Jessie gazed upward to spy Christian's scowling face.

"Good God, man," Ben exclaimed, "but you are as jealous a husband as they come! She's my cousin!" he protested lamely.

Jean Paul laughed, his eyes gleaming still.

"Aye," Christian admitted without qualm, "that I am, Stone, and don't you go forgetting it!"

"Does that mean I cannot congratulate my new daughter?" Jean Paul dared.

"If you mean to embrace her, it does," Christian told him without hesitation. "Father or nay, you're a man first, and I'll not have her embraced by any but me. At least not tonight," he added, and having declared it so, he swept Jessie up into his arms. She squealed, part in laughter, part in protest.

"If you'll excuse us," he said, winking at his wife. "There's a matter of some compensation to be had for my troubles this eve." His smile deepened when Jessie blushed, and he bore her quickly up the stairs, leaving two mouths agape behind them. He didn't bother to offer Ben or his father so much as a by-your-leave.

"But we have guests!" Jessie protested.

"Aye, well, devil hang them both!" her husband proclaimed, and even as he ascended the stairwell, he managed to kiss her soundly, silencing any further protests.

The sight of them brought a hearty chuckle from the pair below.

"Have you ever seen the like!" Ben exclaimed, shaking his head in wonder as he watched the two disappear from the landing above.

"Mais oui," Jean Paul said softly. "But of course." And his look was wistful and distant as he stared up at the empty landing above. Voices could be heard faintly from the corridor, giggles, and then a door slammed shut in the distance, echoing throughout the grand house.

There was a deep hush and an air of profound contentment in its wake.

Tears filled Jean Paul's eyes, but he seemed unaware of them until one slid conspicuously down his weathered old cheek. He swiped at it quickly and turned to see that Ben was staring. *"Pardonnez-moi,"* he said, his voice catching strangely, "but I am an old man, and sometimes I find myself weakened by paltry emotions."

His dark eyes twinkling, Ben assured, "I saw nothing, my friend."

Jean Paul nodded. "And so you've not," he agreed. He placed a hand to Ben's shoulder. "So you've not."

Avon Romantic Treasures

*Unforgettable, enthralling love stories,
sparkling with passion and adventure
from Romance's bestselling authors*

LADY OF SUMMER *by Emma Merritt*
77984-6/$5.50 US/$7.50 Can

TIMESWEPT BRIDE *by Eugenia Riley*
77157-8/$5.50 US/$7.50 Can

A KISS IN THE NIGHT *by Jennifer Horsman*
77597-2/$5.50 US/$7.50 Can

SHAWNEE MOON *by Judith E. French*
77705-3/$5.50 US/$7.50 Can

PROMISE ME *by Kathleen Harrington*
77833-5/ $5.50 US/ $7.50 Can

COMANCHE RAIN *by Genell Dellin*
77525-5/ $4.99 US/ $5.99 Can

MY LORD CONQUEROR *by Samantha James*
77548-4/ $4.99 US/ $5.99 Can

ONCE UPON A KISS *by Tanya Anne Crosby*
77680-4/$4.99 US/$5.99 Can